OPPOSITE SIDES

OF THE TRACK

YOLANDA WILLIAMS

Copyright

Contact Information

Email: ydw@divayolan.com

Instagram: diva_yolan

Facebook: Diva Yolan

Twitter: Diva_Yolan

Editor: Megan Joseph

Editor Email: Josepheditorialservices@gmail.com

Cover Designer: Kylee Wright

Cover Designer Email: kaleidoscopepresents@yahoo.com

Dedication

To every couple who never saw race, size, or financial status, but only saw love in their mate.

Acknowledgements

First and foremost, I give all the honor to God for this gift. I am so appreciative that I am able to follow my passion and bring others some form of entertainment.

Thanks to my family and friends for your continued support and encouragement. Your love, support, and uplifting me keeps me fueled to move forward. I love you all!

To the readers, I am always humbled by your support and the love you show me. I pray I continue to bring some entertainment by way of my books into your lives. Smooches!

Chapter 1

Candy

Jevar: Gone & send me a pic of that fat pussy

Me: Nucca u not bout to have my shit posted on the book or IG

Jevar: Nah bae...4 my eyes only

Jevar, my man of five years, has been trying to get me to send him some nudes lately. After my primary care doctor told me I was a borderline diabetic, I got on the keto diet and has lost a little over twenty-five pounds now. If I worked out a bit more, I am sure I'd lost more by now. At any rate, my Pillsbury dough shape is damn near a Coca Cola bottle shape. Even so, I was still a bit self-conscious of my size.

Don't get me wrong, I'm not ugly at all. I have a gorgeous face that is an exact replica of my momma when she was my age. And even when I was over two hundred pounds, I turned heads everywhere I went. I was and still am a BBW, big body woman. I know how to carry every curve. But it wasn't until I took my clothes off for my man that my low self-esteem kicked in. Jevar was fine with a capital F. He worked out every day, lifting weights and all. With his six-foot four height, chocolate skin and light brown eyes, he definitely caught the eye of every woman he passed. That's why it surprised me when he approached me at Club Mirage five years ago.

My best friend, Shanell and I decided to hit up the new club we had been hearing about. I was oozing sex appeal in an off the shoulder fitted red dress. My body shaper had my curves on fleek and my double D's were pushed up to the sky. A pair of six-inch gold heels dressed my feet to match the gold clutch I carried. My naturally long and curly hair, courtesy of my Choctaw Indian grandmother, was pressed bone straight. Being that I'm not big on wearing makeup, I only wore eyeliner and popping red lipstick. Shanell wore a royal blue fitted jumper and black stilettos with rhinestones on the heel. Her weave fell to her shoulders in a wavy style. Her face was beat for the gawds as always.

We're never the ones to do a line or stand whenever we go out, so we made our way to the VIP line and was about to pay the forty dollars when a crew of guys stepped in front of us. I was about to go off when the one wearing a tailor-made suit told the bouncer we were with him. He then grabbed my hand and led Shanell and me inside the club. It wasn't until we were seated in the VIP that dude spoke to me.

"My name is Jevar. What's your name beautiful?"

"Candice but my friends call me Candy."

"Is that right?"

"It is."

"Well, Candy, I'm liking what I see, and I wouldn't mind finding out how many licks it takes to get to the center of your tootsie pop," Jevar whispered in my ear. *My kitty immediately became moist. As turned on as I was though, I wasn't giving in to him all because he was sexy as fuck and smelled just as good.*

"I'm glad you like what you see," I smiled seductively. *I took a step away from him. Jevar smile and nodded his head at my reaction.*

For the remainder of the night Shanell and I hung out in VIP with Jevar and his crew, dancing, and drinking. Someone lit up and the aroma of weed and a flavored blunt garnished the air. At one point, one of his boys had Shanell over on the sofa feeling her up and whispering something in her ear that had her giggling. A local rapper came in and shut the club down with an impromptu performance. Jevar made his way over and stood behind me while I swayed my hips to the beat of the music. He held onto my waist as I twerked my booty on him. By this time the liquor and weed had taken over me and I was ready to get into some trouble.

"You gone let me take you home?" Jevar asked me. *His hands roamed over my body making their way up to my twins and squeezed. I moaned when I felt his hardness on my ass.*

"I don't know you to be going anywhere with you. For all I know you're a serial killer," I teased as I continued to twerk.

"I'm a good guy, shawty. Besides, you got to take care of my mans since you got him hard as fuck."

"I didn't make you come get behind me. I was over here minding my business, dancing all alone."

"You shouldn't have come here wearing the fuck out of this dress and looking so damn sexy. So yeah, you owe me, and I don't want to wait to collect. I want my payout now so let's go."

Jevar didn't even give me a chance to protest before grabbing my hand and leading me out of VIP and out of the club. He led me to a silver 2015 Cadillac Escalade EXT. He held onto my hand until we were on the passenger side. He opened my door and help me in. I pulled out my phone and texted Shanell just as Jevar climbed inside.

Me: Hey babe, I'm gone with Jevar. Take my car to your house and I'll get it later

Shanell: Bitch, u know we don't leave each other like that but since you with Mr. Fine I'll make an exception.

Me: Bitch the way you attached at the hip with ole boy, I'm surprised you even knew I left.

Shanell: Shit I'm about to be just like you about to be, filled with something nice and right....ooowww!!

Me: roflmao c u 18r

I shook my head and placed my phone in my purse. I looked over at Jevar and he sat staring at me. My face immediately became flush, so I turned away and looked out of the window as he drove.

"Everything straight?" he asked.

"It's all good. I was just letting Shanell know I was with you just in case you decided to kidnap me or something."

"Ha! I told you, I'm a good guy so you don't have to worry."

"I hear you talking. So, tell me something about you," I turned to face him. I crossed my right leg over my left. Jevar watched the motion of my legs and his hand tightened around the steering wheel. He looked up and our eyes locked. The person behind us blew their horn letting us know the light was green. Jevar smirked before he placed his eyes back on the road and pulled off.

"What do you want to know?"

"Everything," I stated.

"Let's see; I'm an only child. My pops is locked up and my mom passed away when I was sixteen. I lived with my grandma for a year before she passed, and I been on my own since."

"What type of work do you do?"

"I'm an entrepreneur," he said running a hand down his face. I knew then he was lying.

"What is your business?" I wanted to see if he would tell me the truth.

"You ask a lot of questions. How about you tell me about yourself now."

"So you're not going to answer my question?" That was a sign that I should cut things off at that moment. My instincts told me so, but I ignored them.

"One day, but not today. So, tell me about you."

"I am the youngest of three. I have two sisters. My parents got divorced when I was nine after my dad was caught cheating with my mom's best friend. My sisters and I went back and forth between them every other week per court orders until we each graduated high school. I too am an entrepreneur."

"Oh yeah, what's yo business?"

"Aht, aht, you don't get that bit of information tonight either," I mimicked him.

"Oh, I see you gonna be a hand full, Ms. Candy."

"Touché, Mr. Jevar."

We made small talk until Jevar pulled up into the driveway of a nice two-story brick house. He pressed a button and the garage door lifted. He pulled into the garage next to an old school Chevy Impala then pressed the button again to let the garage door down. He hopped out then came around to my side and opened my door. He helped me out then held my hand as we made our way to the door.

As soon as he opened the door, the alarm beeped, and he entered the code to shut it off. Once I was inside, he closed and locked the door then reset the alarm. He then led me down a hall that split between the living room and kitchen/dining room combo. "Make yourself at home," he told me.

For some reason my mouth was dry, so I went to the refrigerator and opened it up, in search of something to drink. I grabbed the sprite bottle then twisted the cap off before taking a gulp. I leaned against the marble top island as I took in the décor. The walls were painted a light gray. The appliances were stainless steel. The back splash of the six-burner stove was of different colors of gray from light to dark. The cabinets were an antique white with the top cabinet doors with glass cutouts. The countertops matched the marble island top. A long gray dinette set with a glass top sat over by the huge floor to ceiling window. A set of stairs sat off to the left of the dinette set. Instead of going up the stairs where Jevar took off to, I went back to the living room.

A wall separated the living room from the kitchen, but it was decorated in the same color scheme. The walls were painted the same color. The huge sectional was an antique white with several throw pillows in a variety of light and dark gray. A huge flat screen television was mounted on the wall that separated the living room from the kitchen. A couple of tower lamps were placed in each corner of the room.

"Aye, Candy, come here," Jevar called out to me just as I plopped down on the sofa. I climbed the steps and walked into the room that was off to the right of the staircase. Jevar stood in the center of the bedroom with nothing on but a pair of pajama pants.

"Oh my," I whispered as my eyes took him in. He was so fucking fine. I bit my bottom lip as my eyes traveled from his bowlegged stance to his ripped abs to his handsome face and back down to the nice bulge that tinted his pants.

"I placed a wash towel and a towel to dry off in the bathroom for you," he said breaking me out of my trance.

"*Um, okay.*" *I went in the direction he pointed out as the bathroom.* "*Can you unzip me, please?*" *I stopped at the entrance. I pulled my hair on my shoulder.*

"*Is that all yours?*"

"*What?*"

"*Your hair?*"

"*Oh, yes, it is.*"

"*I can't wait to run my fingers through it,*" *he said as he lowered the zipper on my dress. He then smacked me on my ass.*

"*That shit hurts,*" *I elbowed him playfully in his stomach.*

"*You know you like that shit.*" *He laughed.*

"*What the fuck eva,*" *I laughed and closed the bathroom door in his face.*

I undressed then stepped into the shower and washed up. My intuition was on alert when I saw the dove bodywash in the basket. My first thought was why would a nigga, a thuggish one at that, have dove bodywash in his bathroom. Then I answered my own question. He wouldn't unless he has a bitch. I quickly stepped out of the shower and dried off. I put my dress back on not bothering with the body shaper and stormed out of the bathroom.

"*Nigga ain't no way you got me in yo fucking house and you got a bitch that stay here! That's some fowl shit and I'm not that type of bitch!*" *I huffed as I put my shoes on.*

13

"What the fuck is you talking about? I don't have no bitch staying here. Candy, wait," Jevar called out to me, but I stomped down the steps. I went to grab my purse off the island, but Jevar beat me to it and held it behind his back.

"Nigga, give me my shit so I can go! You got me all the way fucked up!" I barked.

"You need to chill with that damn attitude. I told you I don't have a bitch staying with me."

"Then explain a bottle of Dove bodywash in your bathroom, nigga. That's shit I use my damn self."

I cocked my hip to the side and folded my arms across my chest waiting for the lie I knew his ass was about to tell me. I could see the wheels turning in Jevar's mind as he tried to come up with some bullshit. I knew right then I needed to leave him alone and go on about my business. I knew if I was to fuck with him, stupid dramatic bullshit would follow.

"That's my body wash. I have sensitive skin and that's the only thing that works for me without me breaking out."

"So, you really gonna stand here with a straight face and tell me that bullshit? I can't believe this shit! Nigga yo' ass don't smell shit like that damn Dove bodywash. So, who's Dial men's bodywash is that sitting next to it? Huh?" I shook my head in disbelief at this shit. "I don't even know why I'm standing here arguing with you. You ain't my man and I'm not your lady so it really don't even matter. But we not fucking so which room besides yours can I sleep in if you ain't gonna take me home?"

"Man chill out with that shit! You can sleep in the room with me. It ain't shit you thinking, Candice. I'm not fucking with no bitch and both of em' is mine. So, kill that fucking attitude. Let's go to bed because I'm tired as fuck."

I went and plopped my big ass on the sofa and crossed my arms over my chest. This nigga done lost his mind if he thought I was about to sleep with his lying ass! Jevar stood there looking at me like I was crazy before he turned and went up the steps, my purse still in his hands. Not too long afterwards I heard the bedroom door slam. After about five minutes all the lights cut off downstairs and I sat in the dark.

I'm not sure how long I sat there before I fell asleep. My lids felt very heavy as I tried to open my eyes. A tingling sensation was moving through my body. I couldn't figure out what was causing it. All I know is that it felt good, like I was about to have an orgasm. A breeze crossed over me causing a chill. I could hear myself moaning as the sensation was becoming more intense. My eyes began to flutter open as I became more aware to the feeling. My clit was throbbing, and my pussy was pulsating as I was awakened by an orgasm from Jevar slurping my juices as I came. "Oh, shit! Ah, ah, ah!" I cried out finally awake.

My legs shook as I came a second time when he darted his tongue in and out of my pulsating walls before latching back onto my clit. He spread my legs further apart as he ran his tongue up and down my folds lapping up all my essence.

"Fuck! Suck this pussy!" I arched my back and held the back of his head in place as I ground on his face. "Oh shit, I'm cumming!" I screeched as I gushed in Jevar's face. I felt my juices pouring out of me and onto that pretty, white sofa.

Jevar climbed on top of me and lined the tip of his dick at my opening. I opened my mouth to protest but he slipped his tongue in my mouth as he plunged inside of me. I gasped at the feel of him inside of me. He thrust deep hitting my sweet spot with precision. "Mmm, Candice. You feel so good," Jevar moaned in my ear.

"Sss, ah!" was all I could muster up to say. I couldn't deny that his stroke game felt amazing. I pulled him more into me as we got into a rhythm. I threw my pussy on his dick, contracting my muscles on him with each stroke. "Ooh shit! Fuck this pussy! Damn, I'm about to cum!"

"Fuck, Candice! Shit, baby, give me that shit! Cum on my dick!" Jevar coerced. He pounded fast and hard on me, hitting my spot with precision each time. Within seconds I was cumming so hard I saw stars.

"Oooohhh shit!"

"Mmm hmm, give me that shit. Let it go." Jevar sat up and spread my legs even further apart as he watched his dick move in and out of me. "Fuck that some pretty shit! Damn yo' pussy gushy as fuck!" The look of amazement covered his face as he watched me cumming all over his dick. My juices were splashing out onto his stomach. Jevar thrust a few more times before he released inside of me what felt like a bucket load. "Ah, fuck!"

We lay on the sofa with him on top of me as we caught our breaths. I wanted so badly to be pissed off that I fucked him even after I said I wouldn't. But shit, after that get down ain't no way I could be mad. My body was buzzing just thinking about his sex game. It had been a while since I was sexually satisfied, and this was much needed.

"Do you forgive me now?" Jevar asked.

"I still think you're full of shit, but yeah," I told him.

"Good, now let's go to bed." Jevar pulled out of me, and my pussy pulsated. He stood and held his hand out to me. I took it and we went upstairs to his bedroom.

We became official after that night. Instead of walking away that night like I should have, I let him fuck me good, feeding me that diesel dick and tongue, making me forget the whole damn argument. I should have known what I was up against getting with Jevar. That house he took me to was the one and only time I had been there since that night five years ago. Within three months he convinced me to move in with him. Instead of the house he took me to, he moved me into a condo in Midtown. Coming from the hood, I didn't complain since it was way better than the projects I grew up in.

So now here we were five years in and still going at it. I can't say it was smooth sailing because it was anything other than that. I became one of those females fighting every other bitch about my man, even fighting him because of the lies I knew he was feeding me. But for whatever reason I ignored them and stayed with him. They say love is blind. Well I guess I can be called Ray Charles around this bitch since I seem to always overlook Jevar's bullshit.

For the moment, I can say we were in a good phase in our relationship. We haven't been arguing or fighting and I haven't had to check a bitch in the past six or seven months. I must say, Jevar had been very attentive. He even invested in a building for me to open my own hair salon, using the excuse he was tired of coming home to the house smelling like fried hair and gel. I was cool with that since I didn't have to use the money I had been saving up for the perfect spot to house Candy Land Salon and Spa.

Jevar: Bae stop tripping & send it

Me: U get on my damn nerves lol

Jevar: I kno I do but u still luv me tho....send it to my other phone instead of this one

Me: K

Me: (pic of me laying on our bed spread eagle show casing an up-close shot of my fingers, freshly manicured with purple tip nails, spreading my waxed pussy lips apart, showing my glistening pearl and honey dripping) Here & don't ask me 4 shit else...if you want this pussy then bring yo ass home & get it

"Oh shit!" I exclaimed when I realized I sent the pic to the wrong damn number. I was off by a digit. I sincerely hope whoever got the text disregards and deletes my pic. Just in case I sent a text behind it asking them to please delete the text and to please not post it on any social media.

Me: Jevar fuckin wit u I sent my pic to the wrong damn number. I'm not about to try a 2nd time.

Me: U just have to wait until u get home 4 da real deal....not taking any more chances

Jevar: U on some bullshit I'll c u l8r

I knew Jevar was pissed about me not sending him a nude pic, but I wasn't about to chance it a second time. Because he was so paranoid, Jevar didn't want me to save the burner number in my phone, so I had to memorize it. I was typically on my shit when texting him on that number, so I didn't bother to double check the number. Needless to say, it was after the text had been sent that I noticed it was sent to the wrong number.

Chapter 2

Bryant

I had just shut down my computer for the night after a vigorous, last minute conference call with several business colleagues about a major business proposal. This deal will set up not only McIntosh Conglomerate as the number one app development company, but this deal will have my bank account with an extra set of commas and placing me in an even bigger tax bracket. My personal cell phone dinged, alerting me I had an incoming text message. I didn't bother looking at the message at that time since I figured it was only Trinity.

Trinity Blackshear was my ex-fiancé I broke things off with a month ago after I found out she had been dabbing in heroin as well as sleeping with one of my closest colleagues, Matthew Madison. On one of my surprise pop-ups to her high-rise condo, I was the one who got the surprise of a lifetime when I walked in to find heroin laid out on the coffee table and a trail of clothing leading to her bedroom. I found them ass naked in bed, both of them high as a kite fucking. To say I was beyond pissed was an understatement.

Instead of interrupting their hump session, I took my phone out and recorded them. I then took a snapshot of the drugs for evidence I knew I would later need. I shook my head in disappointment as I left out of Trinity's apartment without being noticed. For some odd reason by the time I was back inside my car, I wasn't as pissed off as I had been upon seeing them. I'm sure any other person would have gone insane had they found their significant other high and in bed with another person. As I drove home, I thought over how Trinity never showed signs around me. But then again, I have been so preoccupied with work that I wouldn't have noticed anyway.

On my drive home, I called Trinity's phone and left her a message telling her to come over for lunch tomorrow. I then made a call to her parents inviting them to join us. My last call was to Dr. Steven Randall, a drug addiction specialist and one of my best friends. He oversees one of the best facilities here in the city. After seeing his mother overdose, he made it his mission to try and rehabilitate as many people as possible of drugs and alcohol. I told him what I walked into popping up at Trinity's place and I asked him to secure a spot for her at his facility with the bill sent to me.

The next day, with everyone sitting around at the table for lunch, I let the cat out of the bag on what I witnessed. Trinity tried to deny my accusations until I showed them the video recording of her and Mathew getting it on as well as the pictures of the drugs sprawled out on her coffee table. I called off our engagement and offered to pay for her treatment at Steven's rehab facility.

At first Trinity lashed out and tried to convince her parents she wasn't on drugs. But with the way her eyes were dilated along with her fidgeting the entire time it was hard to not see she was high at that very moment. Finally, after her mom got on her knees and begged her, Trinity agreed to go to rehab. However, Steven called me a couple of days later saying Trinity checked herself out of rehab and since she went voluntarily, there wasn't much we could do about it.

This week though, Trinity had been blowing up all means of contact for me trying to explain her actions and get back with me. I explained to her too many times, I am not interested in any woman who cheats and definitely not a woman who does drugs. I told her if I had any inkling of wanting to get back with her, the only way I would consider giving us another chance, was if she went back to Steven's rehab facility and got the proper treatment. Trinity refused to go saying she didn't have a drug problem. I then told her there was no more for us to discuss and to stop calling me.

Instead of checking the message, I decided to throw on my gym attire and make my way down to my in-home gym and get a workout in. Working out always relieved my stress of the day and I most definitely needed the stress relief right now. I walked over to the weights and grabbed a fifty-pound dumbbell and began doing arm curls.

I watched my reflection in the floor to ceiling mirror, but my mind wondered to the business proposal that was presented to me. I had so many ideas going through my mind on how the app would be most successful. I made a mental note to call Bradford, my brother and business partner, tomorrow to get his feedback from the last-minute meeting. Although Bradford wasn't into the family business as I was, he was the one with the tech-friendly knowledge that was better than mine. He knew the business in and out but due to our father, he refused to be a part of McIntosh Conglomerate.

I understood both Bradford and Dad's sides of the story and had voiced as much. However, it wasn't enough for either of them. They both felt it was necessary for me to choose between the two, but I refused. As I explained to them, no matter how much I agreed with Bradford that Dad was never there for us as a father, I understood he was busy working hard so that Bradford and I could want for nothing.

I decided to take the long route and work to earn everything I have, whereas Bradford lived off the trust fund we were both granted once we reached twenty-five. The money from my trust fund remains in the bank account untouched Mom and Dad set up for me a long time ago. Bradford said the trust fund was the least Dad could do since he was never there for us physically.

I moved from lifting weights to the treadmill. I hopped on and keyed in to get my cardio on. I set the NordicTrack Commercial X22i Incline Treadmill to an on-demand workout. A digital coach came on gave me a massive workout as he changed the incline and speed for the next forty-five minutes. By the time I was done with my workout, all I wanted to do was shower and give my pillow some head as I slept. I no longer had work, family, or Trinity's ass on my mind.

When I got back to my bedroom, I was stripping out of my clothes when my cell phone dinged with a text message notification. I exhaled loudly as I opened my phone to retrieve my text messages. As I suspected, three of the messages were from Trinity. Then there was a message from an unknown number. I first thought it was from Trinity since she was prone to using someone else's phone to call or text me in hopes of getting me to respond.

I was about to delete the message since it was from a number I didn't recognize, but something told me to open it instead. To say I was speechless when I opened the message and there were two texts that caught me off guard. The first was of a voluptuous woman's pussy. I can tell she was freshly waxed down there. It was a pretty pussy no doubt, but it was her angelic face that caught my attention. She was gorgeous. Her round face, slanted dark eyes, and cinnamon brown skin had me in a trance. Her pouty lips had me rocking up as I imagined them wrapped around my dick, pleasuring me until I exploded down her throat.

I tore my gaze from the pic to read the text included and realized this wasn't intended for me. it was intended for her man or whomever she was involved with. Was it? People were always doing things to get my attention once they realized who I was. If it wasn't some kind of monetary handout, it was using me as clout for some type of association. It was a never-ending misadventure of Bryant Verdell. I chopped this up to one of those incidents even though she sent a second text message asking me to delete her previous text.

I sat my cell phone on the counter. I entered my walk-in shower and proceeded to wash my body. The pussy pic was vivid in my mind as I washed up. I ran the washcloth over my dick as I cleaned it. However, I found myself aroused by Ms. Lady's pretty pussy and gorgeous face. I tried to shake the pic out of my mind but couldn't. It didn't help that it had been three months since I'd had sex. Before long I was jacking myself off to the picture of the mysterious woman and her pussy.

After getting myself off and releasing my load down the drain, I washed up again then got out of the shower. I walked over to my linen closet and grabbed an oversized towel to dry off with. After I dried off, I grabbed my cell phone then moved into my bedroom where I oiled my body down with shea butter before climbing into my king-sized bed butt-ass naked.

After attaching the charger and making sure my alarm clock was set, I pulled up the picture of the beautiful woman and studied it further. She looked like she may have been mixed with something. Her hair was naturally wavy, and I wanted to run my fingers through it. I imagined grabbing a handful as I hit it from the back. I subconsciously moved my free hand down to my man and squeezed the tip. I couldn't understand how my body was reacting to a picture of a total stranger. However, I was once again hard just looking at a pornographic picture, not meant for me I might add, of the most beautiful woman I'd ever seen. I wanted nothing more than to have her in my bed, underneath me as I stroked her pretty pussy to a mind-blowing orgasm.

I hopped out of bed and made my way back to my shower. I stood underneath cold water in hopes of calming the hard on I was dealing with so that I could get to sleep. I decided I would have Aaron look into Ms. Lady. I need to know everything I can about the woman who mistakenly sent me that picture. I only hoped she wasn't on some bullshit. After getting myself under control, I stepped out of the shower and proceeded to dry off and oil my body again. I climbed in bed and fell asleep dreaming of the cinnamon beauty.

Chapter 3

Bryant

I sat in my kitchen enjoying my morning cup of coffee while going over my schedule for the day. My housekeeper, Mrs. Felton, or Momma Fe as we call her, sat a plate of crispy bacon, pancakes, and scrambled eggs in front of me. She walked away only to return a few seconds later with the syrup, and the coffee pot to replenish my cup. I bit down on a piece of bacon just as Bradford came sauntering in through the door.

"Bro, what's up? Good morning, Momma Fe." He stopped next to her and kissed her on the cheek.

"Good morning, Brad. Would you like a plate?"

"Yes, ma'am." Bradford came and sat at the table with me. We bumped fist and I proceeded to eat my breakfast. Momma Fe had a plate sitting in front of Bradford within a few seconds.

"I'm glad you're here. I need your feedback on this latest proposal for this new app. If all goes well, the company will be number one on Forbes as the top-rated computer software and app company." I smiled wide at the thought.

"Yeah, and that would also put you at the top of the list as the richest bachelor. You've been on the list a long time, just not number one. Since your competition is now a married man, you'd finally be number one," he joked.

I laughed at my brother's comment. For the life of me, I seem to always fall in behind Darnell Whitworth. That man is genius in the business world and an all-around good guy. I had the pleasure of meeting him at a conference up in New York last year. We discussed business and even some personal things. He told me his biggest accomplishment wasn't his multibillion-dollar company, but marrying the love of his life, Kayla. He explained to me that being at the top of Forbes list was all well and good, but to go home to her and their children was what life was about for him.

I thought I was going to have that with Trinity. However, the more I thought back on our relationship, I saw she was never the one for me. I was just settling to fill that void in my life. After that conversation with Darnell, as soon as I got back home, I'd proposed to Trinity. She said yes and we had set a date for June 27th of this year. But as fate would have it, that wedding never happened.

"Yo, B! You alright?" Bradford's booming voice broke through my thoughts.

"Yeah, I'm cool. I was just thinking about Darnell and a conversation we had when we met in New York last year."

"Oh? What about it?"

"It was just how he spoke about his marriage and how that was his biggest accomplishment more so than his company. That's all," I shrugged.

"Mmm. I hope that don't have you thinking about getting back with that bitch," Bradford said.

"Watch your mouth!" Momma Fe scolded him.

"My apologies, Momma Fe," Bradford rebutted.

"Nah, I'm done with her. She won't get the help she needs and I'm not in the market to help someone who doesn't want to help themselves."

"I hear that," Bradford agreed.

"But check it, Brad, I know you don't want no parts of the family business, but I need your help on this new app I'm building. You're the only person I know who can get it to the next level and wipe out the competition."

"Nope, nope, nope! I'm not doing it," Bradford voiced. He stood and took his plate over to the sink.

"Come on, Brad. What do you have to lose? Nothing," I answered for him. "Look, just take a look at what I'm proposing and at least give me some feedback on it. I know how you feel about the company and Dad. But he's not in charge anymore. I am and I need my right-hand man with me on this. You're the only one who can perfect this app. You're the only one I trust on this. Can you at least think about it?"

I was now standing in front of my brother. We looked so much alike. At a glance, we could go for twins. But I'm the eldest by two years, with an inch and a half of height over him. Where my eyes were more gray than green, his was greener than gray. We both had wide noses and thick lips. Being that our dad is White, and our mother is mixed with Black and Hispanic parents, Bradford and I were fawn in complexion.

"B, you know I want no parts of the company, regardless of who runs it."

"Well think about this; if it wasn't for this company, you wouldn't have that hefty trust fund that is affording you the playboy lifestyle you're living. I understand your feelings about Dad not being there for our basketball and football games because he was always out of town for business. But had he not been handling business, you wouldn't have all those damn cars you love to go pay cash for, or that mansion across the street your ass lives in."

I was pissed at Bradford's selfishness. For many years, I tried to keep my cool about the situation. Bradford just didn't get that he was being an ass, so I had to finally break it down and give him the real deal. It was time he stopped acting like a boy and start being the man I know he was. My brother had so much potential, and I knew with his brainiac mind and my business sense, we could take the family business beyond the moon.

"Fuck you, Bryant!" Bradford pushed passed me, bumping my shoulder as he stormed out of the house. I leaned against the island and shook my head. I pinched the bridge of my nose as I let out an audible sigh.

"You told him the truth and he knows it. That is why he's so angry. But don't worry yourself, Bryan. He'll come to his senses in due time." Momma Fe patted me on my shoulders. She moved about the kitchen cleaning up around me.

"Thanks. I just hope he gets it together soon. I have to go. Have a good day," I told her while I went and grabbed my suit jacket and suitcase then headed to my garage.

I pushed the garage door button, and it began to lift. I climbed inside of my gold, 2020 McLaren GT sports car and revved up the engine. Before pulling out, I found Aaron's number and pushed the button to call him. After two rings his deep, Barry White voice boomed through the car speakers.

"What's up, Bryant? How you doing my brother?"

"Shit, man. I'm good. How about you? How's that beautiful family of yours?"

"The fam and I are great. I'm sorry to hear about your breakup with Trinity."

"Don't be," I said cutting him off. "I'm not. Trust me when I say I dodged a bullet that would have probably cost me my life had we gotten married."

"Damn! It's like that?"

"Yeah, man," I chuckled as I waited for the gate to my driveway to let up.

"So, to what do I owe the pleasure of your call?"

"Aaron, always getting to the matter at hand, Bostick." We both laughed.

"Hey, man, you know time is money."

"Indeed. So, check it, last night I received a very surprising but pleasing text message from an unknown woman. I'm sure the text wasn't meant for me because of the contents but I want to find out everything there is to know about her."

"And how do you know this is a woman?"

"It was a picture of her in the text."

"Aah, I see. You want the full package?"

"Everything. I want to know the first time she got a visit from the tooth fairy."

"Alright. I got ya. I just got your text of the number. I'll get started right away. Do you think this may one of the Catfish type of ordeals?"

"My instincts are telling me that's not the case and she really did send it to me by mistake. But you never can be too sure, ya know?'

"I feel you. As soon as I have any information, I'll get back with you."

"Alright man, thanks."

"No problem," Aaron said, and I ended the call.

I maneuvered the streets of Dunwoody making my way to the freeway. It was seven in the morning and the morning traffic was in effect. I didn't mind though. This was my time of peace before the demands of the job took over. I usually ran business strategies through my head during my drive into the city. Today, however, my mind is on the mysterious woman who sent that racy and ever so sexy picture.

Chapter 4

Candy

My alarm sounded with the burst of Rickey Smiley's voice blaring through the speaker. I have my clock radio set to his morning show everyday so I can get my laugh in as I prepared for my day. I quickly rushed to turn it off though since Jevar always woke up fussing about him trying to sleep. It wasn't until I turned over to face him that I realized his ass wasn't even in bed. His side of the bed hadn't been slept in at all!

Before I got pissed off, I climbed out of bed, threw on my black satin robe, slipped into my house shoes and headed towards the living room to see if his ass was passed out on the sofa. I sighed when I stepped into the living room and didn't see him. Hell, there was no signs that his ass had even come home. I'm about sick of this shit. I really am getting fed up with niggas fucking over me! I thought Jevar and I were finally headed down the right track, but I see once again I've been deceived.

33

I tightened the tie on my robe while I headed towards the kitchen of our one-bedroom luxury apartment. I went over to the coffee pot and pressed the button to have the coffee start brewing. I pulled my cell phone out of my robe's pocket and hit the number one to speed dial Jevar's number. It rang five times before going to voicemail. I called back again and once again I was sent to voicemail. The third time the call went straight to voicemail. "This muthafucka either blocked me or powered his phone off!"

My pressure skyrocketed and my gasket damn near blew! I was so sick of Jevar and his bullshit! I deserved better! I kept telling myself this, yet I could never find the courage to leave. I've always hated starting over and that's exactly what I would have to do if I decided to leave Jevar. I also didn't like change, even though for my sake change would be the best for me right now. I had to figure this shit out because I couldn't continue on like this.

I shook the madness off and headed back into my bedroom. I went into my walk-in closet and searched for something to put on. Thinking of the number of clients I have booked for today, I chose a pair of denim jeggings and my bubblegum pink business logo fitted tee. I grabbed my Swarovski hot pink Nike Roshe Sneakers and carried the items and placed them on top of my dresser. I opened my panty drawer and pulled out a pair of hot pink boy shorts then grabbed the matching bra out of my bra drawer.

After having my outfit picked out for the day, I made my bed then went into my bathroom and took care of my hygiene. When I stepped out of the shower, I wrapped the towel around my body as I moved over to the sink. I brushed my teeth, then plugged the hair dryer in so I can blow out my hair. My hair is naturally curly but once or twice a week I liked to blow it out so that it was straightened.

Thirty minutes later, my hair was dry and straight. I oiled my body and got dressed. I had just tied up my shoes when I heard the alarm beeping from the door opening. I stood up and placed my hands on my hips. I decided today, I was not going to let Jevar get me upset. Instead, I turned to look at my reflection in the mirror. I was loving the way my shape was slimming down. I haven't lost a lot of pounds as other people following keto has. I've lost mostly inches rather than the pounds. But I'm okay with that because my body was shaping out into that coke bottle figure. I was still a plus size, but I can admit that I looked good.

"You wearing the hell out of those jeans, shawty," Jevar complimented. He stood just inside the entrance. Our eyes met in the mirror. I took him in, noticing he wasn't wearing the clothes he left the house in yesterday. As a matter of fact, he smelled as if he'd just taken a shower.

"Thanks," I said and turned and went over to the bed. I scooped up my handbag and looked through it to make sure I had everything I needed.

"What's wrong with you?" Jevar asked.

"Nothing, Jevar. Nothing at all. Can you move? I have to go."

"Yes, it is. You got an attitude." Jevar scoured at me but stepped aside so I can pass by.

I went into the kitchen and grabbed my favorite tumbler to pour my coffee in. I opened the refrigerator and took out the creamer, bag of Keto blueberry bagels and the cream cheese spread. Jevar stood with his arms crossed over his chest and feet planted wide, watching me move about the kitchen as if he was not in my presence. I knew he wanted to start a fight with me, but I wasn't falling for his shenanigans today. I took a bagel out of the bag, cut it in half and stuck them in the toaster oven.

"What you got going on today?" Jevar asked trying to spark up a conversation.

"Work," I simply said.

"How many of those chicken heads you gotta do?"

"Eight." The bagel popped up. I grabbed them and spread the cream cheese on the halves. I fixed my coffee then placed the creamer, bag of bagels, and cream cheese back in the refrigerator. I wrapped my bagel in a paper towel and stuck it in my handbag. I grabbed my coffee and started for the door.

"What the fuck is your problem? You acting like you don't see me standing here," Jevar stressed gripping my arm in a tight hold.

"Let me go, Jevar. I don't have time for this." I tried snatching my arm out of his grasp, but he only gripped tighter.

"I'm trying to hold a conversation with yo' ass but you acting like a bitch!"

I let out a sigh and glared at him. I used to love the man with every fiber in me. I still do. That's the part that hurt so badly. Why couldn't he just get his act together and treat me the way I deserved to be treated and not like those hoes he's always fucking with?

"Jevar, how do you expect me to act when yo ass didn't come home last night? Not only did you not come home, but when I called your trifling ass, you didn't answer and then just block my calls. On top of that, you come sauntering your disrespectful ass in here like shit is all gravy. So yeah, I'm acting like a real bitch. But I don't have time for this shit. I have to go." I successfully snatched my arm out of his grasp or maybe he just let go seeing the shocked expression on his face.

"Yo, who the fuck you talking to like that? Bitch I will buss your ass in your mouth if you talk to me like that again!" Jevar threatening me would typically send me back into my shell, but today I found some new energy from somewhere because his words didn't faze me.

"Okay, Jevar, do what you feel you want to do, but again, I have to go."

I walked out of the door and down the hall to the elevator. I pressed the button and lifted the tumbler to my mouth when I felt a sting across my face. The tumbler fell out of my hand and coffee splashed across the wall and onto the floor.

"Bitch, disrespect me again," Jevar snatched me by the hair and whispered in my ear. He let my hair go when the elevator dinged. The door opened and one of the building security guards stepped off. He looked back and forth between Jevar and me.

"Miss Carson, are you alright?" Mr. Johnathan asked, concern and anger laced in his question.

"She good," Jevar quickly replied.

"I'm talking to Miss Carson, sir, unless you're a woman with that same name." Mr. Johnathan's British accent was strong.

"I'm fine, Mr. Johnathan. Rushing to get to work and spilt my coffee," I said trying to diffuse the situation. I bent down and grabbed my tumbler then quickly stepped inside the elevator. "I'll see you later, Jevar."

His face scrunched up with anger as Mr. Johnathan step backwards into the elevator and pressed the button for the parking deck.

"I'll see you safely to your car, ma'am," Johnathan told me.

Not once did he try to pry in what happened. I'm sure from the swelling of my left cheek as well as the bruising, he had an idea as to what really happened.

The elevator stopped at the parking deck level and the door slid open. Mr. Johnathan stepped off and checked his surroundings before standing to the side to allow me to get off as well. He followed behind me as I made my way to my assigned parking spot. I clicked the button on my fob to unlock my doors and disable the car alarm. When we reached my 2019 Audi A6, Mr. Johnathan opened my door.

"Thank you, Mr. Johnathan." I lightly touched his shoulder.

"It is no trouble at all, Miss Carson." He closed my door once I was seated behind the wheel and stood off to the side until I pulled out of my parking spot.

No sooner than I pulled out of the parking deck, Jevar was ringing my line. I sent him to voicemail, then did what he had done to me when I called him earlier. I blocked his calls. I wasn't feeling the arguing and back and forth bullshit today. No, I wasn't going to let his negative energy spill over. I turned my radio up and got my laugh on with the

Ricky Smiley Morning Show as I weaved through traffic heading to my salon.

I arrived at Candy Land Salon and Spa with only fifteen minutes to spare before opening. This was the only good thing to come out of this tumultuous relationship with Jevar. Before we met, I was paying booth rent at hair salon but saving my money to buy one of my own one day. After Jevar and I got together, during the first year of our relationship, he purchased some land and had this building built located in Lithonia, now called Stonecrest. It was the perfect location being that it was right by Stonecrest Mall and was easy to get to from the freeway. I liked that it wasn't in a plaza but was a stand-alone spot.

I also loved the fact I was able to have this building built to my imagination. I always wanted a spot that housed a day care my single parents could bring their children to while they got their hair, nails, and any other spa treatments done. Upon entrance of the building, there was a lounge decorated in a variety of light and dark pink and silver. My receptionist, KeKe greeted me with her bubbly smile and personality.

"Good morning, Boss Lady!"

"Good morning Ke," I chuckled.

"Jevar called and said to call him as soon as you got here. It's important."

"Okay, thanks," I smiled and kept it moving. My smile faded as soon as I bent the corner.

I did a quick walk through of all the areas before heading back to my office and sitting my things down on my desk. I powered on my computer as I took my lip gloss, phone and charger out of my bag. I unlocked my file cabinet and placed my bag inside it before securing the lock back on.

I plopped down in my chair and logged onto my computer. Once I was in, I scanned over my schedule for the day then checked some emails. Seeing I had five minutes before my first appointment, I logged off my computer. I stood and was about to head out of my office when my office phone buzzed from the receptionist. "Yes, KeKe."

"Jevar is on the line and demanding to speak to you." The poor girl sounded as if he was standing in front of her with a gun to her head, her voice quaked.

"Put him through," I sighed.

"Yo, Candice. Who the fuck got you losing your damn mind? First you walking around with an attitude then you ignoring my calls. What nigga you fucking, huh?"

"Jevar, you got me losing my mind. You are the reason for my attitude and me ignoring your calls. Don't try to blame anyone but your damn self. Have you thought that maybe I'm just tired of the bullshit you keep putting me through? This is a cycle that will never change and I'm just tired."

"I asked you what nigga you fucking. I ain't trying to hear that other shit you talking. Let me find out who the nigga is and I'm gonna put some lead in both you muthafuckas! Try me, bitch!"

I pulled the phone away from my ear and stared at the receiver. Of all the shit I said, this dummy is stuck on me fucking around when he is the one out doing dirt. Who the fuck does this? Instead of entertaining him any further, I simply hung up the phone. He was screaming hello the entire time, but I didn't care.

I let out a hard sigh and locked up my office. I walked the long hallway and back through the lounge area towards the right. This hallway led to the nail salon that was on the left side, the hair salon on the right, and the glam room at the end of the hallway. The double doors automatically opened to the hair salon, and I stepped over to my workstation. As soon as I pulled my jacket on, my first client of the day came walking towards me.

"Good morning, Mrs. Piercing. How are you today?"

"Good mor—" Mrs. Piercing's words cut off as she stared at me. Her eyes lingered on the bruise on my left cheek. "Candice, what happened to your face?"

"It's nothing, Mrs. Piercing. Come on and have a seat so we can get started." I patted the back of the chair and waved her over. She slowly walked over and took a seat. I took her purse out of her lap and hung it on the hook next my workstation. "So do you still just want the wash and set or do you want to go with something else?" I asked wrapping a towel around her neck. I then placed a cape over her and secured it with the snaps at the back of her neck, making sure not to make it too tight.

"No, I'll just do the wash and set today. But I need you to tell me what happened to your face, baby. And don't lie and say it's nothing because you and I both know it's something."

"As I told you, it's nothing. Come on, let's go over to the shampoo bowl." I patted her shoulder.

Several of stylists who rented booth space had arrived and were staring at me as I passed. A couple of them shook their heads while the others rolled their eyes with disdain. They all knew about my relationship with Jevar and knew to not make a single comment. Yeah, I probably should have covered it up with makeup. But I'm tired of covering shit up and pretending everything is alright. I just didn't feel like reliving the incident over. I positioned the seat and waited for Mrs. Piercing to sit down. She placed a hand on my shoulder and looked at me with genuine concern.

"Baby, just know you are worthy of so much more. You should never settle for anything or anyone less than what you deserve. If he can't see the queen you are, then he is not your king. Let him go. If you ever need me for anything, and I do mean anything, please don't hesitate to call me. Okay?" Mrs. Piercing said all of this to me in a low whisper only I could hear.

"Yes, ma'am," I shook my head as tears streamed down my face.

She gently touched my face where the bruise was before plopping down in the chair. Nothing else was said as I shampooed and conditioned her hair. I dried my tears and wiped my face before I led her back to my workstation so that I could set her hair. I was placing the last roller in when my crazy and loud best friend, Shanell, came bursting through the doors.

"Hey y'all!" She waved stepping over to me. On any given day at any given time, my girl was always beat for the gawds. Being a demanding makeup artist, she never left the house without her face on. She always said her face was her billboard. She was looking good in a purple logo baby tee, white fitted jeans and purple peep-toe pumps.

"Hey, Shan," Lizzette one of my seasoned stylist spoke.

"What's up, girl," Mona replied.

"Hey, boo," Gina waved to her.

"Un un, Candice. What the hell happened to your face?" Shanell's loudmouth belted out.

"Look, it ain't nothing any of you need to concern yourselves with. I'm good and it's not something I can't handle, so leave it and me alone!" I looked around at everyone with a scowl. "Come on, Mrs. Piercing so I can put you under the dryer." I grabbed her purse off the hook and handed it to her.

"Nah, Candice, you can get pissed all you want, but I ain't leaving shi-nothing alone," Shanell said. She cut her curse word off because of Mrs. Piercing. "You my girl and I'm tired of seeing you go through this with that no-good piece of a man! You need to let him go!"

"Mmm hmm," all the ladies in the shop hummed in unison. Mrs. Piercing only looked at me signaling that she had my back without saying those words.

"Come on let me fix your face. I can't have you in here trying to be professional and looking like this," Shanell said. She grabbed my wrist and pulled me with her. "Gina, if her next client shows up before she returns, go ahead and shampoo her for me if you don't have a client in your chair. And I'll hook you up," Shanell told her without slowing her stride.

"Let me go, Shanell." I pulled out of her grasp.

"Candice, if you don't get your ass in my chair so I can cover up that bruise, I'm gonna put another one on the other side of your face." Shanell pointed towards the glam room. That's where you got your makeup done, had eyelashes put on, and got your eyebrows waxed, razored, threaded, or micro bladed.

I didn't bother arguing with her. I stomped into the room and took the seat at her station. No words were spoken as my girl got to work, glamming me up as the pro she was. By the time she was done fifteen minutes later, I looked like I was ready for my Covergirl photo shoot. Unless you saw it with your own eyes, you wouldn't even know there was a bruise hidden.

"Thank you, Shanell. I truly appreciate you." I hugged her long and tight.

"No thanks needed but know you don't have to keep going through this. Fuck Jevar! He don't deserve you. And the sooner you see it, the sooner you can move the fuck on," Shanell said.

"I know and believe me when I say, I'm just about there. Let me get back to my station so I can get these clients knocked out. I'll see you in a bit."

"Okay, girl. Make that money," Shanell said reciting one of our favorite lines from the movie The Player's Club.

"Don't let it make you," I replied.

I got back to the hair salon and the ladies whistled and woo-hooed me as soon as I walked back in. They all clapped and rang compliments my way. I blushed and shooed them with my hands. But I thanked them no less for the confidence. Seriously, everything Mrs. Piercing and

Shanelle said ran through my mind the rest of the day as I busied myself with client after client and a couple of walk-ins in between.

As usual, I was the last stylist in the hair salon. It was eight-thirty when I finished with my last client who wanted a sew-in. She went from a short Fantasia styled cut to a down the back blonde bombshell. Shareta was one of those women who didn't care that you knew she had an extremely short cut one day and hair weaved down her back the next day. Those were the clients I loved because they sat in the chair and let me have my way.

I made sure my station was clean, placing everything in its proper place. I then went back to the laundry and took the load of dry towels out of the dryer and placed the last washed load in. I sat the basket of dry towels on top of the dryer to be folded in the morning. I shut off lights as I made my way towards the entrance. I headed to my office and plopped down in my chair. As tired as I was, I still needed to look over the books and get the checks written out for the bills and payroll. I grabbed a chicken wrap and a bottle of water out of my mini fridge then got to work. By the time I was done with that part of the business, it was two hours later, and the cleaning crew had arrived. I shut everything down and locked up my office, bidding them a good night.

Driving home, I listened to my missed voice messages, bypassing those left by Jevar. One call that had me intrigued was from a company wanting to discuss expanding Candy Land Salon and Spa. I had never thought about doing that. Shit with the demanding schedule at the one location, I knew it would be hell on wheels opening up many more. However, I didn't toss the idea away. Who'd thought a ghetto girl from the hood would have such a successful business that would garner attention from some bigwigs.

I pulled into the parking deck and made my way to my assigned parking spot but when I got there, both spaces were occupied. I called to security, and they advised me the second vehicle was that of a guest. This was a car I had never seen so I couldn't imagine who it was. Jevar probably had one of his homeboys over. I sighed and drove around to the visitors parking area and parked.

I hopped on the elevator and took the ride up to my floor. I pulled my keys out as I walked the hallway to my door. I stuck my key in and unlocked the door. I was confused when the alarm didn't sound off and the lights were off in the living room. I closed the door and turned on the lights. Nothing looked out of place, but it was odd when Jevar's car and a guest's car were in the parking spaces. I sat my bag on the sofa and looked around as I slowly walked down the hall leading to our bedroom. The light to the bathroom illuminated the hall and I peeked inside to see if anyone was there.

Jevar's clothes were on the floor but what caught my eye were a pair of red lace panties, a dress, and a pair of heels next to his pants.

"Those are not mine," I said out loud.

I left the bathroom and made my way to the bedroom. The door was closed and that was definitely unusual. I was about to turn the knob on the door when I heard a woman moaning out in pleasure followed by Jevar's grunts. I slowly turned the knob and opened the door. Jevar was in the middle of our bed giving it to some woman doggystyle. They were so into it that they didn't even realize I was there. The woman moaned out and called Jevar's name. It was then she looked back at him, and I saw her face.

Sharee Gander, the town hoe, bit her lip as she seductively stared back at Jevar. I shook my head and slowly and quietly closed the door. I stood there a few moments in disbelief, not that Jevar was fucking around with some THOT. I couldn't believe he brought the bitch to the home we shared. Then it was Sharee of all people! That bitch done burnt several dudes in the hood and this nigga gone fuck her!

Without a second thought or a glance I made my way to the door, grabbing my bag. I stopped at the front door and turned back around. I went back to the bathroom and opened the linen closet. I pulled the tile off the secret spot I kept my safe Jevar never knew about. I entered the code and once the door clicked, I hurried and took out all of the contents. I closed the door and replaced the tile. I left out that apartment and out of Jevar's life. No longer am I tolerating the disrespect and abuse.

Once I was back in my car, I pulled up Mrs. Piercing's number. I hated to call at that time of night, but I was taking her up on her offer. I only hoped she answered. The phone rang several times. I was about to end the call when she finally picked up.

"Candice, are you alright?" Mrs. Piercing asked. I could hear the concern in her voice.

"No, ma'am, I'm not." The flood gates opened, and I told her everything that happened from the fight this morning to me getting home and finding Jevar and Sharee in bed. I explained to her the only way I would be able to be rid of Jevar is to be able to lay my head somewhere he wouldn't know to look.

"Come on over, baby. You're more than welcome at my home. I'll be up waiting on you," Mrs. Piercing didn't hesitate to say after I was done speaking.

"Thank you so much."

"You're welcome. I'll see you shortly."

Mrs. Piercing lived in Covington, which was about forty minutes East of Atlanta. Since it was late at night and the traffic was light, with the way I was driving I cut that time by ten minutes. Luck was on my side because not one cop car was in sight the entire ride from I-75 South to I-20 East. Following the GPS to Mrs. Piercing's house, I was in awe at the big houses I passed. Even though it was midnight, the streetlights illuminated the subdivision as I maneuvered my car slowly until I reached my destination.

"Okay, Mrs. Piercing!" I screeched as I drove up the driveway leading to a huge white brick house. It was beautiful! I came to a stop in front of a three-car garage and shut my car off. I got out and took the long sidewalk up the three steps to the large mahogany double door entrance. I rang the doorbell and stood back to wait for someone to come to the door. I didn't have to wait long.

"Come on in," Mrs. Piercing waved me in when she opened one of the doors.

I stepped inside and was simply amazed at the beauty of her home. The travertine floor was shined to perfection. The huge crystal chandelier displayed in the center of the foyer was gorgeous. To the right was a formal dining room. It too had a large crystal chandelier dangling. An elegant, silver, eight-seated dining room set took up the space with a matching cabinet. The chairs had those claw feet that you would see in movies.

The living room that was straight ahead and was just as regal as the dining room with a Versailles traditional ivory velvet formal sofa and loveseat set with carved wood. The carpet was the same color. The Versailles Traditional bone white wooden top rectangular coffee table sat smack in the center adding to the loveliness of the décor. A huge floor to ceiling oil painting of who I assumed was a younger Mrs. Piercing, took up the wall to the left of the fireplace.

Sitting above the fireplace was another oil painting of a couple, the same woman in the other painting and a very handsome man dressed in an army military dress uniform. A third large crystal chandelier dangled in the center of the room. I just know not one person was allowed to sit in that room just because. And I'm sure if one was to step foot in that room, they were bare feet.

"Would you like something to eat? I can whip up something for you."

"No thanks. I don't have much of an appetite," I replied.

"Okay, we'll let me show you to the room you'll stay in. I'll give you the grand tour in the morning. Come on."

I followed Mrs. Piercing down the hall to the left passing what looked like an office or library. We stopped at the first bedroom. I didn't have to guess the furniture would be just as beautiful as what I had seen. A queen bed fully upholstered and tufted in a beautiful gray velvet fabric took up the space in the room with a two matching night stands on either side of the bed and a tall five-drawer dresser. To the left was a bathroom and to the right was a large walk-in closet.

"This will be your room. You're welcomed here as long as you want and as long as you are not involved with Jevar. If you have any more dealings with him, Candice, my hospitality ends," Mrs. Piercing told me. The look she gave me let me know she was not playing around.

"I understand and I'm done with Jevar. I called you because I knew he wouldn't think to look for you or even have a clue that I'm here. This lets you know I'm done. Had I called Shanell, as much as I love my best friend, she would tell him I was at her place, and he would make his way there to cause a scene. I knew when I stepped on the elevator this morning, I was fed up with Jevar and that relationship. But you extending yourself to help me made my decision easy. I just didn't know I was going to need that help right away." I chuckled trying to make light of the situation.

"I am here to help. I've been coming to you to get my hair done for as long as I can remember. Even when you were doing hair out of your apartment. I always said you would go places, you would make something out of yourself. Get out of the ghetto. I can't say I was happy with your choice to be with Jevar when I first met him. I knew he was trouble, but it wasn't my place to say as much. I had to let you live your life and go through the trials and tribulations I knew he was going to take you through." She came and took a seat on the bed next to me.

"I had my suspicions that he was hitting you, but until today, you never had any bruises that could be seen."

"That's because I or Shanell would cover them up with makeup," I confessed.

"That explains it then. But I'm just glad you found the courage to leave. Now don't think it's going to be smooth sailing from here. Now, baby, Jevar is going to do everything he can to find you. He thinks he has control over you. Him bringing another woman to the home you two shared together was to try and keep you in line. What he's not going to expect is for you to do the total opposite. You're going to be up against a lot dealing with him so you're going to need to be two steps, hell four steps ahead of him. If you're truly serious about being done—"

"I am," I said cutting her off.

"Then first thing tomorrow morning, you need to get a restraining order put in place. This isn't going to keep him away because he's the type that thinks he's above the law. But you're going to need that on file so that if it comes down to it, you can say you were in fear of your life and did what you felt you needed to do." Mrs. Piercing stood after the comment and headed out into the hallway. She turned back and stared at me. "You didn't bring in any bags besides the one you have on your shoulder," she said pointing to my handbag.

"This is what I left with, only the contents in this bag. I didn't have a chance to grab any clothes since I didn't want to be seen. I just left with the clothes I currently have on my back."

"No worries, dear. You can always replace material things, but your life, that's something you can't replace. That is priceless. Get some rest. We'll speak more in the morning." Mrs. Piercing didn't wait for my response as she closed the door behind her.

I thought about what she said about the restraining order. I'm not a big fan of the cops. Besides, I don't think Jevar would be that stupid since he already had charges on his record. Remembering the contents in my bag, I emptied them onto the bed and looked over all the documents I took out of the safe. Jevar was quite generous with the money he gave me, so on top of the money stashed in several bank accounts, I had thirty grand in cash that was in the safe. I also kept the deed to the building that I convinced the realtor to put in my name instead of Jevar's. Now I'm not a hoe by any means, but I did what I had to do to make sure his name was nowhere near the deed to the property. This included the land and the building itself. I happily fucked who I needed to make shit happen. I wasn't as successful when it came to the condo. Thinking on that though, I'm not tripping on it. There were more bad memories than good. I'll call to the office tomorrow and pay whatever needed to have my name taken off.

Then there was my car. Jevar bought it for me as a birthday present a few months ago but I didn't want him being able to find me. And he would be able to do that with my car. I will just get rid of it and get a new one. Little did anyone know, because of Jevar's controlling ways and wanting to act like he had it like that, all the money I earned in the five years of this relationship from doing hair, I was able to stash it. Once Candy Land Salon and Spa was opened last year, I became a certified millionaire. The money that I put in the account Jevar knew about were pennies on the dollar of what I really earned. I kept separate books, one for him and the other the real books for the man named IRS.

After going over the documents a second time, I stuffed everything back inside my bag. I sat the bag inside the top drawer. I then went inside the bathroom. I looked inside the linen closet and grabbed a face towel and a towel to dry off with. I smiled when I saw a new toothbrush and toothpaste on the counter. When I pulled the purple and silver shower curtain back, there was a bottle of Oil of Olay shea moisture bodywash and a new loofah sitting in the tray.

I turned the knob and got the water to my desired temperature. After my shower, I brushed my teeth and slid between the softest sheets I ever felt. These had to be a thousand thread count. My body melted into them as I got comfortable and drifted off to sleep. I had a lot of pressing matters that needed to be handled at the crack of dawn.

Chapter 5

Jevar

I was bugging the fuck out. But that bitch pissed me off! I knew I was wrong bringing another bitch to Candy's crib. I knew I would get a rise out of her if she saw that it was Sharee's trifling ass. But I needed to put her in her place and show her I can have whoever the fuck I wanted, and she needed to act accordingly. I couldn't lie though. Sharee had that bomb ass pussy all my boys boasted about. That bitch got a death grip that will have you sucking your thumb while balled up in the fetal position.

After my spat with Candice, I called her several times just to get under her skin. I knew she was pissed because I didn't come home last night. Usually, she would have been going off on me as soon as I stepped through the front door. But today she didn't. She acted as if I wasn't even there. I didn't know how to take that, so I poked at her, tried to start a fight with her. I wasn't used to this quiet, nonchalant Candice and it bothered me. Even when I grabbed her arm, I didn't get her normal reaction. She gonna come at me with 'do what you have to do but I gots to go' bullshit. That fucked with my psyche and why I followed her ass to the elevator and slapped the shit out of her. Even so, that bitch still didn't respond how I thought she would.

I called her phone and the job throughout the day but couldn't get a hold of her. So I said fuck it. I'll show her who has the upper hand. I made sure to have Sharee at the house by the time I thought Candy would be home. We started out in the living room, just chilling, smoking a couple of blunts and drinking on some Hennessey. I made some excuse to go take a shower and invited Sharee to join me. Of course, she did. I strategically had her panties placed in eyesight where I knew Candy would spot them right away. When Candy still hadn't made it home, shit, my man was hard as fuck and a pussy was wet and willing, so I had to take that dip.

We started out in the shower, then made it to the bedroom. I couldn't lie, after Sharee swallowed my dick in the shower, I forgot all about Candy at that point. All I wanted was to see if all that talk Sharee had been spitting was for real or for shits. Being that she had been trying to get on my team for several years, Sharee was more than happy to showcase her skills. Believe me, lil baby got 'em.

We moved from the bathroom to the bedroom. I strapped up and slid into her wet, tight, walls. Man, her pussy suctioned the tip of my dick inside her tunnel, and I obliged her. I long stroked that pussy, had her calling my name in every octane. When I flipped her over onto her stomach and start hittin it from the back, shit I damn near fell in love with the bitch. Sharee knew how to put that arch in her back and toot that ass up to the ceiling!

It was then I felt like someone was watching us. I turned to look behind me without breaking my strokes but didn't see anyone. I could have sworn I heard the front door close. But the work Sharee began putting on me quickly grabbed my attention. I felt her cumming as she contracted around my mans. When she looked back at me and licked her lips seductively, I came releasing in the condom right then.

I fell over onto the bed and laid there catching my breath. I smacked Sharee on her ass and she cooed. She reached down and pulled the condom off and sucked me into her mouth. Once again, I heard a door close. I pushed her off me and ran out of the bedroom. I looked through the bathroom as well as the living room and kitchen. There was a faint smell of Candy's perfume lingering in the air, but I took that as just the aroma of the house.

I looked at the clock on the wall and realized she should have been home by now. I went back into the bedroom and grabbed my cell phone. I dialed Candy's number as Sharee crawled over to me and tried to suck my dick. I pushed her away as I got Candy's voice mail yet again. "Baby, where you at? You should be home by now." I ended the call.

"Yo, get dressed," I told Sharee and left out of the room without a second glance her way.

I went and hopped in the shower, washing off any signs of my sexacapade with Sharee. When I stepped out of the shower, she was leaning against the counter with an attitude. I didn't bother entertaining her as I dried off. I passed by her and went back into the bedroom and got dressed.

"So, you just gonna act like we ain't just fuck?" I heard Sharee ask.

"Nah, shawty, but you gots to go," I told her. I sat on the bed and placed my feet in a pair of black-on-black retro Jordans to match the dark denim True Religion jeans and black t-shirt I put on. I went back into the closet and grabbed my A town snap back. "Let's go."

I ushered Sharee to the front and locked up the apartment as we left out. We didn't speak while on the elevator nor did I say anything to her when we reached our cars. I hopped in my truck and left her ass standing there looking dumbfounded.

I drove as fast as I could to Lithonia without gaining the pigs attention enroute to Candy's salon. I had to find out why her ass wasn't home yet. This was the first time she'd ever been out this late without hitting my line, even after we fought. I pulled into the parking lot of Candy's salon twenty minutes later and found it empty. I drove around back to see if her car was there, but nothing. Where the fuck was she at?

I tried calling her cell phone again, but it went straight to voicemail. "Candice, I don't know what the fuck is up with yo ass, but you need to call me back. You got me worried now. Call me back!" I hung up then called Shanell's ratchet ass.

"Who dis?" Shanell asked all groggy.

"Yo, put Candy on the phone," I told her ignoring her question.

"Huh?"

"Don't fucking huh me, bitch! I said put Candice on the phone." She was pissing me off now.

"First the fuck of all, don't be calling my phone with the bullshit. Second of all Candy isn't here," Shanell snapped off on me. I could hear rustling in the background. "Thirdly, I saw that damn bruise you put on her face. Nigga, you gonna make me fuck you up for hitting my girl like that. Don't be taking your bullshit out on her!"

"Shut the fuck up! You ain't gon' do shit but flap those gums. Keep talking shit and I'll put a fucking bruise on yo' face, bitch!"

"Trust me when I say, it will be your last time. I'm not Candice. Put your hands on me and I'll fuck up your whole life. Candice ain't here. I haven't seen her since at work earlier. But for God sake, I hope she finally got some sense and left your ass. Don't call my fucking phone no damn more, nigga."

Click!

That bitch just hung up on me! When I see her, I'm gon' pop her ass in those big ass lips of hers. If Shanell didn't know where Candy was, I didn't know where else to look. I'll wait until tomorrow and check her ass for this bullshit. Right now though, I got some business to handle. I dialed my boy, Dovirs. As I pulled out of the parking lot.

"Yo," this ignorant nigga answered on the first ring.

"You ready to handle this shit?" I asked.

"You already know."

"That's what's up. I'm on my way to scoop you up," I ended the call and turned up the volume to some old school Outkast. I put the shit with Candy to the back of my mind as I made my way to D's house.

Chapter 6

Bryant

As soon as I stepped out of my car at work, it was nonstop. With the stock market fluctuating the way it has been, people have been on edge. The board members called a last-minute meeting first thing this morning. Even though Mcintosh Conglomerate was doing quite well, some of the members still had concerns they wanted to discuss. Well, it was more so Dad than anyone. I honestly thought this was his excuse to come in and check on the day-to-day operations.

At any point, this meeting set my schedule behind, and it was downhill from there. One of our biggest clients, Sterling Jacobs, got wind of this new business deal and was appalled he wasn't asked to be a part of it and set on taking his business elsewhere if he was not a part of the project. I had to ensure him that this new deal will be beneficial for all Mcintosh Conglomerate clients. This on the other hand, had me fuming. I wanted to know who the culprit was that was spilling the details of this deal. I ended up working through lunch and staying over long after everyone else had gone home for the day.

When I looked up at the clock, the time read eleven twenty-five. I sat back in my seat and pinched the bridge of my nose. I swiveled in my chair and looked out over the Atlanta night skyline. This, this calmed me. My city, filled with a lot of craziness, yet I loved everything about it. Born and raised a Grady baby, but don't let my momma hear me saying that or she'd have a conniption. Due to a car accident while she was pregnant with me, they rushed her to Grady since they have the best trauma center. There I was delivered via emergency C-section three weeks early on July 19, 1985.

My cell phone rang breaking my peaceful moment. I sighed and reached for it. Thinking it was Trinity calling, I silenced the ringing. A few seconds later and my office phone rang. I glanced over at it about to silence its ringing but saw Aaron's name and number flash. I immediately picked up.

"Aaron, what's up brother?"

"I just called your cell phone. I hope I'm not interrupting anything."

"Nah, man, I thought you were Trinity. I silenced the ringing not bothering to look at the number," I explained.

"What's understood don't need explaining my friend." We both chuckled at his statement.

"I take it you got some information for me," I said getting down to business.

"Yep. It wasn't hard at all. I sent all the information to your personal email and I'm going to have a hard copy sent to your office by messenger tomorrow morning."

"Damn, that was fast. I wasn't expecting to hear from you for at least a week."

"Aye, what can I say? I'm good at what I do." We both laughed at his reply.

"No doubt. Thanks, I'm pulling it up now. So, tell me what's your analysis. Do you think she sent this unintentionally or is she trying to catfish a brother?"

"I think that text was sent by mistake. If you pull up the information on her boyfriend, you'll see one of his numbers is a digit off from yours. What concerns me about this thing though is his rap sheet. Dude had several intent to distribute an illegal substance charge as well as gun possession charges. The crazy thing about that is he should be locked up in a cage, but each of his charges were thrown out for either lack of evidence or not being read his Maranda rights."

"So, you think he got law enforcement in his pockets?" I asked.

"It appears that way. I had one of my informants go to her salon today and bring me back some intel."

"Really? What info they bring back?" Leave it to this man to go to the extremes but I'm glad he did.

"She said all is not well in Candice and Jevar's home. Several of the stylists and clients were whispering about a bruise that was on Candice's face earlier this morning. My informant said she didn't see a bruise, but it must have been covered by makeup. She also said he kept calling the salon's number for most of the time she was there, but Candice never took his calls."

"Alright, Aaron. Thanks for the info. Continue to keep eyes on her and also put eyes on him."

"You got it. Peace," Aaron said and hung up.

I began reading the attachments he sent me in the email. Brotherman was a beast with it. He indeed found out the first time the tooth fairy visited her. I picked up my laptop and took it over to the sofa. I sat it on the coffee table that made up the lounge area in my massive office. I then went over to my wet bar and grabbed a bottle of water. I started to pour a shot of Jack Daniels but changed my mind. I then pulled out the southwestern chicken salad my assistant, Charlotte, brought me earlier but never had a chance to eat. I sat on the sofa with my legs spread wide as I mixed the ingredients of the salad. After I had my dressing poured out on top of the salad, I scooped up a forkful and took a bite as I began reading over the file.

Candice Larae Carson was born June 19, 1993. She is the third and baby of Charlene and Michael Carson. Charlene was a stay-at-home wife, and Michael was "a kingpin?" I read that last part out loud. He was known as Magic Mike. Hmm, all his arrests turned out to only be misdemeanors or minor offenses that didn't require jail time. "Oh, this means he had some major people on his payroll. Just like her dude. Ain't no way a big-time dealer went that long without a major charge." I did find it interesting that he lived as long as he did in that life without some retaliations by competition or some young thug trying to make a come up.

I continued reading the file. Her sisters' names are Michelle and Cassandra, Michelle being the eldest of the three at thirty-two and Cassandra at twenty-nine. Charlene and Michael were married on December 31, 1985 but divorced eighteen years later due to Michael's infidelities. "Damn, not the best friend," I read aloud.

Charlene and Michael shared joint custody of their girls, so they were back and forth between two households. Charlene currently lives in Macon, GA. Michael was murdered a couple years ago in a drive by shooting. The case is still open. He left an insurance policy worth five million, split between his three girls and Charlene but has been intercepted by his surviving spouse, Betty, citing his will overrides the beneficiaries on the insurance policy. It was in the courts but was eventually cited for Candice and her family since it the will Betty was trying to use against them, was in fact, in their favor. The will Betty had was outdated. The will the judge based it off was signed and dated the same day Michael was killed.

I grabbed a pen and made a note beside that part so I can have Aaron look further into this. It seems to me Betty thought she was going to get everything since she was married to him, but Michael never changed his beneficiaries on the insurance. That woman is pathetic for trying to take away from his children. But the thing that has me chuckling is the insurance policy she took out on him a couple months prior to his death. It looks like somehow, he caught wind of that one and took her name off as the beneficiary and made Candice the beneficiary. She's probably shitting bricks at this very moment knowing she can't get that money. Hmm, what would make her take an insurance policy out on him two months prior to his murder?

I pushed my now empty container to the side then gulped down the entire bottle of water. I kicked my shoes off and toss my legs onto the sofa, crossing them at the ankles. With my laptop in my lap, I continue to read through the files.

Michelle is now married to Timothy Maxwell, and they have two boys, Timothy, Jr. and Michael, and a girl named Makeshia. They live in Riverdale, GA. Michelle is a RN at Southern Regional Medical Center. Timothy is a paramedic. Cassandra is currently serving as a Captain in the air force and is stationed at Buckley Air Force Base, just outside of Denver. She is single with no kids.

Candice currently lives in Midtown, GA. She is a licensed master cosmetologist and owns Candy Land Salon and Spa. "Damn, Trinity frequents that place. She always raved about their spa services. I remember her saying the owner was her stylist. That is not good."

My cell phone rang tearing me away from the files. I looked at it and I be damned if Trinity's name didn't pop up. I let it ring and go to voicemail. Seeing that it was now one thirty, I thought it was best I headed home. I tossed my empty container and bottled water in the trash can, packed up my laptop and some files I needed to look over in the morning. I put my suit jacket on, took one last look around the office then headed out, making sure to lock it.

My cell phone rang continuously as I rode the elevator down to the parking deck. I sighed at Trinity's shenanigans. I'm going to have to put a stop to this. I think I should just change my number, so I don't have to deal with her anymore. The woman is sick and needs help. Unfortunately for her, she refused the help I tried to get her so that was her loss.

The elevator opened and she stood at the entrance. At first, I was startled since I wasn't expecting anyone to be there, especially not her. I quickly got my barrens and moved passed her walking swiftly to my car which was literally five steps from the elevator door.

"Bryant, why do you keep ignoring me? I've been calling you for days," Trinity said.

I was just going to ignore her and leave her standing there but I figured I should tell her to her face one last time I'm no longer interested. When I turned to face her, I could see the woman had really gone downhill. She appeared to have aged some years than the thirty-four years of age she actually was. She had crow's feet in the corners of her bewildered eyes along with dark bags underneath. Her face had sunken in and she was too tiny. I was afraid if the wind blew the wrong way, it would snap her tiny frame in half. She was no longer wearing the clothes; the navy-blue pant suit was way too big. I remember I bought her that very suit and it fit like a glove.

"What do you want, Trinity?"

"You, I want you, Bryant! Can't you see that? I'm getting clean and getting myself together so that we can be together. The least you could do is acknowledge that. You're acting as if I'm a bum on the street!" she explained all of this while scratching her arm and tweaking.

"What facility are you signed up at? I would like to call them and get an update on your progress. I cannot and will not be with a junkie, Trinity."

"Fuck you, Bryant! You're so into your appearance. You're not perfect you know. Don't forget I know what you did. I was there. So, you'd best not take that tone with me, or I'll be more than happy to let the world know who the real Bryant Verdell Mcintosh really is."

"Bitch, your threats don't scare me. But if I were you, I'd keep my mouth shut. Like you said, you were there, and you know what I'm capable of. Besides if you tell, that will implicate you since you were there and never said anything."

I had gotten in her face and spoke those words through gritted teeth. On the outside it looked as if I was just standing close and speaking lowly so that only she could hear, but to the trained eye they would see I was seething. I was happy that her back was to the camera that sat right by the elevator. If her face was visible, they would see how frightened I had her.

"I'm going to tell you this for the last time. Leave. Me. The. Fuck. Alone. We are done. We were done the minute you spread your legs for another man and sniffed, shot, or smoked that shit in your system." I got in my car and revved my engine up. I left her standing there drowning in her tears.

Trinity

I stood there watching the taillights of Bryant's car through teary eyes. Those weren't tears of sorrow or hurt. No, those were anger tears, the kind you have when you're so pissed off that you start crying. Bryant Verdell McIntosh didn't know who he was fucking with. He had no idea that the world of hurt I was about to put on him for turning his back on me! I'm so sick and tired of men tossing me to the curb like I was a piece of trash! They were the reason I am the way that I am, and Bryant was about to feel my wrath!

Chapter 7

Candice

A knock on my door awaked me from my sleep. I stretched my body and let out a yawn. Another knock and the turning of the knob had me rolling over onto my back and staring up at the ceiling. "Candice?" Mrs. Piercing called out to me.

"I'm awake," I said and sat up with the sheet wrapped around my naked body. I rubbed my eyes and let out another yawn before my eyes set on her. Mrs. Piercing stood in front of me with one hand on her hip and the other holding some folded clothes. Mrs. Roberta Piercing was a sixty something year old woman but looked like she was in her forties. She was a beautiful woman, with blemish-free dark chocolate skin, big hazel eyes, full lips, and shoulder length hair. She resembled a short version of Naomi Campbell.

"Good morning," she smiled warmly.

"Good morning."

"Did you sleep well?"

"What little I did get, I slept like a baby," I chuckled.

"I have breakfast ready so get dressed and come eat. Here are some clothes I still had from when I wasn't as slim as I am now. You should be able to fit them with no problems. Then we can discuss what you're going to do about Jevar," she sat the clothes on the bed beside me.

"Okay, thanks. I'll be out after I wash my face and get dressed," I told her.

She turned and left the room. I unfolded the clothes. She had given me a pair of Levi's jeans and cream-colored top with the Levi's logo printed in the center. I sat them on top of the dresser then made the bed. Afterwards, I went into the bathroom. After relieving myself, I stood at the sink and looked at my reflection in the mirror as I waited for the water to warm up. The stress I was feeling was showing on my face. The bruise on my cheek wasn't as visible as it was yesterday, but still noticeable. I shook my head then preceded to wash my face and brush my teeth. After putting back on the underclothing from yesterday, I got dressed in the clothes Mrs. Piercing brought for me.

My stomach began doing summersaults the closer I got to the kitchen. Mrs. Piercing and another older lady were sitting in the eat in area of the kitchen. They stopped talking when they saw me walk in. The look they gave me let me know I was the topic of their conversation.

"Ah, there you are. Ooh the clothes fit perfectly," Mrs. Piercing said, delighted.

"Yes, ma'am they do. Thanks again," I said. I grabbed the clean coffee mug sitting next to the coffee pot I assumed was there for my benefit.

"Candice, this is Margaret. She's my housekeeper. Margaret, this is Candice. She's the guest I was telling you about. She'll be staying with me for a while."

I walked over to the ladies with a hand extended to shake Margaret's hand. The look she was giving made me pull it back in. She looked at me as if our paths crossed and was not a good encounter. Nevertheless, I was taught to respect my elders, that was until they disrespected me.

"Hello, Ms. Margaret." I smiled at the woman even though she was scouring at me.

"Candice Carson? Are you, Candice Carson?"

"Yes ma'am, I am," I replied slowly. Mrs. Piercing was looking back and forth between us trying to figure out what was not being said. Hell, I was curious, too.

"You are Charlene and Michael's baby girl, right?"

"Yes ma'am."

"Lawd, child I haven't seen you since you were a little girl!" Margaret was now smiling brightly. She stood from her chair and came over to me. She gently cupped my face with her hands. "You look just like your momma." Margaret then hugged me. I stood there with my free hand to the side while holding on to my coffee mug.

"Margaret, how do you know Candice and her people?" Mrs. Piercing asked.

"I used to babysit you and your sisters for your momma," Margaret answered Mrs. Piercing but was looking at and speaking to me. She pulled me with her to the table and we all sat down.

"I'm sorry, but I don't remember you."

"No, I suppose you wouldn't. You were a baby then. I was with Charlene when she found out she was pregnant with you. She was so happy. After she had Cassandra, your father didn't want any more children. He was disappointed he had girls. He wanted so badly to have a boy. Charlene thought they should try one last time. When they found out you were a girl instead of a boy, your mother became depressed. That was when Michael became mean."

"I never seen my dad mean to my mom," I countered. I was beginning to get upset with these things this woman was saying about my parents.

"No, he never showed any of that around you girls. As much as he wanted a son, he still adored the three of you. But he treated your mom so badly. He started messing around with that jezebel, Betty Montford. I told Charlene she needed to keep that woman away from Michael because she was not the friend she claimed to be."

"My parents divorced because my dad and Betty had an affair. The ink on the divorce papers weren't even dry before he married her," I told them.

"I can't say that doesn't surprise me to hear. I would never allow that wretched Betty on the porch if she came over to the house when

Charlene wasn't home. But Grant got a new job and we ended up moving to North Carolina. I told Charlene she needed to keep her eyes on them." Margaret sighed as if she was saddened by the news of my parents' split.

"My momma was never right after the divorce. She became cold and mean for a while because she had to share custody with Dad, and she didn't like us being at his house with Betty. She never had a serious relationship after either. I think had she been able to move away after the divorce she would have been okay. Because of the shared custody, we moved out of the house they shared but remained in the same neighborhood for school purposes. Somehow, Dad was able to get the judge to put in the papers that we couldn't be more than two miles apart and that we were mandated to spend every other week at his house until we graduated high school."

"Michael had pull like that. I don't know if you knew this, but Michael was big time back then."

"What do you mean by that, Margaret?" Mrs. Piercing asked.

"He was a drug dealer. His name rang bells in the streets as they say. He had cops, judges, the mayor, and several other high-profile people in his pocket back then."

"My father wasn't a drug dealer. He was a businessman," I corrected.

"I'm sorry, baby, but your father was Magic Mike Carson, the biggest drug dealer in the south for the longest time. Hell, his name rang bells all the way in Charlotte, North Carolina," Margaret countered.

"I remember hearing that name a few times in passing," Mrs. Piercing said.

"You probably heard it on the news when he was murdered two years ago," I sighed. I never wanted to believe the news or Jevar about my father. I tried talking to my mom about it, but she never would speak on my father. My sisters would never tell me anything either. Maybe it was because they knew I was Daddy's girl.

"That's right. That's where I heard it. I remember them reporting on it for, I don't know, how many weeks. Did they ever find the killer?" Mrs. Piercing asked.

I only shook my head. "No. I was with him that day. We were at the corner store. He called me and asked me to come see him because he had something he needed to talk to me about. When I got to his side of town, I spotted him at the store and went over there. While he was pumping the gas in his car, I went inside and grabbed a bag of Cool Ranch Doritos and a bottled water. All of a sudden, shots rang out. I fell to the floor and covered my head. Glass shattered, screams rang loud, and then tires screeching. All I remember was my dad was outside and I need to make sure he was okay. When I looked up, I saw a black car pulling off." Tears streamed down my face as I recalled the day I lost my father. No matter the problems he and my mom had, he always treated his children like princesses.

"I got up and ran outside in search for him. I stopped midstride when I saw his body lying on the ground next to his car. The gas nozzle was lying next to him. Some of the gas has spilled out on the ground around him. I took one step toward him before his car exploded. I woke up some hours later in the hospital and being told my dad was dead."

Now the tears were coming down fast and nonstop. My heart still aches for him. I always wonder what it was he wanted to talk to me about. It still bugs me he never got the chance to tell me. I asked my sisters on so many occasions if they knew and they always had the same answer. They didn't know shit and was pissed he never got around to telling me. When I asked Betty, she claimed she didn't know, but for some reason I never believed her.

"Lawd, Jesus! I'm so, so sorry, Candice! I didn't mean to open up old wounds. I had no clue Michael had passed on, let alone the way he died. Please, forgive me." Margaret came over to me and held me tight as I cried. I felt Mrs. Piercing's hand rubbing my back in a consoling manner.

"I'm okay," I said not even believing myself. I pulled away from Margaret's embrace. Mrs. Piercing held out some paper towels for me. I took them and dabbed my eyes. "Thank you."

For several moments we all sat in silence, deep in our own thoughts. It wasn't until my cell phone rang that the silence was broken. I pulled it out of my back pocket and checked the caller ID. It was Shanell. I sent it to voicemail since I didn't want her to hear the sadness in my voice. She would interrogate me to find out what was wrong. I just didn't feel like retelling that story. I texted her instead.

Me: hey girl wassup

Shanell: U! bitch where r u? Jevar blowing up my phone looking 4 u

Me: I'm safe. Don't worry. I'm done with him and that's that.

Shanell: Shit, I guess

Me: Frfr I'm so done. I can't deal with the disrespect anymore.

Shanell: R U coming in today?

Me: No, I got shit to do. Once I'm in a good place I'll hit u back. I'm gonna B MIA 4 a while

Shanell: Where r u staying?

Me: Don't worry sis I'm good and b4 u ask, no I'm not at moms or my sisters so don't be calling them

Shanell: I understand you don't want Jevar to know where you are but you need to tell me, so I know you're good.

Me: Just know I'm safe. I'll hit you up later. I have to contact my clients and reschedule them.

Me: Luv u!

Shanell: Pls call me asap! Luv u 2

Even though Shanell is my girl, I just didn't want her knowing where Mrs. Piercing stays. I know her and for the right price she would sell me out to Jevar in a heartbeat. I've always known what information to feed her and what not to. From past experience I knew not to give too much about Jevar and me. For one, I know those two have fucked at some point. My instincts have always told me so. If those instincts were wrong then that's my bad, but nine times out of ten, my gut instincts were always right.

For the next forty-five minutes, I phoned my clients, apologized for my last-minute notice, and rescheduled them for the next day. I knew I was going to have one hell of a day tomorrow but today wouldn't be good for me or them to be trying to do some hair. After calling my clients, I made a call to building office about my apartment. Mr. Reynolds words shocked me. Apparently, my name was never on the lease, even though I was paying half the rent and I do remember signing the lease. But it was definitely a relief to hear. Mr. Reynolds wished me well and we disconnected our call.

I finally called my sisters and mom on a conference call. I told them what happened with Jevar and me and where I was staying. I mentioned Margaret and my sisters went crazy! They all remembered her. I even put the phone on speaker so they could all speak to her. Margaret was just ecstatic to hear from them. After Mrs. Piercing invited them all to come over, plans were made for a reunion at the end of the week.

Being that I didn't have any clothes here and I refused to go back to that apartment, I figured now was a great time to go shopping. Instead of taking my car, I asked Mrs. Piercing to borrow hers and she gave me the keys to her 2018 Mercedes-AMG S65 Sedan. The great thing about it was that the windows were tinted so I was incognito.

Not wanting to run into Jevar since he frequented Stonecrest Mall, I decided to take the ride out to Douglasville and hit up Arbor Place Mall instead. It took me almost two hours to get there because of the distance from Mrs. Piercing's house and there was an accident right at the I-285 ramps coming off I-20 going West. I was sitting in traffic waiting for them to clear one of the lanes when I received a text from an unknown number. My first thought was that it was Jevar, and I started to ignore but my curiosity got the best of me. I looked at the number and saw it was not Jevar's number but the one I sent my pussy pic to by mistake. That prompted me to open the message.

Unknown: Good morning beautiful. First let me say, thank you for that pic. You have a very pretty pussy, but it was your face that caught my eye. You are beautiful! Secondly, don't worry I didn't share it with anyone. That is for my eyes only.

I read the text over and over for at least five minutes. I wondered who it could be. All kinds of thoughts ran through my head. I watched that show Catfish a few times. This would be the perfect scenario for some bum ass to try and get over on me. I bit my bottom lip as I contemplated responding. "What could it hurt, Candy? Shit, a whole lot! This could be some kind of serial killer for all you know." I talked to myself. I let out an audible sigh and after moving up at a turtle's pace and coming to another stop, I decided to respond.

Me: GM thanx 4 the compliment…that text was meant 4 my man; he wouldn't appreciate u texting me

Unknown: I'm not concerned about your man but he is a lucky guy to have you

Me: lol u saying that like u know me

Unknown: I don't but I'd like to

Me: But why tho? U don't kno me & how do u kno if that's even me or even a woman who sent u that pic

Unknown: Something tells me you are a woman and someone I want to get to know

Unknown: What do you or I have to lose by holding conversations

Me: I could lose a lot talking to a stranger. Didn't your mama tell u to not talk to strangers

Unknown: Lol yes, she did when I was a kid. I'm a grown man now. I follow my instincts when dealing with people....so far I've had a 98% success rate

Me: Is that right? How u figure I won't make it 97%?

Unknown: I see you're going to make this a long but interesting road

Me: That's the same shit my man said....I'm good u have a great day

I ended that conversation by blocking that number. That was the same shit or something close to what Jevar told me when we met. Nah, I'm not interested. Besides I know this thing with Jevar is not completely over especially how I left. I know sooner or later he's going to catch up to me and when he does, I need to be in the right head space to handle him. Bringing someone new in the picture would only make matters worse. Besides, who's to say this person don't already know me and know Jevar? Nah, I can't risk it.

Finally making it passed the accident, I pressed the gas pedal and made my way to Douglasville. When I got to the mall, I made sure to check my surroundings before getting out the car. I made my way into the mall and hit damn near every store, buying new clothes, shoes, and accessories. I even got a new phone and a new number. I couldn't part with the old number until I made sure all of my clients and employees had my new number. I also grabbed a gift for Mrs. Piercing as a thank you for helping me out. I was so grateful for her and all that she was doing to help me. I ended up in that mall three and a half hours before I walked out and headed back to Mrs. Piercing's house.

Remembering the documents and money I had in my purse, I stopped by Bank of America. I deposited fifteen grand in my bank account and the rest went into my safe deposit box along with the documents. Happy I got some things done, I headed home to rest up for tomorrow's hustle and bustle.

Chapter 8

Bryant

Me: I'm not your man and I'm sure we don't compare by any means.

I was pissed off Candice compared me to that sorry ass thug she called her man. We were far from being anything alike. Any man that puts his hands on a woman to abuse her isn't worthy of being called a man. That's a straight bitch and there ain't no bitch in me at all. People tended to underestimate me because of my good looks and light-skin. I got called a pretty boy, preppy, wigger, and any other derogatory name you could think of when I was growing up.

My mom's family came from the hood so when Bradford and I went to visit them, our cousins and the kids in the neighborhood always tried to jump on us. But they soon learned that our good looks didn't mean shit and we had no problems getting gutter with them. After seeing we were not to be fucked with, they went from foe to friend. My best friend Dontae is from that side of town, opposite sides of the track, my dad's side of the family like to express.

Having experience on both sides of the track had its advantages for me. I had no issues hanging out in the hood and getting down with my family when it called for then stepping into a conference room full of an all-White panel and sitting at the head of the table. Even though my father is White, I was always considered to be a Black man. I had no issues with that because I was told by both my parents that. I gave my dad props how he always handled his White associates who looked down upon him for marrying my mom. He walked away from many of major business deals because one of those muthafuckas got flip at the mouth about my mom. My dad never disrespected my mom or any of her family and he never allowed any of his side of the family or anyone to disrespect her, period. For that, he had my up most respect.

The rest of my day was pretty much routine. Surprisingly I was done with meetings and other minor matters by five. I decided to take advantage of that once in a blue moon free time and leave the office on time. My assistant was ecstatic when I sent her home. I laughed watching how fast she shut her computer down and gathered her things. She was out of the door in record time. I was right behind her.

Not having anything important to do, I decided to take a ride over to Dontae's crib. Dontae and I met at my aunt Lisa's house over in the Westend. We were there to celebrate my cousin Tootie's birthday. He was one of the knuckleheads that thought he could whoop my ass. He called himself stepping to me after I beat his cousin's ass the weekend prior to that. After I put them hands on his ass and he found out it was his cousin who started the fight, he apologized to me, and we had been thick as thieves ever since.

Dontae became like a second brother to me. No matter what, he always had my back, and I had his. My parents have never been a big fan of Dontae because instead of using his smarts to make money the legal way, he got his another route. I understood he did what he had to do to look out for him and his sister, Deidre. Their mom was a single parent who at times forgot she was a parent and left them to fend for themselves. That caused him to turn to the streets to get it how he lived it. I never judged him for it. I just advised him to be smart with his shit and get legit businesses so if one-time came knocking at his door, they would have a hard time making shit stick. He took my advice and invested his money in the stock market. He also opened a real estate company that Deidre runs along with a construction company.

A ten-minute drive to Dontae's house took me forty minutes due to the rush hour traffic. I pulled into the driveway of the house he had custom built by his construction company. Yeah, my homie was truly enjoying the fruits of his labor. The five bedrooms, five and a half-bath, and finished basement home was his prize once he made his first million. He built it and moved his mom in after she suffered a stroke that same year. He made sure he had enough rooms so that each of his three children had their own room whenever they came to spend time with him. Dontae wasn't the type to settle. He had three baby mommas and one on the way by his last child's mother.

I didn't bother calling before showing up because I already knew he would be home. I got out of the car and made my way to the front door. Before I could ring the doorbell, the door swung open, and Dontae was standing there with a big Kool-Aid smile plastered on his face. A blunt in one hand and a beer in the other.

"What's up with you, Bro? Come on in," Dontae said. He stepped aside to let me in. We shook up as soon as he shut the door behind me.

"Ain't nothing. I got done with work on at a decent time for a change and decided to swing by and holla at ya."

"That's what's up. You right on time. Mona just about done cooking. You want something to drink?"

"Yeah, I'll take one of those beers." I followed him into the kitchen where his cousin Mona was standing at the stove. She was taking some fried fish out of the deep fryer and my stomach instantly growled.

"Hey, Mom Dukes! How you doin? What's up Mona?" I leaned down and kissed Dontae's mom on the cheek.

"How you doin, baby?" she asked.

"I'm alright. How have you been?" I took a seat next to her at the kitchen table.

"I'm making it. How's you mom doing? I ain't seen her in a long time."

"That's cause she too stuck up to come around us," Mona said.

"Man, shut yo ass up! Alicia ain't never been stuck up. You just mad because she cussed yo ass out for trying to get smart with her," Dontae fussed.

"You shut the fuck up! And she didn't do shit! She always thought she was all that but she from the hood just like us." Mona turned her nose up and rolled her eyes at me.

"Gul, you need to cut that mess out! I been living way longer than you and never have Alicia acted like she was stuck up. Ya mama and the rest of the gurls was just mad because she had that good hair and didn't need weaves and wigs y'all always putting in y'all's heads, well ya mama anyways. Just like y'all boys used to try and jump on Bryan and Brad when y'all was kids, the gurls in the hood tried Alicia the same way and she whipped y'all asses just like her boys did," Mom Dukes said laughing.

"Why you got to bring up old shit, Mama?" Dontae asked jokingly.

"Well, it's true," she replied.

"Mona, you still doing hair?" I asked her trying to change the subject. I didn't come over here to go down memory lane and I definitely wasn't about to sit here and listen to Mona try and talk shit about my momma.

"Why you wanna know?"

"I'm just trying to make conversation. That's all," I said with my hands raised in the I surrender manner.

"Well, since you asked, it's going well. I'm renting a booth at a nice salon. My clientele is growing," she smiled as she told me this.

"That's what's up. I'm glad to hear that. What salon are you working at? I'll send some people your way. Just don't be catching attitudes with them when they come see you."

"Whatever, nigga. I work at Candy Land Salon and Spa."

"Oh really? What's the owner's name? I heard of that place," I said in a nonchalant manner, but Dontae caught on and tilted his head to the side looking at me.

"Candy Carson and her man, well her ex-man, Jevar Jackson. I don't know how that's gonna affect the salon."

"What do you mean?" I asked, my curiosity now piqued.

"Y'all go wash your hands and come so you can eat!" Mona yelled out to the children spread about the big house. I had no doubt they heard her because she was very loud.

"Yesterday, she came in with a bruise on her face and today she didn't even come in. I've been working there for six months now, and this is the first time she has ever missed a day. And Jevar came in looking for her too. He was pissed when we told him she wasn't there. He got into it big time with her bestie, Shanell. They were going at it. Shit, I thought they were going to start swinging on each other." Mona ran her mouth a mile a minute not letting up.

"What's up, B? You know them?" Dontae asked taking a seat at the table on the opposite side of Mom Dukes. Mona came and sat plates of fried fish, spaghetti, garlic bread, and green beans in front of him and Mom Dukes.

"Nah, I don't. That was the salon Trinity went to. Her ass used to be at that place every other day it seemed like."

"Do you want a plate?" Mona asked.

"I'll take some fish and green beans," I told her. My momma always told me not to eat any female's spaghetti that lived in the hood. She never really explained why but I didn't need to know. If she said not to then that's what it was.

"Okay." She went back over to the stove. A minute later a herd of kids came running in the kitchen and taking seats at the island or at the table.

"You sure that's all?" Dontae asked in between chewing a mouthful of spaghetti. I gave him a look that said it wasn't the time to talk. "Yo, we going down to the basement," he announced. Dontae stood and grabbed his plate and beer.

I stood just as Mona brought my plate over to me. I took it from her and grabbed my beer off the table. "Thanks," I told her.

"You're welcome. You know you need a woman like me and not that twig you deal with," Mona said and licked her lips.

"Nah, shawty, you family," I said and left her standing there.

"Feed them kids and sit yo ass down somewhere," Dontae shook his head.

We made our way down to his basement, a bonafide man cave. As soon as you hit the bottom step, a pool table sat off to the left of the room and a bar sat to the right. Behind the bar was a wine cellar. There was a gym, two bedrooms, a full bath, a game room that would put you in mind of being at Dave & Buster's, a bowling lane, a theatre room, and an office. We entered his office. I took a seat on the sofa and sat my plate and beer on the coffee table while Dontae sat at his desk. We sat eating our food for a few minutes before anyone spoke.

"So, what's up, B? And don't tell me it ain't nothing. I know you and something is going on," Dontae said.

"A couple of nights ago, I received a text message from an unknown number. At first, I thought it was Trinity because she been on that bullshit trying to get back with me. I started to ignore it, but something told me to open up the message and it was a pic of a woman I never seen before."

"Nude?"

"Yeah," I laughed at the look on Dontae's face.

"Let me see it."

"Hell no!"

"Oh, so you and shawty fucking around now?"

"Nah, I don't know her. I thought this was one of those catfish type shits so to be sure I had Aaron check it out and he think it was sent by mistake and was meant for her dude. She is the woman and dude Mona was talking about. He also told me the same thing Mona said about her being abused by her dude. He had someone go to the shop to get their hair done and said everybody was in the shop talking about her face being bruised."

"So, what does this have to do with you?"

"Something drew me to this woman and before you say it, no it wasn't the pussy shot sitting pretty. It was more so her face, her eyes. I don't know but I want to know what it is," I honestly said.

"So, what about her dude? You know his name?"

"Yeah, Jevar Jackson. I need you to get on that for me. From what Aaron pulled up on him, he is big time. He has one-time in his pockets. Dude done had several felony charges that were written up as misdemeanors, and then thrown out for some reason or another. If dude is on some shit like that, I need to know before I make my move."

Dontae shook his head in disbelief.

"Jevar Jackson isn't someone you want to fuck with B. Aaron is right. This nigga is definitely in with the big dawgs. Word is he is connected with the mafia. If that's true, you really don't want to fuck with him. I suggest you leave shawty where she be and move on."

"Come on, D, you already know once my eyes are set on anything, I'm not gonna leave alone until I have it. I want her and I'm gonna get her. If that means moving dude out of the way, then that's what it is."

Dontae sat staring at me. He knew me damn near better than Bradford, so he knew I meant what I said and said what I meant. The one thing Dontae failed to realize about me was that I too played with the big dawgs when need be. My father didn't become a billionaire from being nice. Everything he knew, everyone he knew, I was introduced to. Not all associates were on the legal side either, but Dontae didn't need to know that, best friend or not. You never let your left hand know what your right hand is doing.

"Bryant, you know I'm always down to ride. I just need you to know what you will be going up against stepping on the toes of the likes of Jevar Jackson."

"What's understood don't need explaining. I already know."

"I just hope this broad is worth this shit you about to stir up. I'd hate for you to go through all this for nothing," Dontae frowned.

"I'll put it to you like this, D, I went through the motions with Trinity. I always knew she wasn't the one. I was really settling because she was safe, comfortable for me. But Candice got a pull on me that I never felt before. They always say when a man finds that one, he just knows; it's on instinct; well, that's what it is."

"Shit, I guess. It just ain't in the cards for me bruh. I got three baby mommas and neither one of them bitches ever had me like that. They just got some of the best pussy I ever dipped off in." Dontae's face contorted and he grabbed his crotch. This fool.

"Yo, get you head out the clouds. You and those faces you be making when you in deep thought," I cracked up laughing.

"Man, fuck you," he laughed.

"Nah, I don't do niggas. You better take that shit to one of your baby mommas."

We laughed and chopped it up for a little longer before I headed home. As I drove home, I thought about what Dontae said about Candice being worth the drama that's sure to come. This feeling I've had since opening that text says so. I only hope I was right.

Chapter 9

Jevar

It has been a week since I last seen Candy. I've been calling her ass and at first, I was getting her voicemail. Now, it's saying the number is no longer in service. I been going by the shop every day and she hasn't been there. To make shit worse, the bitch done changed the fucking locks and codes so I can't even get into the muthafucka I had built for her ass.

I hit up Shanell and she swearing up and down she don't know where Candy is. I knew she was telling the truth because when I offered her ass money and this dick, she still was running with the same story. Candy hadn't even been back to the apartment to get any of her clothes. All of her shit was still there. I called her momma and her sisters and neither one of those bitches would tell me anything except she was alive and away from me.

Remembering I had a tracker on her car, I pulled it up and got a ding. "Augusta? What the fuck is you doing in Augusta?" I wanted to hop on the road right then and go snatch her ass up, but I had meeting with the big man. "I got yo ass now bitch. I'm gonna let you be for a while, let you get comfortable, thinking shit is all gravy and then I'm gonna run up on that ass." I spoke out loud as if Candy was actually in the truck with me.

Instead of hitting the freeway towards Augusta, I headed in the opposite direction in route to my meeting. I had to meet up with Marcus about a missing shipment. Those niggas in Chicago got me fucked up. Never have I been the one to fuck up a shipment but between there and Atlanta, the shipment has disappeared. No one seems to know how and by whom. I didn't need this shit right now. Lucky for me though, I still had enough product to hold things up for a minute.

Between this and the shit with Candy, something had to give. I must say though, I'm surprised at Candy's actions. This is the first time she ever pulled some shit like this before. For some reason, though, when she told me she was tired of me and my shit, I felt that. It wasn't only her saying it, but the look in her eyes that told me. I know I ain't shit, but she knew that from day one. I mean, I had another bitch's shit in my crib the night I met and fucked her. She believed me when I told her it was mine. Well only after I put this diesel tongue and dick on her ass, did she believe me.

Either way, Candy stayed with me all these damn years so why front now? Because she fucking another nigga! When I find her and that nigga, I'm fucking both they asses up, on er'thang! I don't give a fuck about what I did or what I'm doing. That's my pussy and she giving it up to another nigga is fowl. Don't no nigga want some other nigga digging off in his bitch!

"You have an incoming call from Dovirs," the voice boasted through the speakers just as my phone began to ring.

"What's up D?"

"Man, where you at? Me and Omar waiting outside the warehouse for you. Marcus and J-Bone are inside."

"I'm getting off the exit now. Chill out!"

"Jevar these are not the people you want to keep waiting. Hurry the fuck up!"

I looked around trying to figure out who the fuck D was talking to. He acting like he run shit. I'm gonna have to put his ass in his place and let him know who the HNIC was around this bitch. I didn't bother responding to him. I hung up and whipped my ride down Thornton Rd towards Lithia Springs. I pulled into the warehouse just off a dirt road ten minutes after D's call. It took everything in me not to laugh at the puffed up faces him and Omar were giving me. These two were going to learn I'm the one in charge and they will need to fall the fuck back.

"Yo, Marcus left," Omar said as soon as I opened my door.

I stepped out and the gravel crunched under my feet. I leaned against my ride looking at these two dumb fucks. How the hell did I end up with idiots as my main men to run this shit with? "Why didn't you tell him I was pulling up?" I asked looking back and forth between the two.

"What the fuck you mean, 'Why didn't we tell him you was pulling up'? How about we did, and Marcus's words were, and I quote, 'Tell Jevar I'm very disappointed he had me waiting'." Dovirs scolded. "I told you he ain't the type to wait on anybody."

I shook my head and licked my lips. I bust his ass dead in the mouth. He fell backwards into his truck. Omar started for me, but I had my heat pulled out and pointed at his head. "Try me muthafucka! I want you to so I can blow your fucking brains out! You two about the dumbest niggas I ever met! I don't know how I even put y'all on. Ya done! And I mean that shit! If I catch you hanging around my spots, I'm gone dead you muthafuckas!"

"This how you gon' do us when we helped build this shit?" Dovirs said spitting blood that landed by my foot.

"Nigga, I built this shit! I brought you bastards on, and you just been in my way, holding me back. I don't need neither one of you!" I walked backwards towards my truck keeping my piece aimed at them.

"That's fucked up, Jevar. Just know this shit ain't over," Omar stated a little to calmly for me. However, I ignored his threats as I started my ride up and pulled off, kicking up dust and rocks in the process.

"Fuck!" I pounded on the steering wheel as I sat at the light. Shit is getting out of hand and Candy is the reason behind this shit! Since her disappearance, shit has been going all the way left. I got to find her ass so I can get this shit under control. I pulled into the QuikTrip and over to one of the gas pumps. I tried to call Marcus, but he didn't pick up. I tried to call J-Bone's phone as well and got his voicemail also.

I went inside the store, went to the bathroom, and took a piss. After washing my hands, I went and grabbed a pizza and a Sprite. I paid for my food and gas. After pumping my gas, I sanitized my hands then grabbed my pizza as I made my way to the freeway. I was headed to Augusta to snatch Candy's ass up.

Chapter 10

Candy

After thinking it over, I made my way to the police department and filed a restraining order against Jevar. Between my mom, sisters, and Mrs. Piercing, I figured it was best to at least give them some sort of satisfaction. I honestly didn't think it would do any good since I had never filed any charges from past fights we had been in. I would always cover up the bruises with makeup or just stay home until any swelling went down. In hindsight, I do see I was crazy for doing that. But what's done is done.

I also drove my car out to Augusta and sold it to a used dealership. Since it didn't have that many miles on it, I got a good penny for it. I'm so glad I did, because the manager advised me there was a tracker on it, I had no idea Jevar had put on. He must have forgotten since a week had passed since we last saw each other. Either way, I'm glad I was able to get rid of it before he actually found me.

The manager tried to get me to purchase one of their cars, but I declined. Instead, I grabbed an Uber and had the driver take me to an Audi dealership. I used mobile upload to deposit the check I got for the car instead of going to a bank. I was taking every precaution to lengthen the time Jevar caught up to me. I knew it would eventually happen. But I wanted to make sure he had a hell of a time with his search. I knew he had pull around town and I knew sooner or later he was going to put the dogs out on a search party to look for me.

After being dropped off at the Audi dealership, I looked around the lot until I found the vehicle I wanted. As soon as a salesman was near, I pointed to the red, fully loaded 2020 Audi Q7 Matador. I asked them to tint the windows. After speaking with one of banks over the phone to have the money transferred, I hit up Geico and got insured. I drove off the lot within four hours of me stepping foot onto the grounds. That was a perk of having good credit and some coins in the bank.

Driving back to Covington, I had the radio tuned in to Sirius XM radio Heart and Soul station. Atlantic Starr's Secret Lovers began to play. For some strange reason my mind wondered to the texts I received last week from the number I mistakenly sent my nude pic to. I was actually curious who that could be. I liked how they kept complimenting me, saying how beautiful I was. It was nice to get a compliment from someone other than my family, friends, and clients, all women. I was in need of a man's touch, but with everything going on with Jevar, I had to lay low.

But it still wouldn't hurt to chat it up. I mean not knowing who it is and not knowing what he looked like was quite mysterious. I should text and see if I get a response. At this point what harm can this do? I reached in my purse and grabbed my phone. I had to remember to get a holder for my phone. The last thing I needed was to get pulled over for having my cell phone in my hand because of the new law. Maneuvering my car with one hand, with the other I typed in the number to the Mystery Man. I was about to press send and call him but thought against it. He may be married or have a woman who answers his calls.

Me: Hi it's the lady in the pic

Unknown: You got a new number? Is this why you haven't been responding to my texts?

Me: Yes and also because I blocked u after our 1st convo

Unknown: I see..so what changed your mind to unblock me and text me now

Me: Idk maybe it's the not knowing who u r part

Unknown: But I want to get to know you

Me: why what was it about my pic that has u so interested in me besides seeing my pussy

Unknown: As I said before it wasn't your pussy shot even tho you do have a pretty pussy

Unknown: it was your eyes that had me

Me: Really? Explain plz

Unknown: 1st can I have your name, beautiful?

Me: Candy

Me: & urs

Unknown: Candy huh? I like Candy

Unknown: Verdell

Me: that's different

Verdell: Make sure you lock me in

Me: lol done

Me: b4 we go any further…do u have a woman or a man? I don't want any issues

Verdell: No and HELL NO! I'm a straight man, a faithful man, if I had a woman I wouldn't be texting you at all

Me: if u say so about the faithful part & I'll take u @ ur word about u being strgt

Verdell: What about you? Do you have a man I need to be worried about?

Me: I actually broke up with him the next day after u got that pic

Verdell: I would be lying if I said this isn't good news. I don't like to share and I would have a problem if you had a man

Me: Well I'm not trying to jump into anything so quickly…I need time to get him out of my system and I'm not sure how long that will be

Verdell: I must share with you that I just got out of a relationship a month ago myself

Me: Really?

Verdell: Yes, really

For the remainder of my drive back to Covington, Verdell and I text back and forth. We went from discussing our last relationships to family to our careers. I wanted to call and hear his voice but was afraid to. He even called me during my drive, but I declined his call. I told him I liked the suspense in not knowing for the moment. He was understanding and didn't put up a fuss.

Once I was back at Mrs. Piercing, she and I sat and had dinner together, something we had been doing since I been there. She and my mom had been talking over the phone and seem to be getting along quite well. Margaret and I were getting reacquainted also. Some of the stories she told me, I vaguely remember but when I brought them up to my mom or my sisters they would go all in with the same details and some extras.

My phone kept going off with notifications and Mrs. Piercing was giving me the side eye. I made it clear to her it was not Jevar, and I meant I what I said about being done with him. She shook her head and went on about her business and I went into my room and read over all the texts Verdell had sent me.

Verdell: I want to see you, touch you, kiss you and feel you

Verdell: And I mean every word

Verdell: Are you home now from your drive?

Verdell: Are you finally home from your drive?

Verdell: Let me know you made it safely

Me: I'm sorry and yes I made it back safely

Me: As soon as I walked in the door dinner was ready so I sat down to eat

Verdell: Good to know you are safe. You are precious cargo

Me: U talk a good game Sir

Verdell: And I can back it up

Me: Lol well I have to get up early in the morning….finally going back to work in my salon

Verdell: Do you think it's a good idea to go back? It's still early based on what you told me

Me: I know but I have clients I need to take care of. I can't just neglect my business

Verdell: May I suggest you find a secret location to take care of your clients and do all the other business as far as payroll and things like that at home

Verdell: Just until you know for sure things have died down with dude. I'd hate for something to happen to you…that would make me go looking for him

Me: I've actually been going to their houses to do their hair

Me: I guess I can find a small space just for them and make sure they don't speak on it to anyone

Verdell: That would make me feel better to know you are safe

Me: Awe u r so sweet for thinking of my wellbeing XOXO

Verdell: I would think and hope your clients would be understanding about your special circumstances

Verdell: If they don't then you should drop them as a client. Your safety is more important than their hair

Me: Look @ u fussing over me....I like it

Verdell: Woman you are going to see I take care of what's mine and I've put my claim on you

Me: Well alright then...but I'm going to say goodnight for now and I'll talk to you tomorrow

Verdell: Fine goodnight beautiful

Chapter 11

Trinity

It's been really hard since Bryant caught me in bed with Matthew and he found out I dabbled in a little bit of heroin. I wasn't a junkie until he put me on blast to my family. I could function rather well after I had a hit. No one knew my secrets until that night three months ago. Before then, I hid it well. I wasn't always into drugs. People seem to not understand that circumstances or events that occur during a person's life can have a major lifetime altering effect. Shit beyond our control, can change the way we see things in the blink of an eye. That's what happened to me one fatal night two years ago and how Bryant and I met.

I was on my way home when I decided to stop by my friend's office to chit chat. Even though today had been hectic dealing with Mother and those catty bitches at a charity function, I wanted to catch up with him since it we hadn't spoken in a while. Gerald Carlyle and I had known each other since before we were born. Our moms' have been best friends since third grade. They were, well, are so close that they were pregnant at the same time.

I made a left onto Peachtree Street off of Tenth Street. I drove a couple of miles down before parking on the side of the street just a block down from the building Gerald worked in. After I paid the parking fee, I sauntered down the sidewalk, my Manolo Blahniks click clacked with each step as I entered the building and took the elevator to the 9th floor. When I stepped off the elevator, I made my way inside the office. Being that it was after hours, the office was empty. I walked towards Gerald's office and stopped when I heard raised voices. I stood off to the side and listened to their arguing. Gerald seemed angry but more frightened.

"You can't do this to me! I made this app, not you," Gerald said.

"I can and I am, Gerald. You don't have to worry; you'll be compensated well for your hard work. But you will give me the codes. We can do this the easy way or the hard way, G. It's up to you," the man threatened.

"Bryant, we can work together on this. Why are you so hell bent on keeping me out of this?"

"That's none of your concern. Now I'm tired of the back and forth. Give me what I came for or else."

"I can't do that Bryant. I'm sorry but I'm not going to put my hard work and my intellectual property in the hands of someone else so they can take the credit for it. I put my blood, sweat, and tears into this app and I'm not just going to hand it over to you or anyone else! So do what you have to do," Gerald replied.

"Fine. If that's the way you want it. Do it," Bryant said.

I looked around to see Bryant holding his cellphone in his hand. The next thing I heard were a woman's screams then silence. I watched as all the color drained out of Gerald's face and tears began to flow. I gasped at the realization that this Bryant guy had someone hurt all so he could get this app he so desperately wanted.

"It's done," a male voice said through the phone.

"No!" Gerald yelled out as he dropped to his knees. He hung his head down and cried like a baby. His shoulders shook as he cried hard.

"Do you still not want to comply, Gerald?" Bryant asked not even caring about him crying. "Are you willing to risk the life of another loved one? Give me the fucking code!"

"I-I," Gerald stuttered between sobs.

"Give me the fucking code. This will be my last time saying this."

Gerald looked up at Bryant through red, teary eyes. He was pleading without asking. Tears streamed down my face watching my friend going through this. I had to do something to help him. Gerald didn't deserve this. He was a good man who worked hard and took care of his family. I don't know how he got hooked up with Bryant, but I just knew I had to help him.

I moved towards the office door gaining both men's attention. Bryant turned with the gun pointing towards me. Gerald took that as an opportunity to lunge for him. The men locked up and began scuffling. Gerald was trying to pry the gun out of Bryant's hand. The gun went off, but the sound was silent. The bullet flew past my head. I ducked down behind one of the chairs that sat in front of Gerald's desk.

The men continued to scuffle until another shot went off. Gerald stepped back holding his stomach. Blood streamed down between his fingers as it dyed his white dress shirt red, dripping to the carpeted floor. His eyes were buck as he gurgled trying to speak. He fell back onto the glass coffee table, and it shattered.

I screamed out but no sound came out of my mouth. I couldn't believe what I was witnessing. This man killed my friend for something he wanted and didn't even get since he was now dead. I had never hated a person in my life until that moment. Whoever this Bryant person was will get his due diligence, this I was certain of. I vowed to make sure that happened.

"Get up," Bryant's voice broke me from my thoughts.

I slowly stood with my hands raised over my head. I knew in order for me to survive this I had to do whatever he asked and not put up a fight. He motioned with the gun for me to come towards him. I took small steps until I was standing in front of him.

"Please don't kill me. I'll do whatever you want, just please don't kill me," I begged.

Bryant said nothing to me. He snatched my right hand and placed the gun in it. He closed his gloved hand around mine tightly forcing my finger on the trigger. The entire time his eyes bore into me with such rage, I feared he was going to shoot me. After a few minutes he released my hand, taking the gun from me.

"Now, if you go to the cops or anyone else, you would be telling on yourself. You are Gerald's killer. Your fingerprints on this gun says so.

Do you want to go to the cops?" He tucked the gun in his pants then buttoned up his suit jacket.

"No." I shook my head.

"Good," Bryant smiled. He snatched my purse from me and pulled my wallet out. He searched through it until he found my driver's license. He pulled it out and snapped a picture of it with his cellphone. "Just a little insurance. Oh, and if you try to change your identity or even leave town, I'll find you and well, we know what will happen. Don't we?"

"Y-yes."

"Good. Let's go before someone comes and find us here. After you," Bryant smiled. He stepped back and waved his hand out for me to walk ahead of him.

I took one last look at Gerald's lifeless body before rushing out of the office. I started to run but Bryant grabbed me by my arm to stop me. He held onto me as we walked at a normal pace out of the office and to the elevators. He held on to me as we stepped on and made our way to the first floor and out of the building. To anyone passing us, you'd thought we were a couple, but Lord knew we were anything but that. Bryant walked me to my car and held my door open for me to get inside.

"You're going to receive a package to your home tomorrow. It will be a reminder of your situation. Is that understood, Trinity?"

"Mm hm," I nodded my head. I kept my eyes forward not looking at him.

"Good. Get home safe and text me to let me know you made it. Oh and that wasn't a request but a demand," Bryant said then closed my door.

I quickly started my car and pulled out of the parking spot. I drove home on autopilot, at least that's how it felt because I couldn't see anything the entire time. My eyes were blurry from the tears. But as soon as I arrived to my condo, I quickly made my way inside and fell onto the sofa. I let out a wail that was so loud, I just knew my neighbors heard me through the soundproof walls.

I hadn't been home five minutes when my cell phone rang. I pulled it out of my purse. It was a number I didn't recognize but I answered. "Hello."

"Didn't I make it clear to call me when you got home?"

"I just walked in my door dammit!"

"Trinity, you inserted yourself in business that wasn't yours. You have no one to blame for that but yourself so now you have to deal with those consequences."

"Don't tell me what I have to deal with! You are the blame! You are the one with greed and willing to do anything to get what you want. Don't you dare place blame on me for what you did!"

"If my recollection is correct, it is your fingerprints on the murder weapon. So no, you are to blame, Dear. But that's done and over with now. You should get some rest. Goodnight, Trinity," Bryant smoothly said before disconnecting the call.

Bowel came rushing up. I ran into the bathroom and released everything I had in my system. I heaved as if I had more to release but nothing came out. I flushed the toilet then stood at the sink and brushed my teeth. The tears flowed freely trying to figure out what to do next. At that point, I was stuck between a rock and a hard place. I had a choice to either go to the cops and be charged for a murder I didn't commit, or I can keep my mouth shut and go on like nothing ever happened. But how could I do either one? Why was I placed in this predicament? I didn't ask for this. Damn, I wish I had just come home instead.

My doorbell rung startling me. I started not to answer, but knowing Bryant, it was best I did. I went to the door and looked through the peephole. It was a pizza delivery guy. I cracked my door to let him know he had the wrong apartment.

"Hi, I have a delivery for Trinity Blackshear," the young man said.

"I, I didn't order a pizza."

"It's from Bryant Mcintosh. He said you had a rough day and wanted to make sure you got something to eat."

The young man pushed the box towards me. I reluctantly opened the door and took the box from him. He held on to the opposite side of the box with a crazed look. I tried to take the box from him but held on. "Can you let go?"

"Something is clearly bothering you. Look, I may have something that could help take off the edge. That's if you're interested," he said just above a whisper.

"What are you talking about?"

"I have weed, Molly, heroin; whatever you like."

"What? Did Bryant set this up as well?"

"Oh, no no. This is, uh, for lack of a better word, just my side hustle," he smirked. "I see people like you all the time when I make deliveries that have that same look you have. You can say, I bring a little extra to help get you through," the young man smiled.

"Come in," I waved. I closed the door behind him and ushered him over to the island. "Have a seat. Would you like something to drink?"

"I'll take a soda."

"What's your name by the way?"

"Caleb. So what is your choice?"

"I'm not sure. I've never done any of it so I'm not sure. Tell me what you think would be best?"

"Weed mellows you out but gives you the munches like a muthafucka. Molly enhances your mood. Heroin gives you an unexplainable rush. So, it's all about what it is you want to feel."

"I want to be able to forget everything and tune it out, at least for a while."

"Then heroin is what you want." Caleb went into his backpack and pulled out a bag of white substance. "This right here is pure, undiluted heroin. It will get you right with one hit so don't overdo it."

I took the small baggie from him. I closed my hand around it tightly as if I was holding on to my life. I exhaled as thoughts of what I was about to do ran through my mind. "How, how much?"

"This one is on me. I'm sure you'll be back for more after this hit. Take my number down and give me a call when you need more." I grabbed my phone and did just that.

After Caleb left, I sat at the island looking at the bag of heroin for a while. I picked it up and examined it over and over again. I ate a slice of the pepperoni pizza and drank a glass of wine. I took the bag and went over to the living room to sit on the sofa. I pulled a credit card out of my purse. I grabbed the book I had been reading and sat it in my lap. I turned the TV on and channel surfed until I came across Scarface. This was one of my faves and right on time for what I was about to do.

I watched Al Pacino's character Tony Montana divide the coke with his hand and snort it. I followed him but divided the heroin with the credit card instead. I placed a finger on my right nostril and snorted the white powder with my left nostril. My nose burned from the inhalation. I laid back on the sofa and let the contents take effect. A feeling of euphoria rushed to my brain then down to my lady parts. My clit began throbbing and my walls began contracting. I was horny. I wanted, needed, to get laid.

I stood and unzipped my dress. I undid my bra then took my panties off. I laid back down on the sofa. I ran my hands down my body. One lingered on my breast, rubbing and squeezing them as my other found its way to my garden. My fingers brushed along my labia, and I could feel how wet I was. I slid one then a second finger inside my tunnel of love. I moved them in and out. Sloshing sounds invaded my ears as my juices flowed out of me with each thrust of my fingers. I rubbed on my pearl as I fucked my fingers, gyrating on them. My orgasm built up so quickly. I inserted a third finger inside me and took myself over the edge as I came hard. I cried out in pleasure as my orgasm rushed through me. I continued to move my fingers in and out bringing on a second orgasm, something I had never been able to do before. After my second orgasm, I lay on the sofa feeling as if I was floating on a cloud. This feeling was like nothing I'd ever experienced in my life. I liked it. I didn't want it to end.

It was on that day I found my solace in what happened. It was that day my life changed forever, and Bryant Verdell Mcintosh was the blame for it. Heroin became a crutch for me. It helped me escape the wrong I involuntarily became a part of. I didn't ask for any of this. He caused my life to turn upside down and he had the audacity to want to throw me away like I was a piece of trash! Oh, hell no! I be damned if he was going to do that to me. Bryant owed me and I was ready to collect. At this point I had nothing else to lose, so it was only right I made a path so that he could join me at the bottom of the barrel.

Chapter 12

Candy

"Candy, who is this guy you've been chatting with? What's his name? What does he look like?" Shanell barked off question after question.

"Why you so damn nosey?" I laughed.

"I need to know because he got yo ass glowing these days. I haven't seen my friend like this in a long time. So, tell me, who is he?"

"Uggh, you make me sick some damn times. I swear! But his name is Verdell. He's an engineer and I-I don't exactly know what he looks like," I admitted.

"Huh? How the hell don't you know what he looks like? So, what y'all met online or something?"

Shanell looked at me confused as hell. As much as I had been going on about this new guy, I'm sure she assumed I at least knew what he looked like. Since I decided to reach out to him, we have kept in touch with each other through texts. We made several attempts to meet up but I was afraid and always chickened out at the last minute. I was afraid of who he might turn out to be or maybe he wouldn't be interested in me once we were face to face.

"One day I mistakenly sent a text message to his phone that was intended for Jevar. I was a digit off on the numbers. Verdell texted me back and it just started from there." I shrugged.

"So, you broke up with Jevar for a guy that you've only been texting with back and forth? That is the dumbest shit, Candy."

"Bitch, first of all I broke up with Jevar because I caught his ass in bed with Sharee's dirty pussy ass! Of all the bitches to fuck, that bastard fucked the town hoe! And you know I ran my ass to the clinic to make sure I hadn't caught anything behind that shit. And because of the fights. I'm just fed up, Shan"

"Oh well, you got a point there. I would beat both their asses for that. Okay, so then why are you just texting this dude and not actually seeing him? Those must be damn good texts."

"He has asked us to meet up, but I'm scared to."

"Why?"

"I'd hate to meet him and then he turns out to look like a dog and alien mix or he catfish me. Besides, after this fiasco with Jevar I'm not quite ready to jump into anything with anyone."

"So, you just gonna live off sexting and a damn vibrator?" Shanell laughed and I couldn't help but to join in.

"Shit for now, yeah."

"Have you found closure with Jevar though? You know he's still searching for you. And when are you coming back to the shop? Everyone misses you."

"I found closure the day I walked into the apartment we shared and found him in bed with Sheree. I was done with him at that point. But I know Jevar can't handle me leaving. He really thought he had me wrapped around his finger and that I would never leave. I know I won't be able to avoid the inevitable, but for now I still need to lay low. Tell everyone I miss them, too. I'll be back there soon."

"I understand, Candy, but damn how long do you plan on hiding? The only way to avoid Jevar is if he was dead! Sis, where are you? Why won't you tell me where you are?"

Shanell sounded annoyed with me, but I still couldn't tell her where I was. I was still staying at Mrs. Piercing's place. I found an empty building in Conyers I bought but placed in my sister's name. I had my clients coming there and had them all sign a nondisclosure agreement to keep my location private. I lost a few clients behind that but my most loyal clients who had been with me for several years had no problem. Once I told them my reasons, they understood and wanted to ensure my safety.

I wouldn't tell Shanell because I didn't want her involved in my issues with Jevar any more than she already was. As much as I loved her, I knew she would tell Jevar everything. I couldn't let that happen. Not right now anyways. What she didn't know was for the best.

"Shanell, I already told you why. I can't risk you telling him where I am. Don't forget, Shanell, I know you damn near better than you know yourself. I don't want you involved so it's for the best," I explained as best I could without hurting her feelings.

"If you say so. But honestly, I think you're full of shit! We're supposed to be best friends but you're not acting as such."

"Shanell,"

"No! Don't Shanell me! Candice, I have your back even when you think I don't! I know I've done some fucked up shit in the past, but you said you forgave me. It's obvious you hadn't so fuck you!"

She ended our facetime.

I couldn't be mad at her. She was right. I was holding the past over her head. It was hard for me to trust her because I knew she slept with Jevar and on several occasions she'd even told him my whereabouts when I tried to get away from him after one of his beatings. I mean, what best friend sleeps with your man and even tell him where to find you when you're trying to run away? Not one that's true and loyal. But as much as that hurt me, Shanell was by my side when I needed her the most. She helped me get through my father's death. She held my hand at his funeral. She literally gave me her shoulder to cry on. She was there when Jevar wasn't. She was there when I couldn't turn to my mom or my sisters. For that I owed it to her and to myself to try and make our friendship work.

My head began to hurt after our conversation, so I took some ibuprofen and laid down. Thinking about my dad and the day he died came to mind. It had been a while since I thought about that fatal day. I didn't want to relive it, especially since his killer still hasn't been caught. I shook my head trying to get the memory out of my head. I grabbed my pillow and hugged it as I cried myself to sleep

I woke a few hours later. My headache was gone, but my eyelids were heavy and puffy from crying. I stretched my body before sitting up. It was a Friday, and I didn't have plans. Normally I'd be at the shop hanging out chatting with the other stylists and clients until closing time. Since leaving Jevar, I only scheduled morning appointments on Fridays so I could get the payroll and other administrative work completed.

I had been cooped up in the house and really wanted to get out. I found several spots to hang out at that I knew Jevar wouldn't think to come to. I climbed out of bed and went into the bathroom. I stepped in the shower and washed up. When I stepped out, I heard my phone ding alerting me of a message from Verdell. A smile spread across my face when I picked up my phone and read his message.

Verdell: Hey beautiful. Wyd

Candy: Hey u! Just stepped out the shower

Candy: wyd hwyd

Verdell: Thinking bout u…just got home

Verdell: wish u were here wit me

Candy: ikr u could help me dry off

Verdell: fr fr I wanna see u, touch u, kiss u, feel u

Candy: oh my word

Verdell: I mean er' word ma

Candy: how are u feeling

Verdell: tired…not getting a lot of sleep

Candy: If I were there, I'd rock u to sleep

Verdell: I don't need u to rock me to sleep

Verdell: I need u to keep this head hard

Candy: I can do both

Verdell: and squirt on it…can u do that

Verdell: I will help

Candy: hmm never been a squirter but a creamer

Candy: but I'm always up for a challenge

Verdell: yes yes yes ma

Candy: look don't be talking that shit to me and I can't come home to it after being at work all day

Verdell: lol

Candy: don't laugh I'm serious lol

Verdell: shit tonight may be the night u skeet like never b4

Candy: but u r not here to make that happen

Candy: see now I'm horny and u not here at attention waiting for me to come say hello

Candy: and I need that right now

Verdell: I need to see it too

Verdell: will u let me squeeze ur booty

Verdell: I'll let u touch me...

Verdell: wherever u want

Candy: is that right

Verdell: yes

Candy: so, squeezing my booty is all u want to do

Verdell: if I'm allowed any special privileges then

Verdell: I won't turn them down

Candy: I'm sure u won't

Verdell: oh, u sure?

Verdell: really

Candy: of course

Verdell: I see

Candy: I don't normally toot my own horn, but beep beep

Verdell: I hear your horn

Candy: you wanna honk it for me

Verdell: yes, if u let me

Candy: mmm

Verdell: I'll push the button with my tongue

Candy: tell me more

Verdell: I just want to take your legs and put them on my shoulders

Verdell: and dive in face first into ur sweet pussy.... lick and suck until u can't take no more

Candy: ooh I can feel ur tongue on my hot box

Verdell: shit Candy when u gonna meet up wit me so we can turn this n2 a reality

Candy: iono 2 b honest.... how will I know if it's really u

Verdell: come on ma.... if anyone come up 2 u wit these texts we been doin

Verdell: then that muthafucka tapped n2 my shit

Verdell: tell me the real reason u don't want to meet me

Candy: 4 all I know u could be a serial killer, or some kind of psycho

Verdell: lmao but u been sexting me all this time ma

Candy: I know that seems cray, but I enjoy our sexting

Verdell: I know u ain't a virgin based off the first text u sent me by mistake

Candy: no, I'm not but after my breakup I'm just in chill mode

Candy: this has been keeping me afloat is all

Verdell: trust me ma I'll have u afloat, on top, above, n da damn air if that's what u want

Candy: lol

Verdell: we both grown.... let's cut the bullshit and meet up...if u change ur mind after then cool

Candy: okay...I guess we can do this

Verdell: come to this address 2nite....777 Lexington Dr

Candy: r u serious? That's n Pioneer Ct.... that's where celebrities live

Verdell: ma I know where I live.... just come to that address at 8

Candy: okay but I'm not coming alone.... I'm bringing my homegirl just n case u on some cray cray

Verdell: rotflmao if that makes u feel better then cool...c u l8r

I clicked on recent and dialed up Shanell. She answered on the first ring. "Bitch get dressed and come go with me to meet Verdell," I ordered.

"Oh, so you finally agreed to meet him, huh?"

"Yes and check it. He lives in Pioneer Ct."

"Un un, you are lying," Shanell said sounding skeptical and a little jealous.

"Well, it's the address he gave me. Put on some damn clothes. I'll be at your house in thirty," I told her and hung up.

I was so glad I just showered so all I had to do was oil my body and toss my clothes on. I chose a blue tennis dress and a matching lace panty and bras set. I slid my feet into a pair of thong sandals, grabbed my purse, phone, and keys before saying goodnight to Mrs. Piercing and heading out of the door. I didn't wear makeup and I always let my natural long hair do its own thing. I felt no reason to do anything differently than my normal routine. Either Verdell was going to take me as I was or not at all.

I was nervous about finally meeting Verdell face to face. I really hoped he wasn't on some psychotic bullshit. All that shit he had been talking via sext messages the past four months had been leaving me sexually frustrated and my dildos just weren't doing it for me anymore. I was craving the touch of a man, the feel of a man's body on mine, and a real dick inside of me.

Exactly thirty minutes later, I sat in front of Shanell's house honking the horn of my Audi. I swear her ass was never ready. I kept perusing my surroundings on the lookout for Jevar. The last thing I needed right now was for him to pull up on me. Shanell came out of the house looking as if she had just stepped off the runway, wearing a maxi dress that flowed with each step she took, a pair of wedges, and make up done to perfection. Like me, Shanell was gorgeous without makeup but that didn't stop her. She never left out of her house without a full face done. She didn't have natural long hair like I did, but she kept her weaves done as if she was a celebrity herself.

"Let's go meet Mr. Verdell," Shanell said once she was in the passenger seat next to me.

I pulled off and drove to the address Verdell gave me following the directions of the GPS. Shanell and I made small talk the whole drive. She didn't mention my new whip, but I could tell the question was on her mind. I wasn't going to volunteer the information either. Within forty-five minutes we were pulling up to the gate of the address I was given. I pushed the call button and a deep voice answered. "Candy, I see you are Miss Johnny on the Spot," the man I assumed was Verdell, chuckled.

"You said eight, right?"

"I did. Come on in." The gate buzzed, then swung open. I slowly pulled forward and followed the brick driveway around until we came up to this mini mansion set on acres upon acres of land.

"Damn, bitch! You done hit the fucking jackpot!" Shanell exclaimed.

Both of our mouths were open, and our eyes were bucked at the site before us. This was old money, not that type of money where someone had just hit the mega millions type of money. Whoever this Verdell character is, was from a bloodline of old school money. The house was brick with a large porch, beautiful, manicured landscape around it. There were several cars that sat in the front that range from and old school Chevy, Mercedes Benz, Range Rover, Porsche, and a Lamborghini.

"Girl don't get your hopes up. Verdell could be the help," I said. I didn't want to get my expectations up.

I pulled my Audi up behind the old school Chevy and shut the car off. All of a sudden, I had butterflies in my stomach. I questioned what I was wearing and worried that I probably should have put on makeup and really did something to my hair. I reached over in the glove box and pulled out my brush and began brushing my hair so that it looked more presentable. What I really wanted to do was crank my car up and get the hell away from here.

"Candice don't worry. You look fine," Shanell assured me. "Trust me, he is going to love everything he sees," she patted me on my leg.

I returned the brush back inside the glove box just as the front door to the house opened. A tall light-skinned man, who could pass for a white guy stepped out onto the porch. He was very tall with an athletic build. His broad shoulders and bulky muscles stretched the black t-shirt he wore. His baggy sweatpants left nothing to the imagination as both Shanell and I zoomed in on the large bulge in the center of his crotch. "Damn," we both said in unison.

I shot Shanell a dirty look and Shanell looked sheepishly. "Hey, I'm sorry, sis, but he got his shit out for a bitch to see and dammit I'm gonna look," Shanell told the truth. I couldn't be mad at that since I would have been doing the same thing had the roles been reversed. "He looks familiar to me."

"Yeah, he does to me, too. I just can't place from where, though," I agreed.

The man stepped off the porch and walked to the car. He opened the door for Shanell first. "Good evening, ma'am," he greeted Shanell then hurried over to my side and caught the door just as I opened it for myself. He stuck his hand out for me to grab as I climbed out of the car. "Good evening to you, Miss Candice. Mr. Verdell is expecting you. Please follow me."

I was rather disappointed that he wasn't Verdell. But Shanell was smiling ear to ear at the revelation. Shit she could care less that he wasn't Verdell. As fine as this guy was, I could tell she was very much down to give him a ride. We followed the man inside of the house into a foyer. The house was just as immaculate inside as it was outside with a huge crystal chandelier hanging from a tall ceiling, perfectly shined marble floors, grand staircase, and expensive vases filled with exotic floral arrangements that let off a sweet scent throughout.

"Mr. Verdell is waiting for you in the dining room," the man said.

He escorted us to the dining room. As soon as we entered, Shanell and I gasped. Verdell was the Bryant Verdell Mcintosh of Mcintosh Conglomerate. He was just named Forbes' Richest Bachelor. Yes indeed, I guess I had hit the jackpot because Verdell was indeed fine and rich! He actually resembled the man who'd escorted us in, looks and build.

Verdell stood and came over to us. He walked right up to me and gave me a hug. He smelled so fucking good. He kissed my cheek before letting me go. "Hey, Candice. You look gorgeous. And you must be Shanell," Verdell said holding his hand out to Shanell. She took it and they shook hands.

"I am."

"Welcome to my home, ladies. This is my younger brother, Bradford."

"Hi," Shanell and I sang in unison.

"Since you told me you would be bringing Shanell I asked Brad to come over and keep her company. I hope you don't mind," Verdell told us.

"Oh, no, it's not a problem at all," Shanell quickly stated. "Come on, Brad and give me a tour while these two lovebirds get acquainted."

I rolled my eyes. Shanell could be embarrassing sometimes and right now I was feeling just like that. Verdell and I watched as Shanell walked over to Brad and placed her arm around his. He smiled down on her and saluted the two of us as he escorted her out of the dining room. When I turned back to face Verdell, his eyes were planted on me.

I fidgeted with my purse strap. I was extremely nervous to be in his presence. Who thought the wrong number would lead me into a billionaire's home? Then my mind started racing as I thought of something. "How did you know Shanell's name? I've never mentioned her name to you, and I only told you I was bringing someone, but I didn't say who."

"Yes, I know. To be honest with you, I researched you after getting that sexy message. I had to see who this was sending me such a message. In my position, I must be careful of those type of situations. I hope this doesn't deter you from us."

I stared at him with no response. I didn't know how I should be feeling after learning all of this. It was too much and too fast for me. A part of me was doing backflips learning his identity. But another part of me wished we were still at the sexting each other without our, well, his identity being known. I was beginning to feel like this was a mistake coming here and turned to leave.

"Wait, Candice. Please, don't go," he said. He sounded panicky. I could tell there was no way he was going to let me get away.

"I am into you woman, not just because of our racy texts, but from those where we talked about any and everything for hours on end. Along with reading your positive posts on your social media pages, watching your YouTube channel, I knew you were someone I wanted to be in the presence of. Your spirit is genuine. I can feel that even now, when you want to run away." He softly stroked my cheek with his hand.

"I'm sorry if my confession makes you uncomfortable. Please believe me, I wasn't, and I am not trying to deceive you. I just have to be careful. People are always trying to find some way to get close to me so they can try and get whatever the can from me. I don't nor have I ever thought this was the case with you."

"Why me? You can have any woman you want. So, what about me has you texting me all day every day for the past four months?" I asked in a shaky voice.

"Everything I've learned about you. From our texts to your social media pages, everything I've learned about you along with how beautiful you are is why you. Yes, I can have whatever woman I want, and I want you." He wrapped an arm around my waist pulling me into to him.

"I'm not sure I'd be a good fit in your world. I'm an around the way girl, straight from the hood. You, you're from the upper echelon. You grew up having the best of everything. I had to take the hand-me-downs from my sisters as we grew. So, Mr. Mcintosh, I'm not so sure we'd be good for each other. I'm not looking for a right now thing. I'm looking for my forever."

"And you don't think I already know everything you just said? I did a full background check on you before I replied to your text. I know where you're from and I know where I'm from. But where we're from has no effect on the right now. You can't stand here and tell me that you don't have feelings for me, that the past four months don't mean anything to you. I want you, Candice Larae Carson, around the way girl and all that comes with you."

He didn't give me a chance to say another word. He leaned down and kissed me before I could utter a word. He pulled me to his body and held me tightly as he deepened our kiss, sucking on my tongue gently then rough. I figured he had to shut my mind off so I could let this thing flow. It worked. I melted in his embrace. I dropped my purse on the floor and wrapped my arms around his neck. I stood on my tip toes to deepen our kiss more, if it were even possible. We sucked and nibbled on each other's tongues and lips. When we came up for air, I was ready for more than a kiss. I was ready to feel that steel between his legs that was pressing against my belly.

"Aah, aah, aah!" Shanell's voice can be heard screaming from one of the nearby rooms. Verdell and I stared at each other with wide eyes before bursting out in laughter.

"Well, we see they are getting to know each other very well," Bryant said.

"Yep, sounds like it," I replied. "Now can we go and do the same?"

"Oh, so eager now, aren't we?" Bryant joked.

"Very," I winked. "By the way, what do I call you? Verdell or Bryant?"

"Bryant or Verdell. Whatever you're comfortable with," he said as he bent down and picked up my purse.

Bryant grabbed my hand and led me out of the dining room and down the hall. We passed the room Shanell, and Bradford were in and could hear their grunts and moans very much so now. I couldn't tell who was putting it down on who because they both were moaning as if they were having the best sex of their lives. But their moans were making me just as horny. I was so ready to be calling out to Bryant the same way.

I couldn't wait until we were in his bedroom. Feeling bold, I tugged on Bryant's hand and stopped him halfway up the stairs. He turned to look at me and I pulled him down to my level. I fondled with his sweatpants, pulling them along with his boxers down to his ankles. I cooed at the site of his dick poking at me as if to say, 'I'm all yours.' I licked my lips then spat on the tip before sucking him into my mouth.

"Mmm," Bryant moaned as he watched me deep throat all of what looked like ten inches of him. I took him to the back of my throat and swallowed. "Sss, mmm," Bryant moaned out again.

I swallowed a couple more times. I took him out of my mouth and ran my tongue along the long vein that strained out. With one hand I massaged his balls as I bobbed up and down on his shaft. I moaned when I tasted his precum. He tasted of cinnamon, and it was turning me on so much that I reached between my legs and slid my fingers through the side of my thong and began playing with my clit.

"Candy, you're going to make me come," Bryant said.

Bryant watching me play with my pussy while giving him head was the sexiest thing ever. When I took him to the back of my mouth again then swallowed and moaned, he exploded in my mouth, squirting his seed down my throat. I swallowed it all without gagging. Bryant coming in my mouth caused me to have an orgasm behind him.

When I pulled him out of my mouth, Bryant had to take a seat on one of the steps. I knew I had his legs felling like noodles from my head game. I was still playing with my pussy, rubbing my nectar around my clit and pussy lips. I stood and pulled my thong off. I then pulled my dress off followed by my bra.

I stood before Bryant naked and vulnerable. I wasn't in the best shape. I still had a small pudge from when I was overweight. At one point I was over two hundred pounds but within the past year I'd lost over fifty pounds. I went from a size sixteen down to a size twelve. I made sure I rubbed coco butter on my body every day to keep the cellulite down to a minimum and only had three that just wouldn't go away. By the way Bryant was looking at me, I could tell he didn't care about any of that. The way he was staring at me made me feel as if I was the most beautiful woman in his eyes and seeing me naked had him rock hard in record time.

"Come here and sit that pretty pussy on my face." He pulled me to him as he leaned back on the stairs.

I straddled his face and moaned as soon as his tongue made contact with my now sensitive clit. I wrapped a hand around the railing and rode his face. He expertly lapped my honey as it oozed out of my honey cone. He had one hand on an ass cheek while the other stroked his dick. Verdell literally was putting his mark on my pussy as he spelled out his entire name on it.

"Ooh shit, yes Ver-uh-dell," I called out forgetting he said to call him Bryant. He only got to the 'E' in Verdell when I began coming on his tongue. "Aah, yes!" I rode his face faster, smearing all my juices over his face. That didn't stop him from continuing to fuck me with his tongue. I tried to lift up of him, but he refused to stop until he spelled out his full name on my pussy. By the time he got to the last letter in his last name, I had come two more times.

Verdell tapped my butt cheek and I lifted up off his face. I slid down and positioned my pussy at the head of his dick. I plopped down as he pumped up inside of me. "Uuh," we both said.

Right on the steps, Verdell and I fucked each other hard. I rode him fast and hard in a rowing method, moving back and forth as he pumped up in and out of me with that same intensity. Verdell latched on to one of my nipples and sucked on it. Having my breast suckled on always drove me crazy and the way Verdell was latched on had my fourth orgasm taking over.

"Damn, Candy! Ride this dick, baby! Fuck this dick!" Verdell said.

I rode his dick faster and harder. My legs began to shake as I came long and hard on his dick. My muscles clamped down on him and he damn near exploded too, but he held out.

"I don't want to come just yet." He waited until my legs stopped shaking before he lifted me off him and got behind me. "Here, put your knees on this so you won't get rug burn." Verdell pulled his t-shirt off, and I put it on the step.

As soon as I was situated, he plunged in me from behind then pulled out. "Aaah!" I cried out.

I wondered if this position was what had Shanell screaming out like this. Verdell repeated the process a couple more times then dug off in my pussy with quick but long strokes that hit my spot from every angle. "Oh god. I'm about to come again," I called out.

Verdell smacked my ass and I lost it. My legs shook faster than earlier. My walls sucked Verdell's dick in and latched on as I came. His dick had become a prisoner inside my cove and wouldn't be free until I came down from my sexual high. He continued to thrust in me, and I could feel his nut coming up.

"Squeeze harder on this dick. Make it yours, baby," Verdell said as he thrust harder in me. I squeezed my muscles harder around him and sucked him in further. "Shit, baby! Oh, Candice, I'm about to come in this pussy!" Verdell released in me what felt like buckets of his semen. Just like I did with my mouth when he came down my throat, my pussy sucked in all he released.

Verdell fell over on me and rain kisses on the side of my face. We were spent. Our bodies were dripped in sweat. We lay with him on top and still inside me as we tried to get our breathing under control. "That was great!" I admitted.

"That was miraculous," Verdell countered.

"It was a spectacular show, too," Shanell called up to us.

Verdell and I looked down to see Shanell bent over the table that sat smack in the center of the foyer with Brad behind her hitting it from the back. I guess they were on their way to his room when they were halted by Verdell and me getting our freak on, on the stairs. Knowing

Shanell's freaky ass, watching us having sex turned her on and it didn't take long for Brad to bend Shanell over on the table and enter her.

"Well damn," Verdell said as we were now viewers of a live porn flick. We watched as Brad placed one of Shanell's legs on the table and rode her fast. Shanell held on to the edge of the table tossing her ass back on him.

I could feel Verdell growing hard inside me so I squeezed my muscles around him. "Mmm, you ready for another round, too?" Verdell asked as he slowly moved in and out of me.

"Yes, but can we go on up to your room?" I said not taking my eyes off the other couple getting it on.

"Yes, but I want you to come on my dick first. That shit feels so damn good," Verdell moaned in my ear. He pumped harder and before you know it, there were nothing but moans and groans coming from both couples as we watched each other fuck to our next climaxes.

Shanell was the first to come followed by me. Just hearing Shanell's moans made me come but it was Verdell's thrusts on my g-spot that took me over the edge. I was pleasantly surprised at how he learned of my g-spot so quickly and knew just the right amount of friction to put there and on her clit at the same time to bring me to a mind-blowing orgasm. With both Shanell and I crying out in unison making a beautiful ballad, both brothers released inside of us at the same time.

"Shit, Candy!"

"Fuck, Shanell!"

We all were done. I couldn't believe we just had sex in front of each other that way. At the same time, I was thinking how exotic it was. After several minutes of catching our breaths, each couple ventured off to their respective rooms. Verdell and I went into his bedroom and took a long hot shower together that consisted of round three before we fell asleep in bed in each other's arms. I'm not sure what went down with Brad and Shanell after we parted ways but I'm sure they went another round or two before they too fell asleep in each other's arms.

The next morning, Verdell woke me up by way of his face buried between my legs. As soon as he brought me to a mind-blowing orgasm, he slid in me and fucked me to another one. Afterwards we took a shower and got dressed. I put back on the clothes I'd worn over the night before while Verdell put on a tailor-made power suit. We met Shanell and Brad in the dining room where we all had breakfast together and made small talk. Bryant's housekeeper, Momma Fe, was kind to us. She actually reminded me of Mrs. Piercing. Once we were done eating, the men escorted Shanell and me to my car and kissed us goodbye, promising to see us later.

"Bitch, I'm so glad your ass sent that text message to the wrong damn number!" Shanell exclaimed once we were on the road heading home.

"Who you telling? Girl, me too!" I shook my head. My pussy pulsated just thinking about last night and this morning's events.

"That was the best sex I ever had!" Shanell ranted. "And who'd thought you had some freak in you? Yeah, I saw you checking me and Brad out."

"What did you expect? Shit y'all were butt ass naked on the damn table getting it on! Hell yeah, I was looking, and that shit turned me on! You know I never was into porn flicks but watching y'all did something to me. But then again, I did have a big dick that was still inside my pussy at the time. Hell, I'm with you on that best sex ever. Verdell fucked me better than any other guy I've been with and I'm not afraid to say he got a bitch hooked!" I ranted and raved.

Shanell and I laughed and discussed last night on the way home. I had just pulled up at Shanell's house when both of our phones chimed. We looked at each other, then their phones.

Verdell: Hey beautiful. I had a great time last night and this morning.

Candy: Hey handsome. So did I

Verdell: Can I see u 2nite?

Candy: Of course…what time?

Verdell: I'll pick u up at 7:30. I placed a little something in your purse…

Verdell: go get something nice to wear to a gala function, but don't wear panties

Candy: Oh wow! Thnx babe and don't worry, I'm gonna be classy and sexy for ya muah!

Verdell: I can't wait to see u

I looked over at Shanell typing away message after message. I assumed it was Brad the way that smiled filled her face. I leaned over on my door and waited until she was done. "So, what he say?" I asked.

"Nosey ass," Shanell joked. "But since you're the reason for all this, I guess you can read them." She handed me her phone.

Brad: Hey sexy...so glad u came with ur girl last night...wasn't expecting that

Shanell: Hey urself....so glad I came as well...wasn't expecting any of that either

Brad: I wanna see where we can take this...you down or was it just a fun nite 4 u

Shanell: Oh, I'm down.... funny how the wrong number turned out to be the right number

Brad: ikr....so I want u to go to this gala with me tonight...u down

Shanell: Sure

Brad: b at your girl's spot....my bro and I will pick y'all up there.

Shanell: aight

Brad: I'm gonna have a courier bring u something.... go get a sexy as dress for tonight

Shanell: Well alright then!

Shanell: I'm gonna b so sexy u just might want to give another live performance

Brad: lol I'll c u 2nite sexy

Shanell: indeed handsome

"Damn, you turned his ass out, huh?" I joked.

"Candy, we have officially arrived, thanks to your wrong number ass!" Shanell joked.

We chopped it up for a few more minutes then hugged it out. I pulled off on my way home for some much-needed sleep. As I drove, I thanked my spiritual maker for crossing my path with Verdell's. I didn't know if what we had would last long, but this time around I decided not to worry about the what ifs and just live in the moment. Shit had I not sexted the wrong number, I would not have gotten sexed the way I did last night and this morning.

My gas light dinged and popped on. "Shit!" I was so excited about meeting Verdell, I forgot to fill up my gas tank. I pulled up to the pump at the first gas station I came to. Being that I was still in the hood, I checked my surroundings before getting out of the car. Living in this area for most of my life, I knew how it could go down if you got caught slipping. I would just get enough to get me to my side of town. I took my credit card out of my wallet and got out. I just placed the nozzle in the tank and started it when a tall, dark-skinned woman walked up on me.

"What were you doing at Bryant's house? And don't lie. I saw you pull out of his estate a little while ago."

I looked the woman up and down. It took a minute, but I realized who she was. I hadn't seen her in several months. Even before everything going on with Jevar, she hadn't been to the shop to get her normal full day spa services. Now I see why. Trinity Blackshear was a junkie. One of my nail techs had expressed their concern after seeing track marks between her toes while giving her a pedicure. I explained to the technician as long as she wasn't doing in my place of business and she had the money to pay for her services, it was none of our business. However, I did hold a meeting and reminded all of my employees who frequently provided her service to wear gloves and to use caution. I did her hair and from the looks of it, she hadn't been back since I last did it about six months ago.

I was wondering what her relationship to Verdell was. I decided to play it cool and feel her out. Something was telling me though, her questioning wasn't going to go over well with the answers I provided.

"Trinity, hey! I haven't seen you in a while. You haven't been to the spa in a long time. How have you been?"

"I'm great! I've been busy. Now answer my question. What were you doing leaving Bryant's house?"

"How do you know Bryant? Have you spoken to him about why I was there?"

"Bryant is my fiancé and I need to know if you're sleeping with him! Because if you are, I'm gonna kick your ass!"

"Whoa, Trinity. It's not that type of party. I was there with Shanell. Bryant and I have nothing going on. I was just keeping him company while Shanell and Bradford were getting to know each other." I thought it was best I tweaked the truth a little bit. I didn't want to set her off and I certainly didn't want to be fighting.

"Oh? Really now. Then why didn't you ride in her car instead of you driving yours?"

"Since I drove over to her house, I just decided to drive instead of us switching cars. It was no biggie." I turned and stopped the nozzle. I placed it back on the pump and placed the cap back on the tank. "Well, it was good seeing you, Trinity. Take care of yourself."

I didn't wait for an answer. I just hopped back in my car and locked my doors. I put my seatbelt on and started my engine. I put the gear in drive and was about to pull off when she knocked on my window. I let the window down half-way to see what she wanted.

"Just so you know, if I find out you're lying to me, we will have a problem," Trinity said.

"Just so you know, I don't take kindly to threats so don't come for me unless I send for you."

"I wonder if Jevar knows you're creeping around on him. Maybe I should let him know what you're up to."

"Trinity, before you go flapping your gums about something you know nothing about, you need to rethink that thought. I'd hate for you to come in contact with a bad batch of the shit you been shooting up. I'd hate to watch the news and see a story about you overdosing. Now you have yourself a good rest of your day." I pulled off with a fuming Trinity standing there looking stupid.

I couldn't believe my ears! Did she really say Bryant was her fiancé? Surely there had to be some mistake. Why would he lie and tell me he wasn't seeing anyone? This was the type of shit I wanted to avoid and why I wanted to stick to the texts. I had to find out for myself. I pressed the one on my phone to speed dial Bryant's number.

"Hello, Beautiful," he said. I could hear the smile in his words.

"Something interesting just happened to me."

"Oh and what was it?"

"I ran into your fiancé, Trinity Blackshear, at the gas station. She saw me leaving your place and followed me."

"Oh my god. Candice, I assure you, Trinity and I are no longer engaged and have not been for six months now. She cheated on me and she was, well still is, on drugs. I tried to get her help but she refused. Because of that I couldn't be with her," Verdell explained.

"I could tell she was high. She looked so different. She used to frequent my spa and I did her hair. Look, Verdell, I mean, Bryant, I have to get used to calling you that. But I can't do this with you. I have a lot going on and by the looks of it, so do you. I don't need anything else adding to my drama. She threatened me, you know."

"Baby, I promise you, I will handle Trinity. She will not bother you again," Verdell assured me.

"Please don't make promises you can't keep."

We remained on the phone in silence as I drove. I could hear him typing on his computer. I didn't want to hang up and I guess he didn't either. It was too early in this situationship to be having drama. Hell, it was too early in the morning for drama period. That's how it started with Jevar and me. I refused to go through that again. It was in my best interest to end it.

"Look, Bryant, it's best if we parted ways now. I can't go through another toxic relationship. We aren't even in a relationship and we're already in some mess. I can't do that again. So, I respectfully decline your invitation for tonight. Thanks for last night. It was definitely one I'll never forget."

"Don't I have a say so in the matter?"

"No. This is my decision."

"That's not fair to me, Candice. I like you and I want to see where this thing goes between us. It's only right we pursue it. I don't know why Trinity told you we were together, because we are not. I can't let you walk away like this, not after last night."

"I hear you, Bryant, but"

"But are you listening?" He asked cutting me off.

"I'm listening as well, but the fact remains that you have some baggage that needs to be handled. Once you get that taken care of as I too handle my baggage, there is no us. It's too much and I can't deal. Goodbye, Bryant." I hung up before he could say another word.

Chapter 13

Shanell

Brad: Hey sexy...so glad u came with ur girl last night...wasn't expecting that

Me: Hey urself....so glad I came as well...wasn't expecting any of that either

Brad: I wanna see where we can take this...you down or was it just a fun nite 4 u

Me: Oh, I'm down.... funny how the wrong number turned out to be the right number

Brad: ikr....so I want u to go to this gala with me tonight...u down

Me: Sure

Brad: b at your girl's spot....my bro and I will pick y'all up there.

Me: aight

Brad: I'm gonna have a courier bring u something…. go get a sexy ass dress for tonight

Me: Well alright then!

Me: I'm gonna b so sexy u just might want to give another live performance

Brad: lol I'll c u 2nite sexy

Me: indeed handsome

"Candy, we have officially arrived, thanks to your wrong number ass!" l joked.

We both laughed and hugged it out. I told Candy I'd see her later then hopped out of the car. I ran inside my townhouse and tossed my purse on the sofa. I started stripping out of my clothes as I made my way to my bedroom. I had just stepped out of my panties and was walking in my bathroom when my doorbell rang. My first thought was Candy turned around and came back for something. But the banging on my door and the ringing of the bell at the same time told otherwise.

I grabbed my robe and wrapped myself with it as I padded to the front door. I let out a groan when I looked through the peephole and saw it was Jevar. I didn't tell Candy, but he had been coming by almost every day now looking for her. He refused to believe I knew where she was staying. I kept telling him I didn't know but it seemed his patience was running out. I hoped he didn't see her dropping me off.

I know I did some fowl shit in the past by fucking with Jevar. But I blame Candy for sharing the business on how he was putting it down in the bed. Hell, I was curious and wanted to see if she was just talking shit or if it was all facts. She wasn't lying at all! Jevar can lay some pipe and hooked a sista up when I wasn't kicking it with someone at the time. After Candy found out, though, I realized how fucked up of a friend I was. She stopped speaking to me for a while behind my actions. She didn't deserve that from me. She had always been there when I needed her most. I stopped fucking with Jevar after she found out. But he always made attempts to get at me. I've refused his advances and that was pissing him off even more.

"Open the door, Shanell. I know you're there," Jevar called out.

"What do you want, Jevar?" I swung the door opened. I stood there with my hands on my hips mean mugging him.

Jevar was fine as they get. His thugged out swag made him even sexier. But to know he was abusive made him so damn ugly. He never hit me while we were messing around but the bruising on Candy told me all I needed to know. That was definitely another reason I stopped fucking around with him. I wasn't Candy and I wasn't about to be his punching bag. I'm a different kind of crazy and would hate to end up behind bars because of his bitch ass.

"I came to check on you and see if you heard from Candy. I don't believe you saying you don't know where she's at. It's been damn near six months and you trying to tell me you don't know where she staying at."

"That's exactly what I'm telling you. She only text me from a blocked number. I've tried my best to get some information out of her as to where she's staying but I get nothing."

I gave Jevar a good look as he paced back and forth on the porch. He wore a black Atlanta Falcons jersey, baggy black jeans that hung off his ass, and a pair of throwback black and red Jordans. His handsome face bore a scowl. But he actually looked concerned more so than angry. I've been trying to wrap around my mind why he wants Candy back so badly when he only mistreated her when he had her. Men are so full of shit! They never miss a good thing until it's gone.

"Look Jevar, I have to go."

"Shanell, you need to stop lying to me about Candy. I know your black ass know where she at. I just don't understand why you keep feeding me this bullshit! You really think I'm one of those dumb muthafuckas you be fucking with."

Jevar stopped pacing and stood glaring at me. He hands were balled into a fist at his sides and for the first time I was afraid of him. He had a look I had never seen before, like a maniac.

"I'm sorry you think that but I'm telling the truth. And you know I don't lie. I'm sorry Candy hasn't told me anything. I don't know where she is, Jevar. I got to go." I stepped back so I could close the door when he shoved his way in.

"Since you won't tell me where she is, I have a way to bring her to you," Jevar said.

He slapped me so hard across my face knocking me to the floor. I felt dazed. My right cheek swelled up immediately. I scrambled to get up but was stopped by a kick to my face. The back of my head hit my hardwood floor hard. Jevar began kicking and punching every part of my body. At one point I could no longer hear in my right ear and my left eye was completely shut from the swelling. Before long I could no longer feel the punches or kicks and not too much longer, I passed out.

Jevar

I tried to stomp a whole in that bitch! I knew she was lying. As much as Shanell and Candy talked, I know at some point Candy mentioned where she was staying at. Even if she wasn't lying, I still needed to put her ass in her place. I stomped and kicked until I was out of breath. Then I pulled my gun out of its holster, took the silencer out of my pocket, screwed it on, and put two bullets in her head.

As I looked down at Shanell's lifeless body in disgust, I unscrewed the silencer before placing it and my gun back in their holsters. I turned to leave and when I noticed her purse. I grabbed her purse off the sofa, stuck it under my shirt, and made my way back to my truck. Once I was inside my truck, I unzipped the purse and poured the contents onto the passenger seat. I grabbed her cellphone and tried to open it but it was locked.

"Fuck!" I banged my fist on the steering wheel. I just can't catch a break!

I tossed the phone back on the seat then pulled off. I pulled into the gas station to go take a piss and grab a bag of chips. As soon as I stepped out, some homeless chic was in my face. I had to put my hand to push her as away from me. I almost punched the bitch because I thought she was trying to rob me.

"Back the fuck up!"

"I'm, I'm sorry. I need your help," she said.

"Here." I pulled out the money from my pocket and peeled off a fifty. I tossed it to her. "Now get the fuck away from me."

I started to for the entrance when she bent down to pick up the money from the ground. She ran behind me as I entered the store, thinking she was about to go buy her ass something to eat, but she followed behind me towards the bathrooms.

"What the fuck you following me for?" She bumped into my back when I abruptly stopped walking. I spun around to face her with a scowl on my face. "What the fuck do you want?"

"I have information about your bitch."

"What bitch?"

"Candy."

Now this got my attention. I looked her over and noticed the oversized suit she wore that looked expensive. She probably got that from the Goodwill or some shit, but looking at her face, I could tell at some point in her life, she kept her appearance up. She was skinny as hell, and needed to get her hair done, but she didn't smell the way she looked. One would have thought she'd smell like ass but she didn't. As a matter of fact, she looked familiar.

"You hungry?"

"Y-yeah."

"Let me take a piss then we can go eat."

I turned in went into the bathroom. Standing at the stall, I whipped my mans out and relieved myself. I wondered what information she had on Candy. I tried not to get too excited since I didn't know what she knew. But the thought of finally getting a step closer to finding Candy made my dick hard. I shook my shit then placed him back inside my boxers and zipping my pants. I walked over to the sink and quickly washed my hands. When I left out of the bathroom the chic wasn't there and I was about to be pissed off that she dipped but I found her ass leaning against my truck.

I popped the locks with the key fob and we hopped in. We rode in silence as I made my way to the nearest Waffle House. When we got there, we took a seat in the booth in the back. The waitress came over and took our orders. I waited until the waitress came back with our cups of coffee.

"Aight, talk," I commanded

"I went to my fiancé's house last night, but he didn't answer. I knew he was home because there was an unfamiliar car in the driveway. So, I sat outside of the gate to see who it was that came out the next day."

She stopped talking as she stirred in the creamer and sugar she'd just poured into the coffee. It was like she needed to concentrate strictly on that. I scooted down in my seat and ran a hand down my face. I was one with little patience and this was starting to work my nerves.

"This morning, Candice and her friend that does makeup came strolling out the front door, doing the walk of shame with Bryant and Bradford trailing them. Bryant kissed Candice before she got in her car and left. I followed her to her friend's house, then to the gas station we were just at."

I sat staring at this broad taking in what she just said. So both of them bitches done started fucking some other niggas and Candy fucking him? First, she does a disappearing act, then she pops up with another nigga? I knew Shanell's bitch ass was lying. I'm so glad I dead that trifling hoe. When I say my blood was boiling. I was seeing red. But then a thought ran through my mind.

"So, how the fuck you following somebody but now you on foot? And if yo ass got a car, why you walking around here looking like a bum?"

The waitress came over and placed the Texas cheesesteak melt with hash browns scattered, covered, smothered, and capped in front of me before placing the pecan waffle and scrambled eggs with cheese Infront of ole girl.

"Y'all need something else?" The waitress asked.

"I'll take some more coffee," Ole girl said.

"Nah, I'm good," I told her with a mouthful of hash browns.

"I just told you I sat outside of Bryant's house all night, so I haven't changed clothes yet. And I never said I didn't have a car, nor did I say I was homeless. You just assumed that." She smirked.

She spread the butter over her waffle with the butterknife. She then poured a shit load of syrup over it. My blood sugar shot up seeing how much she poured. I gulped the remainder of my coffee down as she ate. For some reason I was now having mixed emotions about the shit she

148

was telling me. Like for starters, what was the reason she was walking around looking homeless if, in fact, she wasn't? And how did she know me and Candice? This was starting to feel like a setup. For her sake, this bitch better not be on some bullshit, or her ass will be joining Shanell.

"What did you say your name was again?"

"I never said, but it's Trinity."

"Trinity, how do you know me and Candice?"

"A while back I used to frequent Candyland, and Candice used to do my hair."

"Really? Well, what the fuck happened to you that got you looking like that?"

"Life."

"What do you want from me, Trinity? Because you saying it's about your man, but I feel like you have another agenda. What kind of shit you up to?"

"I'm loyal. I'm extremely loyal and I expect that back. So, like I know something about Bryant McIntosh that could crumble his whole empire and fuck up his pristine reputation."

Trinity forked up the remainder of eggs and ate them. She eyed me as she chewed her food and swallowed. She sat the fork on her now empty plate, then wiped her mouth with a napkin.

"I also know you were just at Shanell's house. I saw you push your way through her door. And fyi, you might want to get rid of those shoes you're wearing as well as those jeans. You have some blood on them."

She leaned over the table as far as she could and whispered so low, I barely heard what she said.

I nodded my head, never changing my facial expression. I had no clue as to how, why, shit just kept going left for me. It was one thing after another. Trinity must not have known who the fuck I was and that I wasn't the one to be fucked with. There's something in the air these muthafuckas inhaling that got them acting out of character. I see they testing my gangsta and I'm not having it. It's time I show these fuckas who the fuck Jevar is.

"Oh, so you blackmailing me or something?"

"I think we can help each other with a problem or more so, a person we both have a problem with. You're looking for your woman and I can lead you to her. You will have her, and I will have him. I see a win-win for the both of us," Trinity smiled deviously.

"And you think telling me you saw me at Shanell's house will make me help you?"

"Well, I think that would push you in the right direction to want to help me. I mean, if you had done something to that woman, you wouldn't want anyone finding out and being that I am a witness, well." She hunched her shoulders.

"Well, what? What you fail to realize about me, is that I'm a real G. I have no problem making sure you're not a witness and I can do that without helping you do a damn thing."

I reached in my pocket and peeled off a couple of twenty- dollar bills. I stood and placed the rest of my money back in my pocket. The waitress came over with the ticket. I handed her the money and told her to keep the change. I leaned down to Trinity who still sat in the booth. I whispered in her ear so that no one heard what I said.

"Bitch, if you even dream about me being at Shanell's house today, I'll kill you and send your body in pieces to your family. Keep your fucking mouth closed." I stood straight then patted her on the back. "It was good seeing you, Trinity. Take care of yourself."

I left her ass in the restaurant, hopped in my truck, and spun off out of the parking lot. I headed to get rid of the clothes and boots I wore and to do some research on this Bryant McIntosh dude. I already had plans to get rid of Trinity, but not until I got the information she had on him. This could be my ticket to the top.

Chapter 14

Candy

Me: U r not gon believe what happened after I dropped you off. I know u sleep so I'll hit u up l8r

I didn't bother to check my phone to see if Shanell responded to my message because I knew she was sleep within fifteen minutes of me dropping her off. I plugged the charger into my phone then sat it on the nightstand. I stripped out of my clothes, then tossed them into the hamper. I turned the water and shower nozzles on, and as I waited for the water to get hot, I stepped over to the sink and began to brush my teeth.

When I finished rinsing my mouth with mouthwash, I stepped into the shower and welcomed the feel of the hot water beating down on my body. The way the water hit my body sent chills down my spine with thoughts of Verdell and what we did last night and just a little while ago. I could still feel his hands all over my body, and the things he did with his tongue, my damn! My kitty clenched when flashes of that big pole of steel crossed my mind.

My body was immediately aroused by those thoughts, and I gave it my attention, grabbing my breast and squeezing them. I pinched my nipples and moaned at the sensation. I ran a hand down my belly and to my hotspot, slipping two fingers inside of my sugar walls. I rotated my hips gyrating on my fingers at the same time I moved them in and out. Quickly finding my g-spot, I gave it the attention needed, stroking my fingers there with just the right amount of pressure. I steadied myself with my free hand on the shower wall. I grind my pussy on my fingers faster, feeling my orgasm making its way to the forefront. My toes began to tingle, and my legs began to shake just as my orgasm shot through me with a vengeance pushing my fingers out of me.

"Oh, mmm," I let out, creaming all over my fingers. My sensitive bud throbbed from the pleasurable orgasm. I placed both hands on the shower wall as I got my breathing under control.

"Whew," I shook my head.

I grabbed my loofah and body wash and began to wash up. Once I was done, I dried off and oiled my body down. I went back into the bedroom and pull a black tank top that had "It Girl" in pink and the matching boy shorts out. I put them on then dived in bed pulling the covers over my head. Within minutes I was asleep.

Someone shaking me and calling my name caused me to stir from my sleep. I slowly moved the covers from over my face to find Mrs Piercing standing next to my bed with tears streaming down her face. I immediately became fully awake and sat up.

"Mrs. Piercing, what's wrong?"

A myriad of emotions flashed across her face, but sorrow and fear seemed to be the two that were noticeable. She was struggling to get her words out. It was as if she was trying to speak for the first time but didn't know how to form her words. She finally plopped down on the bed, holding her hands to her chest while rocking back and forth.

"Mrs. Piercing, please, what is it? You're scaring me."

"Shanell, oh Lord!" She shook her head back and forth.

"Shanell? What about her Mrs. Piercing? Tell me what's going on."

"She's been murdered!" Mrs. Piercing blurted.

"No! What are you talking about? We were just together, and she was fine. That must have been someone who looked like her," I said. I grabbed my phone and input my passcode to call Shanell but stopped when I heard Mrs. Piercing's next set of words.

"It was her, Candice. Shanell Turner is the name they said. Someone beat, then shot her."

"No, no, no. That's not true!" I shook my head at her. Tears poured down my face. Mrs. Piercing saddened eyes told me everything.

"I'm so sorry, Candice."

My phone lit up in my hand indicating I had a call. I always placed it on silent when I slept. Shanell's mom's, Gertrude, name popped up on my screen and I knew then Mrs. Piercing's announcement was confirmed. I slid my finger across the screen to answer and slowly raised the phone to my ear.

"Momma Gertrude?"

"Candice, she's gone! My baby's gone!"

The phone dropped from my hand, and I wailed out a sound that was so painful, my body shook. Mrs. Piercing slid up so that she could wrap her arms around me in an embrace. Once again, I cried on her shoulders for the pain and drama that has taken over my life. I knew this had Jevar's name written all over this. There was no other explanation behind her sudden death. My friend died protecting me.

I didn't tell Shanell where I was staying, hoping this would keep her out of my drama with Jevar, but apparently that didn't work. He knew how close we were and that we told each other everything so I am sure he never believed her when he asked her of my whereabouts. Jevar has really underestimated me. I knew how he got down and knew drastic measures had to be taken to be rid of him. However, I underestimated him not thinking he would harm Shanell. I definitely didn't think he would kill her.

"Hello," I heard coming from my phone. I ended the embrace with Mrs. Piercing and scooped my phone back up placing it back to my ear.

"I'm sorry Momma G. What happened? Does the police have a suspect in custody?"

"I went by to take her some of this new coffee I came across and to check on her since I hadn't seen her in a few days. You know I always ring the bell instead of using my key, but she never came to the door."

She let out a sigh before she continued.

"I used my key to let myself in and I found her laying right there on the floor. There, there was so much blood," she said that last part in a whisper.

"The police said it was someone who knew her that could have done this since there were no signs of an invasion. I don't know who would want to do this to her. Do you know who could have done this, Candice?"

There it was. The question of the day I knew everyone was going to turn to me looking for the answer. I will no longer be able to hide from Jevar after what I am sure he is responsible for. I had to do what I had to do to make sure my friend received the justice she deserved. Yes, we had our ups and downs, and yes, she violated the sister/friend code and slept with my man, but I forgave her. Regardless she didn't deserve to be killed all because Jevar was controlling and abusive towards me. But because I knew he had some cops in his pockets, I didn't want to reveal him just yet. I needed to carefully plan out my next moves so that I can make sure he is held accountable and will serve real time for her death.

"Momma Gertrude, I am trying to figure that out just like you are. If I find out anything, I will definitely take it to the police. Who is the detective assigned to her case?"

"A Detective John Shingles. I gave him your name and phone number so I am sure he will be contacting you soon."

"Oh, okay. Do you need anything? Do you need me to come to you?"

"Nah, baby. What I need, no one can give me. I just want my child here and alive. Plus, Rashad and David are here with me. I'll keep you posted on the arrangements." She immediately began to sob.

"Momma G take care of yourself and I'll see you at the service. You call me if you need me for anything, though okay?"

"Okay, baby."

We hung up from each other and I just sat there numb from it all. I couldn't wrap my mind around the fact that my best friend is no longer here. Like we were just together, spending a glorious night with two of the finest and richest men. And just like that, with a snap of my fingers, she's gone. Now who will I be able to talk to and spill all of my insecurities, all my dreams and desires to, and not get judged? My sisters and I aren't that close so they're not an option. My mom is too fragile to talk to about my issues, and as much as I love Mrs. Piercing, she's a second mother to me so she was out of the question as well.

"Did Jevar do that to Shanell?"

My head snapped up to look at Mrs. Piercing at the question that came out of nowhere. Her face was contorted into a scowl. She looked as if she was about to pull out on him and let it rip. Her eyes were red and swollen from crying. But they were also cold. Her usually made-up face was makeup free, but she still had a gorgeous face. However, I could also tell she had been through some shit in her life.

"Don't lie to me. Did. Jevar. Do. This?"

"I believe so," I answered honestly.

"Do you understand the realms of this situation, Candice? This man is doing whatever to get to you. He did that to her because he knew that would bring you out of hiding. He's desperate at this point now. He won't stop until he finds you. Are you ready for whatever he's going to come with now? For the past few months, you've been going about your business as if you're not on the run from this fool and now he's about to be on your ass! Now, I gave you a place to stay, but this right here, I don't know."

I looked confused at what she just said. I have taken every precaution to keep my whereabouts hidden. Did she not understand that was why he killed Shanell? Because she didn't have any information to give him about me?

"What are you saying, Mrs. Piercing? Do you want me to leave? I assure you I haven't been doing anything besides working and being here. Last night was the first time since I've been here that I actually went out. The last four months of my life have been to the hideaway shop to do hair and coming back here. Shanell never knew where I was staying, nor did she know about the shop because I knew he was pressuring her to give him some information. But if you feel like this too much for you, I'll leave. I never wanted to bring you any drama, and I do not want anything to happen to you."

"I don't want you to leave, Candice. What I want is for you to understand what is really going on. Let me tell you. I was married twice. Once briefly before my marriage to Stanley. I thought Harvey was the love of my life. We met my junior year in high school. My dad was in the military, so we moved around quite a bit. Being the new girl in school all eyes were on me as I made my way down the hall trying to find my class. Harvey came up to me and introduced his self to me.

I was smitten. He had dark chocolate and smooth skin. He was tall and muscles galore. And that smile! Oh, that smile melted my panties off. From that day, we were the it couple. I became popular just by being his girlfriend and when he graduated high school and went off to college at NCCU, that made me more popular for having a boyfriend in college." She shook her head at the memory.

"Anyway, what looked good on the outside was anything but that. It started one night after one of the football games. It was against our rival high school. The game was intense as the teams were going toe to toe with touchdowns. The other team was a point ahead because the kicker missed one of the field goal kicks. There were just seconds left in the fourth quarter and we had the ball. The ball was snapped and one of the guys on the other team rushed Harvey knocking the ball out of his hand before he could toss the ball. It caused a fumble, and the other team recovered the ball. That was the play that caused us to lose that game.

Harvey was pissed and he took his anger out on me. I tried to console him on the loss, but he was not hearing anything I said. For every positive word I spoke over him, he had some negative to refute me. And as soon as we got to his house, he went in on me. His parents were out for the night, so he had free reign to manhandle me. He slapped me so hard across my face, his handprint was left. I was in total shock. I had never seen that side of him before. I was speechless."

By now Mrs. Piercing was up and slowly pacing my room. Tears slowly streamed her face. I sat in silent listening to her pouring her soul out to me. To say I was shocked about what she was telling me was an understatement. I never would have imagined her to be in an abusive relationship, especially not while they were in high school. I couldn't fathom how anyone would want to hurt her. She was one of the nicest and most down to earth people you'd ever meet. So, for anyone to hurt her physically, hell verbally, would make anybody want to mess up some stuff behind her. However, I patiently sat in my bed waiting for her to continue her story.

"After that day, whenever he had a bad game or day, he took all his frustrations out on me. My best friend, Tanya was the only one who knew and she begged me millions of times to leave him, but what she didn't understand was I had to get to a point where I was sick and tired. It wouldn't be until we were married six months and I was eight weeks pregnant, that I was sick and tired.

Harvey came home from work, angry about something that happened between him and a coworker. He walked in and slammed the door. From the smell of the alcohol spilling out of his pores, I knew he stopped by the bar before coming home. Sweat poured down his face and his clothes looked disheveled.

He came into the kitchen where I was preparing dinner and began to go in about the food smelling like shit and slapped all the pots onto the floor. Food and the juices splattered everywhere even getting on my face, clothes, and hair. The heat left a scar above my left eye for a long time. But before I could react to the burn from the food on my face, Harvey backhanded me.

I went flying to the floor and that's when his boot came down on my face. He stomped, kicked, and punched my body until I lost consciousness. When I woke up, I had been in the hospital for a week. Tanya and my parents were there. They broke the news to me that I lost my baby. That was the straw that broke the camel's back. Out of the bitter, nasty situation I was in, the baby was what brought sunshine and rainbows to my life. The fact that it was taken away from me by that man's hands enraged me."

She finally stopped pacing and sat back on the bed. She turned and folded one leg on the bed with the other hung off with her foot on the floor. The anger that spewed from her scared me. This was a first. Her face contorted into a look I can't even describe. Her chest heaved up and down as she breathed heavily. My mouth opened and closed to speak but no words came out.

"Do you know that bastard didn't come see me once while I was in the hospital? Not once! But you know, I wasn't even upset. I put all my attention and time into getting well. When I was finally discharged from the hospital, I went to stay with Tanya. I went to the courthouse and filed for a divorce, a restraining order, and submitted paperwork for a weapon's permit. I then went and bought a gun. I went to the gun range and learned how to shoot. I knew I had to be ready for Harvey when he came for me.

When he received the divorce papers, he started blowing up my phone leaving nasty threatening voicemails. I saved every last one of them as proof I knew I was going to need in the future. When he finally caught up to me, Tanya and I were out to lunch on one of her rare days off. Harvey made a scene about the divorce paper and the restraining order. I had Tanya call the police since he violated the restraining order.

He wasn't supposed to be within a hundred feet of me, yet he was in my face calling me every name but what it was.

The police came and arrested him, but he was out the next day. A week hadn't past before he began to stalk me. But I was ready for him."

"What do you mean by that?"

"What I mean is I was ready to dead his ass for what he did to me to make me lose my baby. I waited until it was dusk and made my way to the park. I dressed as if I was working out. I had a fanny pack with my gun, permit, license, a copy of the restraining order, and my key in it. I put my headphones on my ear and I began to walk around the trail. I spoke to everyone I passed. I even held a conversation with a police officer who told me I had an hour to be out of the park. I assured him I was just going to do one lap around the trail since I knew I was late getting out there. He advised me he'd wait until I got back around before he left. That was all I needed as I got my walk on.

I was half-way around the trail when Harvey jumped out of the bushes in front of me. He cursed me out calling me all kinds of bitches. He went in on me. I allowed him to beat my ass, strip my jacket off me, and when he had me on the ground, I pulled my gun out of my fanny pack and shot him in his chest."

I gasped at that. I mean, yeah, I should have figured that was going to be the end result, but I didn't think she was going to actually confess that. My hand automatically went to my chest on my heart as I tried to calm my fast-beating heart down. My mouth was open and became dry all of a sudden. Mrs. Piercing reached over and grabbed my free hand and held it in her hands.

"Candice, I did what I had to do to be rid of Harvey. After the gunshot went off, the police officer I talked to earlier came out and helped me. I told him what happened even though him seeing me beat up and, on the ground, pretty much told everything. That restraining order and the arrest report got me off with self-defense. They didn't press charges since there was a paper trail. That's my story and my truth. What is yours?"

I raised an eyebrow wondering what she meant. Was she telling me to kill Jevar? I'm no killer. Heck, I've never held a gun in my hand. Jevar has done me wrong, and I knew I needed to be away from him, but killing him was something I could not do, and I told her so.

"Mrs. Piercing, I can't kill Jevar. I'm not a killer. I'm too afraid to even pick up a gun."

"I'm not telling you to kill anyone. But think about this; if it came down to your life or his, and you're going to find yourself in that position sooner than you think, are you willing to lose your life or take his in self-defense? Just think about it." She patted my hand then stood and stretched. Without another word, she left my room, quietly closing the door behind her.

I sat in my bed with so many questions running through my mind and so many emotions flowing through my body. I ran a hand through my hair thinking back on how I ended up here in this moment. As much as I want to blame Jevar for everything that has happened, I can't. I have to admit that had I left the moment I found that woman's bodywash in his bathroom, I wouldn't be in this predicament. I'm no dummy. I knew he was no good for me, yet I stayed in that relationship.

That's the biggest mistake we as women do. We stay in an abusive relationship or in a relationship we're not happy in but for what? For love? Shit, Tina was right to ask 'what's love got to do with it'. The signs were always there but instead of acknowledging those signs, we put on those rose-colored stained glasses to block our visions of them. We ignore the red flags waving at us, warning us of what was ahead. And just like Mrs. Piercing's situation, we don't get a wakeup call until we're placed in an it's either you or me type position.

I don't want to be with Jevar anymore. I'm done with the fighting and arguing over nothing. I want to be loved, to love back, and be in love. I want to come home to a peaceful sanctuary, be welcomed by the sexy smile of my man whose adores me. I want to welcome him home in nothing but an apron and a pair of the sexiest stilettos. Then we'd have a romantic, candlelight dinner before we curl up on the sofa to watch our favorite show before our hands start to roam each other's bodies. That would lead to a little bit of fourplay then a night of lovemaking. That's what I wanted, deserved. But that was just a dream that has yet to come true. The ding of my phone indicating a message came in brought me out of my thoughts.

Verdell: Are you okay? I just heard about Shanell on the news.

Me: No not okay...my best friend is gone

Verdell: where are you

Me: home

Verdell: Can I come see you? I don't want you to be alone

Verdell: Or you can come to me

Me: I'll come to you

Verdell: bring an overnight bag. I'm gonna take good care of you tonight.

Me: don't you have the gala tonight?

Verdell: I'm not going. You are more important

I got tired of texting and pressed the button to call him to finish the conversation. I put the phone on speaker and began to make up my bed. The phone rang only once before he answered.

"Hey, beautiful."

"Hey."

"I'm finishing up here at the office and will be heading home in about thirty minutes to an hour."

"Okay. You don't have to skip out on your plans for me. Isn't that for business?" I asked between sniffles.

"It's a charity event my parents started for troubled youth. My parents will get over it. I just want to be there for you."

"You are too sweet, but I don't know Verdell. After running into Trinity earlier, I just don't want any added drama. I have too much going on." I shook my head side to side as if he was sitting in the room with me.

"And like I told you, I'll take care of Trinity. You don't have to worry about her coming at you again."

"How do you plan to take care of her?"

"I'm going to talk to her. Candice, don't worry about Trinity, alright?"

"Okay, fine. I'll take your word." I rubbed my temple still not too sure if this was the right thing.

"Good. Let me finish up here so I can be on my way home. I can't wait to see you."

"That made me smile," I admitted.

"Oh? Well, wait until you see what I have in store for you tonight, beautiful. I'll see you in a bit."

"Okay. Bye."

"Bye, baby."

I ended the call and just stood there holding the phone in my hands. A giddy feeling rolled around in my belly.

"Who is that?" Mrs. Piercing's voice made me jump. I didn't hear the door open nor hear her come in.

"He's a friend I've been conversating with for a few months via text. I mistakenly texted him one night something meant for Jevar. Last night was the first time we met in person. It was the last time Shanell, and I spent together." I plopped down on the bed, sadness creeping back in.

"Does he know about your situation with Jevar?"

"Yeah, he does. I mean, he doesn't know who Jevar is, but we held a very long conversation about each other's last relationship. I pretty much told him everything. As a matter of fact, he was the one who suggested I get a temporary spot to bring my clients and have them sign nondisclosure forms."

"He sounds like he's really into you. Just be careful."

"I know and I will. He was calling me about Shanell. He saw on the news what happened. He wanted to see how I was doing."

"Do you mind telling me about him?"

"Um, well, he's totally opposite of Jevar in the way he carries himself. He's a prominent businessman, very good looking, and he makes me feel special. He shows his concern for me."

"I hope I get to meet him soon."

"You will. I promise."

"Alright. I came in here to tell you Margaret made you a sandwich."

"Okay, I'll be out after I shower and get dressed."

"Okay."

As soon as Mrs. Piercing left, I went into the bathroom and handled my hygiene. Once I was dressed, I packed my overnight bag, or not the walk of shame bag, Shanell and I used to call it. I then made my way to the kitchen where I joined Mrs. Piercing and Ms. Margaret at the breakfast nook. I sat with the ladies and ate my sandwich while they gossiped about the news, some of the people at the senior center they frequent, and the church picnic that was coming up. I shook my head at these two ladies who have become a big part of my life in a short period of time. I almost choked on my sprite when they turned their attention to my overnight bag and began reminiscing on their days of going out and keeping their overnight bags in the trunks of their cars. I wasn't trying to hear any of that. I finished off my sandwich and soda, then quickly left. I texted Verdell to let him know I was on my way.

Chapter 15

Candy

It was the evening rush hour traffic and as usual, I-20 was moving at a turtle's pace. I was anxious to get to Verdell and be in his arms. For some reason I felt that's where I would be the safest. As much as I fussed about not wanting to deal with him after the encounter with Trinity, I was lying to myself about staying away. After last night and the way he made me feel, I couldn't let that go. I needed that, wanted that. Even with all this damn drama going on, there was no way I could resist him.

These past few months of us getting to know each other over the phone was what really made me go ahead and meet Verdell in person. He listened to me and never judged me on things I knew were dumb. Instead, he helped me find solutions to my problems and gave his advice. He made me laugh with those corny jokes he loved to tell. The best part of it all were the nights we just held the phone listening to each other breathe.

A giddy feeling built up in the pit of my belly. I smiled at the thought of a repeat of last night. My kitty clenched in anticipation of what I was sure to come. My body began to tingle with want. I subconsciously licked my lips thinking about having that big slab of meat in my mouth. Verdell was definitely a better lover than Jevar. He made sure I got mine before he got his. He caressed every part of my body, making sure no part was left untouched.

Honk! Honk!

The horn blowing brought me back to the now. I didn't even realize I had zoned out. Shaking my head, I moved forward as the speed picked up, finally. It took me an hour and a half to get to Verdell's estate. I scanned my surroundings to see if Trinity was somewhere lurking. If she was, I didn't see her. Shrugging, I pressed the call button.

"Hello, beautiful," Verdell's baritone voice blasted through the speakerphone.

"Hey, handsome." My face heated up at the sound of his voice.

The gate opened, and I pulled forward. As if this was my first time coming here, my mouth fell open in awe of the beautiful mansion and landscape. I waved at the men who were manicuring the lawn as I drove up the long driveway and around stopping in front of the house. I smiled seeing Verdell standing on the porch waiting for my arrival. That giddy feeling returned, and my cheeks heated at the site of him standing there in the suit pants and shirt he wore this morning minus the suit jacket and tie. The top two buttons were undone.

Lord that man was fine. On the day God created Bryant Verdell McIntosh, he took his time and perfectly molded him. From the curly sandy-colored hair to his dark eyes, Jackson 5 nostrils, Colgate smile, down to his chiseled muscular frame, this man was among the gods. I watched him descend the steps and make his way to my door. He opened it for me and held his hand out for me to take. I placed my hand in his and stepped out of the car. We said nothing to each other as we embraced for a hug. Damn, he smelled just as good as he looked.

"Hey, baby," Verdell kissed my forehead.

"Hey, yourself."

He opened the backdoor and grabbed my bag. He slung the strap over his shoulder then grabbed my hand. He held it as we made our way up the steps and into the house. Being in the foyer, my mind went back to last night's events of Verdell and I on the steps while Shanell and Bradford were on the table. I shook my head.

"How was your day?" I asked, following Verdell into the family room.

"It was busy. I had meeting after meeting. When I finally texted you, I had just finished the last one for the day. I think I still would have bailed on going to the gala. But now that you're here, I'm good."

He sat my bag on the floor next to the sofa then turned to face me. I stood in front of him and placed a hand on his cheek. I caressed the side of his face as we stared into each other's eyes.

"Awe, babe. Thank you for thinking of me. I'm glad to be here with you as well. With all that has transpired, being here with you is a much-needed distraction."

I stood on my tip toes and placed a soft kiss on his lips. Verdell placed one hand on my waist and the other behind my neck, pulling me closer to him, deepening the kiss. Our tongues played a game of 'tag, you're it' in our mouths. I tilted my head to the side to welcome more of his tongue into my mouth. I pulled away and sucked his bottom lip into mine gaining a moan from him. The hardness of his man pressing on my belly moistened my panties.

Without breaking our kiss, I undid his pants and pushed them along with his boxers down. I stroked the massive eggplant up and down. Verdell was already big in length and girth, but he grew even bigger in my hand. At the same time, he pulled my dress up and pulled my panties down. He brushed his fingers along the folds of my wet box. My kitty awarded him with my juices spilling out onto them. My hips began a slow grind in sync with his fingers stroking my clit.

"Mmm," Verdell moaned in my mouth. "You missed me, baby?"

"I did and I can say the same for you."

"Hell yeah. I couldn't wait for you to get here."

Verdell hoisted me up and I wrapped my legs around his waist. I wrapped my arms around his neck as he lined my pussy with him then slid me down on him. He pushed up and I cried out from the pain and pleasure.

"Oooh, ssss," I moaned.

Verdell was stupid big. It felt like he was about to split me open upon entrance but just as quickly his thrusts began to feel amazing. I tightened my arms around his neck and began to bounce up and down on his dick meeting his thrusts.

"Shit," Verdell grunted.

"Fuck," I said at the same time.

I continued to bounce on his third leg as he turned towards the sofa and laid me down on it. He spread my legs wide, tossing my left leg over the back of the sofa and putting my right leg on his shoulder. Verdell's eyes bore into mine as he began slow but long thrusts into my wet tunnel. I returned the favor matching him stroke for stroke. I tried to keep my eyes open on his, but the euphoric feel of his magic stick was making that a hard task.

"Aah! Oooh, mmm," I moaned.

"Nah, beautiful, open your eyes for me."

They immediately popped opened and were back on his. But just as quickly they closed as my orgasm began to build up. I pushed him further into me. I spread my left leg further back on the sofa welcoming him balls deep. My walls began contracting around him quickly. My legs began to shake. I pressed my head into the armrest as I came hard.

"Ooooh, Verdell! Shit, baybeeee!"

"Open your eyes, Candice. I want to look into your eyes while you cum all over my dick," Verdell said.

Somehow, I managed to open my eyes back up as I continued to orgasm. He smiled then bit down on his bottom lip. That had me cumming again. I pulled his face down to me and kissed him lightly on the lips, our eyes still open. He pulled back and thrust deeper in me.

"Goddamn!" Verdell let out.

"Shit!" I replied.

"Let me get this from the back." Verdell said but continued to thrust in and out.

When he finally pulled out, I winced. However, before I could move to turn around, he dipped down and sucked my clit into his mouth. My eyes rolled to the back of my head as he ate my pussy. He ravished me with his tongue, licking, sucking, nibbling, on every inch of my most sacred place. I placed a hand on the back of his head and arched my back as I squirted my honey all over his tongue and face. My heart beat so fast, and my breathing raced as my body shook with pleasure.

"Oh, my fucking god!" I blurted out.

I dug my nails in the back of his head. Shit, that orgasm was so intense I pulled my own hair with my other hand. I rode the wave of my orgasm as if I was a surfer riding the highest wave on his surfboard. My orgasm shot through my body like an electric current. My body reacted as if I was being shocked and convulsed as Verdell sucked on my sensitive bud a few minutes more before coming up for air.

"Damn, you're so sweet, just like Candy." He licked his lips.

He held a look of satisfaction on his face, swiping his pink tongue across his lips with his eyes closed. With his eyes still closed, he double tapped my leg for me to get on all fours. I obliged him and turned onto my belly, then hiked up on my knees. I arched my back and tooted my ass up to the ceiling. My breathing picked up in anticipation of him entering me again. Like I said, it was pain upon entrance, but oh so pleasurable once he was inside me.

I felt Verdell's hands spread my ass cheeks apart then his tongue circling my asshole. I moaned at the amazing feeling he blessed me with. He licked my pussy and ass again before bringing me to yet another explosive orgasm. I couldn't ever remember having as many orgasms in one night as Verdell had given me. And he still hadn't bust his first nut. My damn!

"It's my turn now, beautiful," Verdell whispered in my ear.

"Mmm, then get it, daddy." I wiggled my ass and he smacked it. I moaned.

"Damn, look at that shit jiggle." He smacked my other cheek. "That's some pretty shit!"

He rubbed the mushroom tip along my folds and my pussy automatically began to suction it. She was hungry for some meat and he wanted to tease her. I pushed my ass back into him, causing that big dick to enter my honey cave.

"Mmm," we said in unison.

"Fuck me, Verdell," I whined.

And he did just that. He fed me that meat with quick, long thrust, hitting my spot from different angles with each thrust. I bounced my ass back on him with each thrust. Sounds of our bodies smacking against each other along with our moans and groans bounced off the walls of the room. The smell of our sex fragranced the room. That turned me on even more and I began to play with my clit. At the same time, I felt Verdell's thumb invading my asshole, thrusting in when his dick pulled out of my pussy.

"Oh shit, baby! Fuck!" I screamed out. I'm sure the workers outside heard me.

"Fuck, Candice. I'm about to cum in this pussy," Verdell grunted out.

I bounced my booty back on his thumb and dick while rubbing on my pearl. He stroked me and I bounced on him until we both reached our peak and came together. Fireworks went off and the sound of a band playing Auld Lang Sing was all I saw and heard as I had the biggest orgasm ever. My entire body went numb and then everything went black.

When I came to, I was laying in Verdell's bed. I heard bath water running in the bathroom. My body buzzed from our lovemaking. I felt so sleepy. All I wanted to do was close my eyes and fall back to sleep. I started to do that until Verdell came sauntering out of the bathroom naked. As wore out as I felt, I was more than willing to go another round seeing him in all his glory. That man was fine for no reason whatsoever. I bit my bottom lip as my hooded eyes roamed his body from head to toe then back up to that monstrous dick.

"You're awake."

I nodded my head.

"Come, beautiful, let me wash you up."

He picked me up bridal style and carried me into the bathroom. He had candles lit up around the bathroom. Some fresh fruit and a bottle of chilled wine sat on a serving tray next to the spa tub that was filled with rose petals. Verdell stepped inside the tub then placed me on my feet. I grabbed ahold of his arms at the same time he held onto my waist when my legs buckled underneath me.

"Don't worry, baby, I got you. I won't let you fall," Verdell reassured me.

I looked up to see the seriousness in his demeanor. I smiled up at him then wrapped my arms around his waist into a hug. I knew from the intense look on his face and the way he spoke those words, he was telling the truth. That was the moment I fell in love with Bryant Verdell McIntosh.

"Come."

That one-word command had me doing as I was told, and I sat down in the tub with my back pressed to his chest. I exhaled at the of the hot water feeling so good against my skin. I relaxed against him and felt so content. I felt like I was asleep and dreaming, but the dream felt all too real. It was a dream I did not want to wake up from. This right here was pure bliss. Verdell was pure bliss, and I was here for it!

"You good?" He broke me out of my thoughts.

"Mmm, I am much better now. Thank you."

"It's my duty to please your booty."

"Ha! Okay, Samuel L. Jackson as Shaft."

"Awe, look at you knowing your movies."

"I love watching movies and ole Sam is one of my favorite actors."

"Uh huh. Let me find out you got a thang for Samuel L. Jackson."

"Do I detect a bit of Jealousy, Mr. Verdell?" I lazily made swirl patterns on his leg enjoying our little banter.

"Nah, baby. He ain't got shit on me. Besides, he's old enough to be your daddy and mine, too," Verdell joked.

"Hmm, maybe I like them seasoned."

I couldn't get that out before I broke out laughing. Verdell joined in on the laughter as well.

"Okay seasoned. Hey, let me ask you something."

"Okay."

"Why do you still call me Verdell instead of Bryant?"

"Because that's how you introduced yourself to me. Besides I like Verdell over Bryant. It's unique."

"That makes sense. For a second, I thought you were going to say you didn't remember it."

"I know you told me to call you Bryant, but I just like Verdell. Again, Verdell is who I had been texting back and forth with. Does it bother you that I call you Verdell?"

"Nah, baby. I kind of figured that was the case but instead of assuming, I thought it was best to ask."

He swirled a rose petal around my nipple, causing it to harden. His other hand traveled down my belly, disappearing under the water, and landing on my sweet spot. He rubbed my pearl, awakening my sensual nerves. My back arched and my legs spread with want. But it wasn't his fingers I wanted inside of me. I turned to face him. Water splashed all around us with my movement. It was definitely about to slosh more. I grabbed ahold of his already erect penis and stroked him. I squeezed the tip before straddling him. I positioned him at my opening and slid down until I was completely filled.

Verdell gripped my butt cheeks as I began to slowly rotate my hips, grinding on his delectable dick. I wrapped my arms around his neck and threw my head back, enjoying the feel of him. I swear he fit me perfectly as if his man of steel was made just for my golden paradise. I felt complete and never wanted this feeling to ever go away. I bounced faster. Verdell spread his legs wider, opening me up more.

"Aah," I called out.

Verdell pushed up matching my stride. He latched on to a nipple and sucked on it. The swirling of his tongue around the hardened pebble had me in overdrive. Water was splashing all around us and onto the floor. I didn't care. I was on my way to another explosive orgasm that was ripping through my body.

"Shit, Bryant!" I called him by his first name.

This caused a groan to escape him. He took control of the pace as he tightened his hold on my ass cheeks and pounded up inside me as he slammed me down on him. My fingers dug into his shoulders when the pain became too much but I couldn't stop him. I didn't want to. I let him have me the way he wanted me.

"Say it again," he demanded.

"Bry-ant! Bryant! Baby I'm about to cum!"

My orgasm shot through me so fast and so intense. My legs became numb. My words got caught in the back of my throat. That didn't stop him from continuing to fuck me senseless. All I could do was hold on for the ride of my life. He stood up, holding me, and continued to bounce me up and down on his dick. The slapping of our wet bodies invaded the bathroom. The sound reminded me of when I used to dive in the pool at the rec center when I was kid. But this was way fun and better than diving into a pool.

"I'm about to cum in this pussy. I want you to cum with me."

"Mmm, okay," I sang more than spoke.

Verdell found my sweet spot and pounced on it, thrusting frantically up in me. I clasped my pussy muscles down on his dick and contracted them. We became as one when our eyes locked, and we rhythmically began to cum at the same time. We both let out loud grunts and moans, cursing our way to the finish line. Not once did we take our eyes from one another. In that moment, it felt as if we were floating in the air. I could hear harps playing loving lullabies as bursts of stars gleamed all around us.

"I love you," I let out before my brain even registered the words I spoke.

Verdell smiled a big Kool-Aid smile at that. He then slammed his lips into mine and kissed me fervently. Our tongues danced a sexy tango that would have scored a perfect ten from the judges of Dancing With the Stars. Tears of joy flowed from my eyes. This was home. This was my saving grace.

When I got with Jevar, I knew I was settling. I blame myself for some of the things that went wrong in that relationship. First of all, I should have been done with him the night we met, but I settled for him simply because I didn't want to be alone. I wanted to be in a relationship. I had the mentality that a piece of a man was better than no man at all. Secondly, Jevar showed me the type of man he was from the beginning. I ignored the signs because I was desperate to be in a relationship. I accepted anything from him not really knowing my self-worth. It took me a long time to really embrace who I am and to understand my worth. Once I realized I deserved better, I wasn't afraid to leave him.

This issue I knew was going to come about me leaving is that Jevar thought he had me in place. He was controlling and could not fathom the idea of me going against him. What he failed to realize was that once I started to get tired of being sick and tired, there was nothing he could do to stop me from leaving. Walking in my home and finding him in bed with another woman, was the straw that broke the camel's back. I dealt with a shit load of his infidelities but Jevar bringing that into the bed I slept in every night was the end.

Now here I was in the arms of a man who has shown me so much love, care, and respect, all because of texting the wrong number. Who'd thought this would be possible? I surely didn't. I am so grateful I stepped out on faith and responded back to Verdell. The four months we've taken to get to know each other over the phone not knowing what the other looked like, well, me not knowing what he looked like, helped strengthen our bond. And once we made love the first time, it was hook, line, and sink. He had me.

"The truth is I love you, too. Your picture had me as soon as my eyes landed on it. It wasn't your pretty, hot, and wet snatch that caught my attention either. Well, at first it did."

We both laughed at that. Still holding me, Verdell carried me over to the walk-in shower. He stopped just outside of it then placed me on my feet. He curled his finger under my chin so that I was looking up at him.

"But it was your angelic face and your eyes. Your eyes had something in them that made me want to protect you. I want to always protect you. I know this thing between us is unconventional in how we met, but I'm happy we found each other. So you don't have to worry about anything, not even ole boy. I protect what's mine, and you, Candice, are mine."

Well damn.

"Okay," was all I could muster up.

"Let's shower. Mrs. Felton should be done with dinner,"

"Wait, she was here when we were getting it on downstairs?" I asked just as the shower head rained down on us.

"Yeah, but she was busy prepping dinner, so she wasn't going to disturb us."

"How do you know? She could have had an emergency and you had my ass up in the air."

Verdell chuckled but I didn't see anything funny. I didn't need anyone thinking I was a hoe especially when they learn of how we met. I shook my head and turned away from him. We washed up and made small talk in the process. Once we were done, we oiled each other's body down, then got dressed. We headed downstairs, and I couldn't help my blushing face as thoughts of our rendezvous on the staircase came to mind. Then Shanell and Bradford getting it on the table at the same time, brought a melancholy mood over me.

I did my best to shake the feeling, not wanting to bring the mood down. We made our way into the kitchen just as Mrs. Felton was pulling a pan of macaroni and cheese out of the oven. With the lovely aroma floating in the air, my stomach loudly announced it was ready to enjoy the meal that had been prepared. We all laughed at its announcement.

"Well, yes ma'am, dinner is served," Mrs. Felton replied to my growling stomach.

"That makes my belly really happy," I chuckled.

"Have a seat, you two. Your plates are on their way. What would you like to drink, Ms. Candice?"

"Sprite if you have any, and please, just call me Candice."

Verdell and I sat at the table and within seconds, Mrs. Felton had our plates in front of us. Everything looked delicious from the mac and cheese to the string beans, fried chicken, and cornbread. My mouth watered in anticipation of chowing down on this feast. She came back with two glasses of water, a beer for Verdell, and a bottle of Sprite for me.

"Here you go, Candice," she smiled politely at me.

"Thank you."

Verdell and I held hands as he said grace. Just as we finished, Bradford came walking in looking somber. He wore a pair of baggy black jeans, black t-shirt, and black Lebron James XVII 17 Black Global Currency sneakers. He slowly came over and plopped down in one of the empty chairs.

"How are you feeling, Bradford?" Mrs. Felton asked. She rubbed his back in a soothing manner.

"I'm not sure really. When I got news of what happened, I didn't want to believe it. It's crazy we were all just together this morning and now Shanell's gone."

"I know. I couldn't either. I still can't believe she's gone. Her mom is devastated. I'm devastated. Shanell was my best friend and now she's gone." The tears streamed down my face.

"I'm sorry, Candice. I wasn't trying to make you cry," Bradford said.

"It's okay. I've been shedding tears ever since I found out. Anything and everything is making me cry." I dabbed my eyes with a paper towel.

"Do they have any clues as to who did this?" Mrs. Felton asked, placing another a box of Kleenex on the table next to me. She then rubbed my back the same way she had just done Bradford.

"They don't but I do."

"Who?" they all shouted in unison.

"Jevar."

"Who is Jevar?" Bradford asked.

"My abusive ex-boyfriend who has been looking for me for the past few months."

"So, you're telling me he killed her to get to you?" Bradford interrogated.

"I believe he thought Shanell was lying about not knowing where I've been staying. I didn't tell her, thinking her not knowing would have kept her safe from his rage. But as you can see, it didn't."

"Please forgive me for asking, but what the hell do you have going on?"

"Brad, chill," Verdell scolded.

"No, babe, it's okay. I'm tired of hiding and with what happened to Shanell, it doesn't matter anymore to keep it a secret." I placed my hand in the palm of Verdell's hand.

"Okay, Bradford, four months ago, after enduring physical and mental abuse in my last relationship, I left him. He came home after being out all night, picking a fight. I tried to ignore him because I was finally tired of the shit. He couldn't take me not wanting to argue with him so he kept poking a fight until he hit me in my face. I made up my mind at that point that I was done. I go to my hair salon to work and after I got home, I walk in on him screwing a known hoe in our bed. I didn't even let it be known that I was there. I just grabbed some important documents and cash I kept in a hidden safe, then left with only the clothes on my back. I've been staying a friend's place who welcomed me into her home when she saw the bruise on my face."

"So, you left your dude when you met Bryant?"

"Me leaving Jevar had nothing to do with Verdell."

"But how did y'all meet? I mean, bro, you never even told me."

"I mistakenly sent him a text that was meant for Jevar. I was texting one of his burner phones but input the number wrong and it went to Verdell's phone."

"I reached out to Candice after getting the text and we began a texting relationship until I finally convinced her to meet me, which was last night."

"Okay, I guess I'm just having a hard time understanding why you didn't want Shanell to know where you were staying."

"Shanell was my best friend, but Shanell also slept with Jevar while he and I were together. Shanell knew about the abuse and there were times I tried to leave and told her where I was, and she then told Jevar where I was. When I left him, I was determined to be rid of him. I knew it wasn't going to be easy since he's very controlling, but I never imagined he would go so far to kill Shanell or anyone for that matter."

"You need to go to the police about this," Mrs. Felton said.

"I'm sure they will be looking to talk to me soon. Momma Gertrude, Shanell's mom, told me she gave the detective my number. I'm surprised he hadn't called yet."

"Did she say who the detective was?" Verdell asked.

"Yeah, she said it was uh, Detective John Shingles."

I noticed the exchange between Verdell and Brad when I said his name.

"What?" I asked.

Verdell rubbed a hand over his face. That named seemed to have both men shaken up. Bradford got up from the table and went over to the walk-in pantry and came out with a bottle of Hennessey Black. Mrs. Felton followed behind him with tumblers. She sat the glasses down on the table. Bradford poured some of the Hennessey in each glass. Mrs. Felton was the first to grab a glass and toss back the brown liquid. My mouth opened and closed at that. The brothers downed their glasses as well.

"Um, can someone tell me what's up?"

"Yeah, baby. Detective John Shingles is one of those people who makes his mind up without any real investigation, that you are the guilty person. But I thought he retired."

"Nah he didn't after that fiasco with Greg's death and how he went harassing Darnell and Kayla about it. And yeah, then he harasses the hell out of you to the point you damn near want to commit murder and kill his ass—" Brad was cutoff.

"Then walk into the police department and turn yourself in, waive your rights, and sign a written confession," Verdell finished off.

"What happened?"

"My son, Frederick, was hanging with the wrong crowd. He was a good boy but made some bad decisions." Mrs. Felton clutched the dish towel to her chest as she leaned against the island, sadness all over her face. "He went out with his friends and one of them decided it was a good idea to rob the gas station. Freddie and his best friend, Josh were standing outside of the store, while the other three boys were robbing it, unbeknownst to them. Well, once the shots rang out and the boys ran out of the store, Freddie and Josh took off to running as well.

Security cameras caught all of them. Detective Shingles tried to say Freddie and Josh were lookouts for the others, but that wasn't true. They were just standing outside talking. Once they found out our family was connected to the McIntosh family, he began harassing Freddie and even tried to get the other boys to say Freddie was the mastermind behind the robbery. If it wasn't for Bradford and his lawyer, Freddie would be locked up now."

"Yeah, he's a real dick," Bradford stated.

Mrs. Felton smacked him on the back of his head with the towel. "Watch your mouth."

"Sorry," he chuckled.

"I don't want you talking to him without a lawyer present. He won't be able to change your words around then."

"Okay, I won't. I'm willing to do what needs to be done to get justice for Shanell. I want Jevar to get what he deserves." I pushed my plate away from me, no longer hungry.

"You should try and eat a little bit. You need to keep your strength up," Mrs. Felton said.

"I don't have an appetite anymore. I'll just sit my plate in the microwave and come back for it later."

I move to get up, but she placed a hand gently on my shoulder stopping me. "No worries, dear, I got it."

"Thank you."

"Aye, so B, I've been thinking about you asking me to help you with that app."

"Really?"

"Yeah, I decided I'll help you with it."

"What changed your mind? I mean you damn near bit my head off when I brought it to you."

"I know and my bad for that. I was just so wrapped up in how Dad was never there because he was so consumed with business. It took a minute for me to truly understand he was working hard for the life we now live."

"I'm glad to hear that. And look, we can just take things slow with you and only let this project be your main focus for a while. When you're ready for some more responsibilities, we can add on to this."

"Thanks, Bryan."

"No problem at all. Thank you. With your expertise, we about to take over the digital world!"

I smiled as the brothers did some special handshake then embraced in a brotherly hug. Bryant and Bradford were two of the most gorgeous men I'd ever seen. They could easily have careers as models and would be on the cover of every magazine and billboards. It makes sense they would date supermodels. Hell, they are the only ones to compliment these men's good looks. That thought had my self-consciousness rearing its ugly head into view. I tried to shake it off but it pushed its way closer.

As the men sat and began chatting about the app, I excused myself and walked around the mansion. Even though the house held a lot of history, the décor was modern throughout. Everything was in either white or gray tones and had clean lines. Beautiful artwork was strategically placed about. I'm sure they cost way more than I would see in a lifetime. I took the steps down into the basement. The lights automatically turned on as soon as I took the first step. When I reached the bottom, my eyes lit up at the massive gym to my right. It held everything you could think of to get a good work out in and right now I needed that. So I sprinted back up the steps to go find something to put on. I just got to the top when Verdell appeared.

"There you are. I was wondering where you snuck off to."

"I gave myself the tour but as soon as I saw that gym, I wanted to work out. I'm headed upstairs to change."

"Cool, we can work out together if you don't mind."

"I'd like that."

We made our way upstairs and began to change into workout gear when my phone rang. I looked at the number but didn't recognize it. I started to decline the call but something told me to answer. I swiped the green button to the right.

"Hello."

"Hello, I'm trying to reach Candice Carson," the male voice stated.

"May I ask who's calling?"

"Yes, I'm Detective John Shingles."

"Oh, yes, Detective, I've been expecting your call."

"Good, then can you come down to the station so we can talk?"

"Sure. I can come down tomorrow. What time?"

"How about nine a.m.?"

"Okay, I'll see you then."

"Thank you and have a good evening."

I ended the call and plopped down on the bed.

"What did he say?" Verdell asked.

"He asked me to come down to the station to talk and I told him tomorrow. We meet at nine in the morning."

"I'm going with you, and I'll have my attorney meet us there."

There was no need to protest because it was evident in his tone that I had no say so in the matter. All I could to was nod my head in agreement.

"I don't mean to sound commanding. I just don't want Detective Shingle coming at you with the shits. You understand that I have your best interests at heart?"

"Yes, Bryant I do. I know and trust you only want the best for me." I pulled him so that he was standing in front of me. "Thank you for looking out for my best interest."

"I got you, sweetheart." Verdell bent down and kissed the top of my head.

"I don't feel like working out now. I just want to go to bed," I expressed.

"Whatever you want my love. But I do want to ask, if you want to go to bed or did you have something else in mind?" He playfully lifted his eyebrows.

"You're so silly, but sorry, babes, I really just want to go to bed."

"Okay, well can I at least rub on that big, sexy booty?"

"Oh my goodness, what am I going to do with you, sir?"

"Touch me, tease me, feel me and caress me. Hold on tight and don't let go. Baby I'm gon' lose control," Verdell belted out the chorus to Case's song. My mouth fell open at how great he sounded, then I burst into a fit of laughter at his horrible dance move.

"Wow, you sound great. I see you are a man of many talents."

"Stick with me kid and I just might teach you some things," he winked.

I shook my head and got undressed. I slid under the covers and melted. A yawn escaped me and my eyes grew heavy just that quickly.

"I'll be back. I'm going to make sure everything is locked up. I left Brad and Momma Fe in the kitchen, too."

"Tell them I said goodnight."

"Sure thing."

I must have fallen asleep as soon as Verdell walked out of the room. A tingling sensation flowing through my body stirred me awake. Verdell had his face buried between my thighs feasting off my juicy peach. Once my body was awakened, it responded to his every lick and touch. I moaned out in pleasure as I climaxed, my back arching pushing my pussy more into his face. Verdell lapped up every drop of my liquid sugar until I had no more to give.

"Mmm good," he said as he climbed on top of me.

I spread my legs further apart, welcoming him there. He rubbed the mushroom tip of his dick up and down my wet folds before pushing it inside of me. We both moaned at the feel of our connection. He placed both of my legs on his shoulders and thrust deeper inside me.

"Ah," I let out.

Verdell found his rhythm and worked me over. He felt so amazing. I ground my pelvis to meet his strokes. Somehow in the darkness, he found my mouth and sucked my bottom lip into his mouth. We kissed passionately, not as intense as our previous kisses. This was more sensual, meaningful, loving. Before I knew we had stopped fucking and were just kissing. I felt our souls connecting in that moment and it was a feeling I would never let go of.

"I love you, Candice."

"I love you, Bryant."

He placed his forehead on mine, and we just lay there, connected, with him inside of me and my legs still on his shoulders. I could feel his dick pulsating and that made me wetter. I clinched my walls around him, beckoning him to finish what he started. I felt him smile at my action knowing what I wanted. He obliged me and began his thrusts. He went fast and deep, just the way I liked it. I pulled him in deeper, throwing my pussy back on him. My body began to shake at the feel of my orgasm brewing. My walls began contracting and I climaxed for a second time. I screamed out like a banshee, raking my nails down his back.

"I know, baby. Give it to me," Verdell whispered in my ear, and I came again.

He removed my legs off his shoulder and turned me onto my side. He slid back inside me from behind and began fucking me. He held my leg up in the crook of his arm, opening me up more and I was in pure bliss. I threw my good girl back on him, meeting his every thrust. We fucked our way to explosive orgasms that left us both happy and spent. He removed my leg from his arm then wrapped his arm around my waist and we fell asleep.

Chapter 16

Bryant

My driver, Felix, pulled over to the curve in front of the Atlanta Police Department. Candice let out an audible sigh as she wrung her fingers around her scarf. I leaned over and pecked her cheek. She responded with a smile. Felix exited the car and came around to open the back door. I stepped out onto the curb then held my hand out for Candice. She placed her hand in mine and stepped out.

"I got you, babe. No need to be nervous," I reassured her.

"I know. I just want all of this to be over," she buried her face into my chest.

"Bryant," my attorney, Philip Moore, called out from behind us.

"Phil, thanks for coming. This is my lady, Candice Carson. Babe, this is my attorney, Phil Moore."

"It's nice to meet you," Candice extended a hand.

"The pleasure's all mine," Phil took her hand, and they shook.

"Before we go in, can you tell me what to expect?"

"Yes, ma'am. Detective Shingles tends to be a hard ass. He's going to try and get you to confess to something you didn't do. Just tell the truth and you'll be okay. I'll be right by your side so no need to worry."

Candice shook her head and started towards the entrance. Phil and I followed behind her. It was loud and busy inside the precinct. An officer was struggling with a prostitute even though she was handcuffed. An old drunk man sat on a bench attempting to sing but his words were coming out slurred. A few officers spoke as we passed them. We stepped up to the concierge desk and waited for the officer to finish up a phone call.

"Sorry about that. How may I help you?"

"Yes, we're here to see Detective Shingles. He's expecting us," Phil told him.

"Alright, one moment." He picked up the receiver and pushed in a few numbers. "Yeah, Detective, I have some people here to see you. They say you're expecting them. Yeah, uh huh, uh huh, okay." The officer ended the call and turned his attention back to us. "He'll be right down. Aye, Mackey, show these folks into interview room one."

"Sure, right this way folks."

We were led down a hall and into the first room on the left. It was the typical interrogation room with the mirror wall a table and chairs on opposite sides of the table. I pulled a chair out for Candice. She sat down and placed her purse on the table. Phil took the seat next to her. I stood back and leaned against the wall with my arms folded across my chest.

"Can I get you something to drink?" Mackey asked.

We all declined, and he left the room. Not too long after, Detective Shingles entered the room and looked surprised when he saw Phil and me. I smirked at that dumbass look on his face.

"Well, I wasn't expecting this to be a party," Detective Shingles said.

"I just want to make sure my client isn't coerced into anything. We know how you do," Phil replied.

I chuckled at that and Detective Shingles turned red in the face.

"I assure you all I want is the truth from Miss Carson."

Detective Shingles took a seat across from them. He placed a manilla folder in front of him. He then pulled out a notepad and a pen from the inside pocket of his suit jacket.

"Well, now, Miss Carson, as I'm sure you already know, I'm investigating the death of Shanell Turner. Can you tell me about the last time the two of you were together?"

"Shanell came with me to Bryant's house. That was the day before yesterday. We spent the night at his place, and I dropped her off at home yesterday morning. That was around seven-thirty."

"Did you see or talk to her any time after that?"

"No. Once I arrived home, I sent her a text message, but she didn't respond back. I figured she had already fallen asleep, so it wasn't a red flag or unusual for her not to respond."

"Do you know anyone who had a beef with Shanell?"

"No, but I know my ex-boyfriend, Jevar Jackson, kept going to her looking for me. I believe he may be the one who killed her."

"And why would he kill her instead of you?" Detective Shingles placed his hand under his chin.

"He's been trying to find me. He and I had a fight and I left him. That was four months ago. He kept going at Shanell thinking she knew where I've been staying, but she didn't know. I didn't tell her because I was trying to keep her from being involved in our mess. He must have thought she was lying. I know that Jevar is very controlling, and he's pissed that he hasn't been able to find me. I believe he's now at the point where he's willing to do anything possible to bring me out of hiding, so he killed her."

Candice started crying and it pissed me off, not her crying but that fucking idiot that was causing her anguish. I moved and stood behind her. I placed my hands on her shoulders for support. I could feel the tension leave her. Detective Shingles looked between us questionably.

"You two are very cozy. How long has this been going on?" He waved his fingered back and forth.

"We just started dating. And no, Bryant has nothing to do with the issues between Jevar and I. It was Jevar's infidelities and abuse that was our problems. I got tired of his shit and left him. I knew when I left I had to really fall off the grid. I couldn't go too far because of my business but I made myself inaccessible to him. I'd like to keep it that way," Candice explained in between sniffles.

"Do you have an idea as to where we can find Jevar?"

"Sure, give me a piece of paper and I'll write down all his addresses. I'm sure you will find him at one of them. If not, you can look up his friends, Dovirs Daniels and Omar Baker. He's always hanging with them."

"Alright, thank you Miss Carson for coming down and cooperating with us. While you're writing down those addresses, include yours should I need to reach you. Or should I assume you're staying with Mr. McIntosh?" Detective Shingles asked sarcastically.

"If she is then what?" I asked.

"Ain't nothing. I just wanted to know where I can reach Miss Carson if I need to," he shrugged.

"I put the address to where I'm staying. If Jevar finds out where I am, I know it would be because of you," Candice told Detective Shingles with lots of attitude as she slid to paper to him. That shit made my dick hard.

"Thank you. I'll follow-up on these addresses you gave me. Now, are you sure you don't know of anyone else who would want to harm Shanell?"

"As far as I know, she wasn't beefing with anyone. Jevar is the only person I can think of that would do something like this."

"My client has answered all of your questions. If you have any more, contact my office first. Don't try and go around me to talk to her, Detective," Phil said.

"Yeah, yeah. Thanks for coming in Miss Carson."

Everyone stood and we all filed out of the room. As we got towards the entrance, Trinity walked in. It looked like she tried to clean herself up, but she missed the mark. She wore a dress that was a size too big. It really looked like it hung from a rack. Her shoes looked worn. Her hair had thinned out and was pulled back into a straggly ponytail. As soon as she saw me, she tried to pep up her step.

"Well, hello, Bryant."

"Hello to you Trinity."

"Ah, Ms. Blackshear, thanks for coming in on short notice," Detective Shingles said. He extended his hand out to her and she shook it.

"It's no problem. When I saw the news about Shanell I wanted to do whatever I could to help."

"What do you know about Shanell's murder?" Candice asked. I could hear the desperation in her voice.

"Wouldn't you like to know," Trinity smirked.

"Bitch, don't play with me."

"Ladies, ladies, no need for the hostility," Detective Shingles stood in between them.

"Trinity, what's going on?" I asked.

"What's going on, Bryant, is you and how you've mistreated me! I've been by your side for three years and you just throw our relationship away. And for this, this hood rat!"

I pinched the bridge of my nose to keep from snapping on her. "Trinity, you and I both know the reason we are not together anymore is because of you and your drug problem. Candice wasn't even in the picture when all of those problems started."

"Why do you insist on embarrassing me, Bryant? I have suffered enough don't you think?"

"I'm not embarrassing you. You're doing a pretty good job of the that yourself. Just stay away from Candice and me. Are we clear?"

"No!" She leaned in and whispered where only I could hear her. "Don't forget I was there when you killed Gerald. How about I discuss that with Detective Shingles?"

"Bitch, you are crazy," I laughed out loud before leaning back in and telling her, "But it's your fingerprints on the gun. Don't fuck with me or Candice and I won't make your life any more pathetic than it already is."

I grabbed Candice by the hand and escorted her past a crying Trinity and out of the precinct. Trinity just enlightened me on what I know I now have to do.

Jevar

I sat on the edge of the bed watching the news while I rolled a blunt. They been running the story on Shanell all damn day. I somewhat felt bad for what I did to her because I knew she didn't know where Candy has been staying. However, Shanell was just a casualty of war. I needed to find Candy and I needed to find her ass soon. I know once I had her ass back, shit would get back in line.

I lit fire to the end and inhaled that loud. I blew the smoke through my nose, enjoying the high I was enhancing. Movement behind me grabbed my attention. Sheree slid over to me and took the blunt from me then placed it between her lips. That shit turned me on. I took the blunt back from her then grabbed the back of her head. I guided her head towards my soldier, and she happily opened her mouth to take him in.

Just as I started to enjoy Sheree's head game, my phone rang. "Yeah," I answered a bit agitated.

"I found her. Check your text message for the address," the voice stated then hung up.

My phone dinged and I opened the text up to an address. My dick got harder knowing Bae and I will soon have a reunion. I fell back onto the bed and enjoyed Sheree's head game.

Chapter 17

Candy

One week later....

"Let not your heart be troubled: ye believe in God, believe also in me. In my Father's house are many mansions: if it were not so, I would have told you. I go to prepare a place for you. And if I go and prepare a place for you, I will come again, and receive you unto myself; that where I am, there ye may be also."

Pastor Lennox stood at the podium and read the scripture as we entered the church. Shanell's family and I made our way down the aisle to our seats. Being that Shanell was an only child, Momma Gertrude wanted me to escort her since we were like sisters. It was difficult walking towards the closed casket that sat at the end of the aisle knowing that was Shanell laying inside. I hadn't been to a funeral since my dad's, and it was bringing up memories I had buried for years.

Momma Gertrude let out an excruciating wail once we were at the front. Her knees buckled and we almost fell. Luckily, her brother and nephew were behind us and caught us before we hit the floor. Uncle Mike had to help Momma Gertrude in her seat. Once she was seated, I took mine next to her and the rest of the family followed suit.

Tears streamed down my face as the program of the service began. To take my mind off the sniffles all around me, I admired the décor of the church that was all made up for Shanell. Momma Gertrude went all out to send her off in style. The church was decorated in pale pink and white tule and flowers. Shanell's casket was a pale pink with the most beautiful bouquet of white roses sitting on top. Several pots of plants and flowers surrounded the casket as well. There was a poster sized framed picture of Shanell wearing a pink flowy maxi dress, her hair done up in a curly weave, and her makeup beat for the gawds. She displayed her biggest smile. She was beautiful. I remember taking that picture the day we went to the Funk Fest in Orlando. We had a great time as always.

After the choir finished up their rendition of Never Would Have Made It by Marvin Sapp, Shanell's cousin, Keisha, went and read off a poem she wrote in tribute to her. It was beautiful and had my tears flowing faster.

"You were the sister I never had. The one who came to my aide when I was down and sad. You helped me out and taught me so much. You showed me genuine love and a true sisterhood of such. You taught me how to apply my makeup, always telling me a lady never leaves the house not made up. You lit up the room whenever you entered, your smile, your style will always be remembered. I miss you so much and you haven't been gone long, but I know we'll see each other again before long. So, rest well my cousin, my sister. I'll forever love you and treasure our moments together."

"My baby! My baby!" Momma Gertrude yelled out when Keisha came over and hugged her.

"Next, we will have a few words from Shanell's best friend, Candice."

Uncle Mike softly patted me on the back to encourage me to go up to the podium. I took a breath and stood. I took slow steps up to the podium, my mind all jumbled. Last night I finally wrote out what I wanted to say but left it at home. When I realized I didn't have it, I almost spazzed out. Just speak from your heart, Candice. I gave myself a pep talk as I stood before the congregation. When I spotted Verdell and Brad sitting towards the back, he gave me a slight head nod that gave me some encouragement. But then I spotted Jevar. That smirk on his face that he always wore when he was on his bullshit. That smirk that always told me a slap, a punch, or a kick was about to be thrown my way. That smirk I hated just as much if not more than I hated him. That was the last thing I remembered before feeling my heart beating fast then everything going black.

Bryant

I jumped up so fast at seeing Candice fall to the floor, I got a bit light-headed. I raced down the aisle to get to her almost knocking down the pastor when I reached the alter. I placed two fingers on her neck to see if I could feel a pulse. Luckily, it was strong. I took off my suit jacket, balled it up and placed it under her head. "Come on, baby. Wake up," I coerced.

"I called 9-1-1. The ambulance is on the way. I heard someone say.

"Alright everyone, let's keep the aisle clear for the paramedics. Have a seat and let's bow our heads in prayer," Pastor Lennox directed. "Lord, we ask you to lay your hands on Candice right now."

"Yes, Lord," a woman cried out.

"Lord pour strength back into her body and breathe life into her as well. We all are mourning the loss of Shanell, and I see how much of toll it's taking on her closest friend. But Lord we ask you to heal Candice's heart as well as us all here to celebrate Shanell's life. Don't take another young soul from us right now, Lord. Let her light shine. We thank now and ask these things in your precious son, Jesus's name. Let the church say, amen, amen, and amen again."

"They're here," Pastor Lennox tapped me lightly on my shoulder.

I stood and backed away from Candice to give the paramedics space to work on her. They quickly placed an oxygen mask over her nose and mouth and just as quickly hooked her up to an IV. They picked her up and placed her on the gurney before securing her to it. One of them called out some medical sayings through a radio mouthpiece as they hauled her out of the church. Brad and I were on their heels behind them.

"Take her to Emory, I told them."

"Yes, Mr. McIntosh," the younger of the two men replied. I watched as they placed Candice in the back of the ambulance. I stood there watching them until they pulled off.

"I advise you to walk away from Candy before your world gets fucked up, Mr. McIntosh."

I heard a voice behind me. I turned to face the person who spoke them and all but snapped when I was met face to face with Jevar Jackson. He stood with a sinister smirk on his face. Dude was dressed in a black t-shirt, black baggie jeans, and black J's. The snapback he wore was turned backwards on his head. I wanted to knock that smirk right off his face but being where we were at the moment was his saving grace. Bradford pulled up beside us and waited for me.

"Today is your lucky day, Jevar. You get to live." I pointed my finger at him. "I'm going to say this to you only once. Stay the hell away from Candice. Whatever you had with her is over. She doesn't want to be with you anymore. She's with a real man now," I pound my chest with my fist. "She doesn't have to worry about getting beat or cheated on. You think you're so tough, beating on a woman, but you ain't shit!"

"Oh, so you think you can beat my ass, nigga?" Jevar stepped closer up on me.

From the corner of my eye, I saw the funeral service coordinators walking out of the church with a few people behind them carrying some of the potted plants and flowers. One of the guys looked our way and I could see his body tense up. I took a step back to put some distance between Jevar and me. As bad as I wanted to kick his ass up and down the street, now wasn't the time.

"Bryan, let's go." Brad called out to me. I backed away from Jevar and made my way to the car.

"I'll see you again, preppy," Jevar said.

"Indeed."

I hopped in the car and slammed the door. I was seething. My vision was blurry, and I felt the headache creeping up on me. I needed to calm myself down before we got to the hospital. I didn't want Candice to see me in this state of mind. I needed to be there for her right now, not add to the stress she was already dealing with.

"Yo, Bry, you're going hard for this woman you just met. What's up with that, and who is that guy?" Brad asked, breaking me out of my thoughts.

"Candice and I just met in person, but we've been chatting for several months now. That's her ex that she has been hiding from. You heard her talking about how she believed he is responsible for Shanell's death. He's been looking for her for months, but she's been in hiding. I think the shock of seeing him is what caused her to pass out."

"Bryant, I'm going to say this and then I'm done. Please be careful. There are three sides to every story, you heard only one. I'm not saying Candice didn't tell you the truth or every detail of their relationship. I just want you to tread carefully and keep your eyes and ears open. I don't want to see you hurt, physically or mentally. You have too much at stake. I mean, I've never seen you go this hard for Trinity, and you were engaged to her."

"I know, Brad. Something deep within me attached to her and I can't let go. I'm not dumb. I know there aren't things she hasn't told me, but I believe her when she said he beat her. Hell, he didn't even deny it when I brought it up. Trust me I did my research on Candice and everything she's told me matched up to what the background I had done on her."

I looked out the window watching the cars as we crept along with the traffic on our way to the hospital. It hurt me to see Candice going through this shit with Jevar. What was really bothering me though is that she didn't know she literally had been sleeping with the enemy for a long time. I want to tell her what I found out but didn't know if, one, she would believe me, and two, how she would handle the information. I wanted to get Brad's opinion on this, so I turned to face him.

"So, check it. The background check I had done on Candice revealed that her stepmom had a million-dollar insurance policy taken out on Michael, Candice's dad, a couple of months before he was killed. He somehow found out about the policy and had Candice named as the beneficiary and took his wife's name off it."

"Do you think he may have suspected she was up to some fuck shit?"

"I'm thinking so if he had her taken off and put Candice on it."

"Explain how Jevar plays into this," Brad's impatient ass said.

"I'm getting to that. Jevar is Betty's brother. They have the same dad. It seems he was a rolling stone even in his old age."

"You don't say," Brad chuckled.

"Betty didn't learn about Jevar until their dad passed, and she met Jevar and his mom at the funeral. My theory is she plotted to have

Michael killed to get both insurance policies, but it didn't go as she planned since her name wasn't on anything and from what I read his last will still had Candice, her siblings, and their mom listed as the beneficiary of everything."

"Damn, so you think she had Jevar get with Candice to try and get the money that way?"

"I believe so. I mean, it's too big of a coincident that Jevar gets with her."

"That's cold," Brad shook his head.

We finally made it to the hospital. Brad drove around the parking deck before finally finding a parking space on the third level. I opened the door to get out, but he placed a hand on my arm halting me.

"That's some heavy shit you just told me, bro. If what you're saying is true, then Candice's entire family is in jeopardy. I think when you tell her this, you should tell all of them together so they can get some type of security in place, especially for her mom. If Jevar was so comfortable killing Shanell, then he won't have any qualms offing her family members one by one until he has her."

"I know and I'm already working on a plan to get them somewhere safe."

"I got your back bro. And I know this is going to sound crazy coming from me, but I think you need to tell mom and dad as well. You don't want them to be blindsided by all the shit that's about to hit the fan."

"You're right. Let's go by there once we leave here."

We got out and made our way inside the ER of the hospital. We walked over to the reception desk and inquired about Candice. She told us to have a seat and she would get the doctor. As soon as I sat in an empty seat, my phone buzzed. I reached in my suit jacket inside pocket and pulled it out.

"Hey, baby. How are you? We're here in the waiting area now."

"I'm okay, just a little dehydrated, but I'm okay."

"Okay, good. You scared me."

"I know but I'm alright. They're running some tests just to make sure there are no underlying issues, but I'm sure they won't find anything."

"Okay, do you need anything?"

"I would like you to be in here with me, if that's possible."

"Your wish is my command my lady."

"The doctor is here now. I'll let them know to bring you back."

"Cool."

We disconnected the call, and I relaxed a bit. She sounded well but I wouldn't be able to fully relax until I laid eyes on her. I sat thinking how our lives collided all by a damn text. I was putty in her hands the moment I opened that text and saw her picture. She had no idea. It's hard to understand how someone could just feel a connection to another person not knowing anything about them, but that is how it was when I saw her picture. My heart skipped a beat, my palms became sweaty, and my breath was taken away.

Some people may say she isn't my type because they only saw me with model type of women, such as Trinity pre-drugs. The thing is, those women were just easily accessible. Not that I couldn't get any woman I wanted anyway, but they were the ones that seemed to be around me. Candice isn't skinny like a typical model. She has curves for days and even with the small pudge, she is the finest of all the women I've ever been with. It turns me on even more that she doesn't look like them, but like a real woman. She's a natural beauty, no makeup needed at all.

Not only is she beautiful, but she's also business savvy as well. She has both street sense and business sense. Now that's a perfect combination in my book. She kind of reminds me of my mom. She was from the opposite sides of the track, but unless you knew her personally, you would never know; that is until she was placed in a situation that made that side of her come out. My mom was and still isn't nothing to mess with once you pissed her off. Candice has that fire in her but being with Jevar took away some of it. If she will let me, I planned to help her get that fire back.

"Mr. McIntosh?"

Brad and I stood at the sound of a woman's Asian accent. We met her at the receptionist desk.

"I'm Bryant McIntosh," I said extending my hand out to her. She took it in hers and gave me a firm handshake.

"Hello, I'm Dr. Kim. You can follow me back. Miss Carson is asking for you."

"How is she?" I asked her as Brad and I walked with her.

"She'll fine. Miss Carson gave me permission to talk to you about her medical condition. She had a panic attack that was very intense and caused her to black out."

"Is this a common thing for her or was this the first time?"

"Based on what she's told me, she had episodes like this after she was hospitalized from the explosion at the gas station and the drive-by shooting that killed her father. She remembered this happening quite a bit after that, but over time the therapy helped with it."

"Is there some specific care she will need at home?" Brad asked.

"Miss Carson needs to be in a stress-free environment. She needs to rest the next few days and drink more water. I am going to release her. I think she's well enough to go home as long as those things are put into play. She will be fine."

We were standing outside of Candice's room as Dr. Kim told us that bit of information. I shook her hand and thanked her for the details. I was relieved it wasn't anything too serious, but I also knew Candice wasn't going to get the peace she needs until everything about Jevar, Betty, and her father's death was out in the open and people held accountable.

Chapter 18

Jevar

This nigga just don't know who the fuck I am! I watched him and his bitch ass brother drive away. My trigger finger was itching to blow a hole through his fucking skull, but there were too many witnesses and those were problems I didn't need. I bobbed my head up and down and rubbed my hands together as thoughts of how I'm about to cause havoc in Bryant McIntosh's life went through my mind. I stepped off the curb making my way to my car when my phone vibrated. "Yo."

"Have you found that gul yet?"

"Yeah, but the bitch passed out in front of the congregation at the funeral," I replied hopping in my truck. I started it up to let the AC kick in because it was hot as fuck for it to be the beginning of October.

"Look, I need you to do what you got to do to get at her. I'm running out of time, and she has what I need."

"Don't worry. I got you."

"Have you taken care of your business with Marcus?"

"No, and Dovirs and Omar is in the wind. I haven't been able to get up with those niggas or any of my peeps," I told her.

"Jevar, handle your fucking business! We need to get this shit wrapped up soon."

"Don't worry, Sis. I got you."

"You better. I have plans to be laid up in Jamaica within the next couple of months. Handle this bitch and let's tie up these loose ends, bro."

"I'm on it."

I disconnected the call and pulled out of the parking lot. Time was running out and I needed to get all this shit together.

Trinity

I sat on my sofa reading a mystery novel and nursing a glass of Riesling. I was just getting into the meat of the story when my doorbell rang. I wasn't expecting anyone, but I assumed it was more than likely my mom who seems to keep popping up every other day. She keeps trying to get me to go back to rehab and I shut her ass down every time. I don't need rehab. I need revenge. Bryant fucked up my life and I want him to pay for it. He owes me and I intend to collect while bringing him down.

Ding dong!

I laid the book down on the table and reluctantly hopped up to go answer the door. I let out an audible sigh as I made my way to the door. I stood at the door with my hand on the knob saying a silent prayer my mom didn't come with the same shit she keeps preaching. Tonight, just wasn't the night. The pounding on the door jerked me out of my thoughts, startling me.

"Who is it?"

"Jevar, now open the fucking door."

"How do you know where I live?" I asked as I opened the door.

Jevar stood there with a scowl on his face but looking sexy as hell at the same time. His hands stuffed in the pocket of the baggy jeans he wore. The crisp black tee and ATL snapback he wore to the back enhanced his swag. For the first time in a long time, my girlie parts were fully alert.

"I have my ways of finding out what I want to know," he shoved me to the side as he stepped inside.

"To what do I owe the pleasure of your unwanted visit?"

I slammed the door and followed him into my living room. He plopped down on the spot of the sofa I was just sitting in. He picked up the book I was reading and read the title before dropping it back onto the table. He grabbed the bottle of wine and took a swig of it before getting comfortable with arms spread on the back of the sofa and his legs spread wide. I wanted to hop on him and take a ride. Damn!

"I need you to tell me everything you know about Bryant McIntosh, and don't leave out any details."

"What do you plan to do with this information and what do I get out of this?"

"I plan to take the nigga down and you get to live. Now speak," Jevar demanded.

"You waltz your ass in my house demanding information and have the audacity to say I get to live! You have some nerve!" Fuck how good he was looking and how my yoni was pulsating. This asshole was crazy!

"Look, bitch, I'm not in the mood for your shit. You can either give me the information voluntarily or I'll beat it out of you. I suggest you choose wisely."

Jevar hopped off the sofa and was in my face in the blink of an eye. I took a step back and he stepped back in my face. He was so close I could feel his breath on my face. It was then I saw the venom in his eyes and knew he was stone killer. It reminded me of that same look Bryant had on his face the night he killed my friend. Jevar and Bryant were one in the same. The difference is their outer appearance. They would do whatever and to whomever to get what they wanted, even if that meant taking a life. I was sick of men treating me like shit to get to the top. This shit stopped now.

"You don't scare me with your threats. What? You gonna beat my ass or better yet kill me like you did Shanell? Go ahead and do what you have to do. Just know that little threat you spewed isn't going to get you shit out of me unless I get what the fuck I want."

I stood toe to toe with Jevar, my chest heaving up and down with my breathing, my hands balled up into fists. I no longer gave a fuck about any of this shit. If he was going to beat my ass, I was going to put up the fight of my life. I don't know if Shanell did, but he was going to have a hard time kicking my ass. Jevar nodded his head and took a step back. He ran a hand down his face before back handing me.

The blow sent me back into the wall. My head hit the frame of the picture that hung and I immediately got a headache. I shook my head trying to gain my composure. Jevar cocked his fist back and attempted to punch me in the face but I ducked to the left, and he hit the picture instead. I scrambled over into the middle of the room and got in my fighting stance.

"If you think I'm just gonna let you beat my ass, Jevar, you are sadly mistaken. Come on motherfucker, let's dance!"

He charged at me, and I did a punch and round kick combination sending him backwards. To say he was shocked was an understatement. He made another attempt to charge me again and again I did a punch and round kick combination. This time I switched hands and leg. Along with ballet, I also took up Tai Kwon Do as a kid. I'm a certified black belt. Until now though, I never had to use those training skills. Jevar must have caught on to me because he changed up his stance and got into fighting position.

"As you so put it, let's dance." He said.

Jevar came at me with different hand combinations that I matched. We went at it like this until I swung, and he ducked. He was able to grab me and place an arm around my neck. I struggled to get loose, grabbing for his shirt, his hair, anything to help me get loose. When I realized that wasn't working, I began kicking his leg. I then used my weighed and put my foot on the wall then pushed off sending us backwards landing on my coffee table. His grip loosened from around my neck. We both quickly jumped up to our feet. Jevar swung hitting me across the face. That blow had me dazed. He took that opportunity to come back-to-back with quick punches before kicking me in the stomach, sending me to the floor.

I landed on my knees heaving, trying to catch my breath. I had my arms wrapped around my midsection from the pain and when I looked up all I saw was the bottom of Jevar's shoe as he kicked me in the face. I fell backwards and it was downhill from there. Jevar stomped every part of my body, breaking bones in the process. I thought the best method was for me to lie there and take the beating praying he didn't kill me before I passed out.

Jevar

I give it to the bitch. She had balls. I underestimated her. The last thing I'd ever think of Trinity Blackshear was that she knew martial arts. But there was no way in hell I was going to let a crackhead, bony ass bitch whoop my ass. One of the things my mom did to try and keep me out of trouble when I was a youngin, was to put me in karate classes. That just made my ass even badder. But yeah, Trinity had me fucked up. I didn't get to finish her ass off though because I heard the police sirens. One of her nosey ass neighbors must have heard the commotion and called the cops. I tried to stomp the life out of her and prayed I did. Even if I didn't I did enough damage to show her I wasn't the one to be fucked with.

After my run in with Bryant at Shanell's funeral I wanted to hit up Trinity to find out what she knew about that nigga. I mean, since she came to me about him and Candy, I figured she would be more than happy to give up the info. To my surprise she wanted to talk as if she was in a position of power over me. Ain't no bitch got no power over me, not even my sister, who thinks she's calling the shots. Maybe I shouldn't have threatened her, but fuck it, that's how I roll. And if she didn't know before, I guarantee she knew now.

I had to get out of the area and lay low for a bit until I can figure out my next move. This would be the perfect time for me to hunt down Dovirs and Omar. I got too much shit going on and it's all Candy's fault! If the bitch just stayed in her place none of this shit would be happening. She decided she wanted to get bold and gain a backbone and dip on a nigga. And to find out she fucking some other nigga! Oh she done lost her mind.

I don't know why I can't just let her go and move the fuck on. Nah, I know why; no bitch ever leaves me. I leave them when I'm done with them. I wasn't and still ain't done with Candy. She has something that I've been wanting and until I have it, we ain't done. She owes me. She been living and acting as if she a broke, hood bitch when she's loaded. I've had to go along with this fake ass relationship to find out where the money is and haven't been able to get to it. Her ass has been playing that role very well. I be damned if some other nigga swoop in and get access to all that bread. I pretended to like that fat hoe all to help my sis get the money that's rightfully hers, what Mike was supposed to leave her. I wanted my cut from my part in this whole charade. I wasn't going to stop until Candy gave me what I wanted. And I got something for her, that bitch nigga Bryant McIntosh, Trinity, and anyone else who gets in my fucking way.

Chapter 19

Bryant

"Along with being in a coma and her broken arm, she also has a broken jaw, four cracked ribs, a broken nose, a concussion, and she suffered an orbital fracture in her right eye that she needs surgery for," Trinity's mom wearily explained.

"Do they know who did this?"

"Not yet, but they were able to get a good shot of him from several of her security cameras."

Rachel was a regal beauty. Everything about her puts you in mind of Diane Carroll as Dominique Deveraux in that tv show Dynasty. She always portrayed so much grace and class. For as long as I've known her, I've never heard a curse word come out of her mouth, nor had she ever spoke negatively about anyone or anything. Even though Trinity and I broke up, Rachel still called me on Sundays and pray for me.

She scrambled through her purse and pulled out her cell phone. She pecked on it a few times then held it out to me. I took it from her and without even seeing his face, knew it was Jevar. But what was their connection? Was he Trinity's dealer? Were they messing around? What have you been up to, Trinity? All these questions flooded my mind.

"Do you know that man, Bryant?"

"Unfortunately, I do. He's the same guy who killed the lady whose funeral I attended a few days ago."

"What? What is going on? Why? How do you know this man? Is this about you?" She began to cry.

I walked over to her and placed a comforting hand on her shoulder. I honestly didn't know how to answer her question. I knew Jevar was pissed about Candice, but I was not sure why he attacked Trinity. I wasn't sure if this was random or not. But at the same time, something in the back of my mind was telling me that wasn't the case. There was more to this incident, and I needed to find out what that was before someone else was hurt or seriously injured.

"My Lord! She's awake!" Rachel hopped up from the chair and ran to Trinity's bedside. She pressed the nurse button and told the nurse that answered Trinity was awake.

Trinity's left eye bulked as she ran her free hand over her mouth and jaw line. She made a squeaky noise and tears streamed down her face. My heart ached for the pain that I could see she was in. She peered over at me, and the look she gave me read so many emotions in that one eye. Pain, anger, fear, sorrow, were what I saw. I only wished she could speak so I could find out what happened. Since she was left-handed and that was the arm in a cast, it was going to be hard for her to write so that was out of the question for now.

A couple of nurses rushed into the room and began assessing her vitals, asking Trinity questions, and having her blink one or two times as a response. A few minutes later the doctor entered the room and asked Rachel and me to wait in the waiting room until he was done. As we sat in the waiting room, my phone pinged of a text notification.

Candice: How is she?

Me: She's awake…doctor examining her now

Candice: I'm glad to know she's alive. How are u?

Me: I'm pissed! Jevar did this to her

Candice: What?! OMG! Why?

Me: IDK but I will find out

Candice: Babe I'm so sorry for dragging you and Trinity in my mess. I really feel it's best if we cut ties until they catch Jevar. I don't want to see anyone else get hurt.

I stood and started pacing after reading her last text. I read it over several times and had to woosah to get my anger under control before responding. Instead of replying by text, I called her because I wanted, need Candice to hear me when I said what I had to say. The phone rang twice before she picked up.

"Hey, babe. What's up?"

"Candice, why do you keep trying to end us? Why do you think running away is going to solve your problems?"

She sighed and cleared her throat. Silence ran through the line about a minute before she finally responded.

"I'm not running away."

"Bullshit!"

"Can you let me finish please?"

"Oh, sorry. Go ahead."

"I'm not running away. I have a plan in place that will get Jevar to calm down, but just enough to get him caught by the cops. The good cops anyways because he does have some of APD in his pockets."

"I'm listening."

"Let's not talk about this over the phone. How about you come over to where I've been staying. You can finally meet Mrs. Piercing. I'll fill you in on my plan then. Okay?"

The doctor entered the waiting room and headed towards Rachel and me.

"Babe, let me call you back, and yes I'll come see you when I leave here, okay?"

"Okay good, love you."

"I love you too."

I ended the call and placed my attention on the doctor.

"Given the circumstances, I'd say she is doing great. I don't see any major issues. Now that she's awake, we'll do a thorough exam on her eye to see if she will still need surgery or if it's healing on its own. If it is, then surgery won't be needed. We are going to keep her here because of her fractured jaw. We need to monitor her to make sure it heals properly. If she progresses well within the next couple of weeks, we can talk about releasing her only if she will have someone to care for her around the clock."

"Oh, thank you Doctor! Thank you, God," Rachel said pulling the doctor into a hug. He graciously patted her on the back.

Once they pulled away from their embrace, he turned and left the waiting room. Rachel waved her hand around praising God for the news before turning to me with her tear-filled eyes gleaming.

"Isn't that wonderful news, Bryant? My girl is going to be fine."

"Yes, ma'am it is."

Her expression turned serious, and her eyes went cold. She walked over to me and stood closely so that only I could hear what she was about to speak.

"I want you to find that man and drag his ass for the filth he is. Do whatever you have to do. Do you understand me, Bryant?"

"I do."

"Good, now I'm going back in to sit with her. Handle your business."

With that, Rachel turned and left me standing in the waiting room shocked as hell at her request. To know Rachel is to know that those words that came from her mouth were the last thing you'd ever expect from her. This is the first time I have ever heard her speak a curse word in the many years that I've know her. To hear her say to do any type of harm to another person is out of her character. This is proof that when people are stuck between a rock and a hard place, they will do whatever needs to be done to get them out of that situation. I can't say I'm a stranger because I've been there and have done some shit that would end my career as well as my family's reputation if it ever got out.

For a brief second, I wondered if Trinity ever let the cat out the bag. But she couldn't, wouldn't, if she wanted to continue to live her life. I needed to find out why Jevar was at her house and what their connection was. Right now wasn't the right time with Rachel here. She was going to smother the lady with her presence. I'd just have to come back later and get answers from Trinity then. Now I needed to get over to Candice and see where her head was at with this plan of hers to bring Jevar down.

Chapter 20

Jevar

I've been laying low since I fucked oh girl up. She put up a good fight but there was no way she was gone whoop my ass, no matter how much martial arts training she had. My damn picture has been plastered all over the fucking news outlet since Shanell's funeral, and they have identified me as a person of interest in Trinity's assault. This just goes to show no matter how much you paid the pigs, they will still fuck you over. Even with Shingles grimy ass. He gave the info on where Candy's ass was staying but he was the main muthafucka on TV talking about I'm a wanted man.

I've drove over the address Shingles gave me hoping to snatch Candy up, but the neighborhood was too lively during the day with bad ass children everywhere and elderly people doing yard work. I even went back in the middle of the night a few times, but it was too illuminated with the streetlights, then they ass had the neighborhood watch people out and about. One muthafucka had the nerve to come knock on my damn window to see if I needed some help. I would have popped his ass, but there was another nosey muthafucka standing guard across the way. With my face all on the news, there was no way I would be able to snatch up Candy. Damn! I had to find another way.

And on top of that, Marcus has been blowing up my phone every day for the past three weeks. They still haven't found out what happened to that shipment a few months ago, or at least I don't think they have. Shid, I jacked that muthafucka up and used it to get more dough in my pockets. It was time I ventured off and really became king of this city and not some worker under another nigga who didn't even live here. Marcus was generous with his prices, but it was time I was boss and not working under him. I even went to him man to man, and he came at me ignorant with his response. So, fuck him. I did what needed to be done to solidify my spot on top. Shit would have gone smoothly had Dovirs and Omari fell in line and followed my lead. These two bitches was loyal to Marcus and not me; that was a problem.

Even with the problem I had right now though, I really needed them right now because I didn't trust any of these other niggas; not even the niggas that helped me jack the shipment. Another problem I had, was I didn't think I could trust them anymore after how I talked shit to them. At this point I needed to reach out and see what it was, so I can get back to business. My cash was low, and I needed to reup. I had no choice at this point. So, fuck it. I pulled my phone out and dialed Dovirs' number.

"Yo," he answered on the first ring.

"What's good my nigga?"

"Who dis?" I ran my hand down my face, annoyed by his question.

"It's J nigga. Who you think?"

"Oh, damn. I haven't heard from yo' ass in a minute shit. I forgot what you sound like. What the fuck do you want?"

"What's been going on? I haven't heard from you or O in a minute. What, y'all just said fuck me?"

"Nah, you said fuck us, so we don't rock with you now. But if you haven't already, I advise you to get with Marcus and straighten that shit out about that missing shipment. He's still pissed about it and looking for yo' ass."

"Mane, fuck Marcus for now. I need to get up with you and O asap. I need to make a visit to Verna and need y'all to roll with me on this."

"You know, you got some balls calling us to help you. What happened? You don't have clout like you thought? Or is it that your shit has finally caught up with you and now you need the niggas that's been holding you down from day one to come to your rescue?"

This is why I didn't want to hit his ass up. He got to act like a bitch about shit. I don't have time for this shit. I knew I should have called Omari. He was more level-headed and rational. Dovirs always had to go deep in shit. For the most part, it worked to my advantage, but right now wasn't the time.

"Hello."

"Yeah, nigga, I'm here," I told him.

"Yo check it. I'm willing to look past your bullshit if you admit you were the one who had something to do with that shipment. Just admit that shit and we can move like nothing ever happened. Also, O and I get a fifty percent cut you make off Verna. No exceptions."

I held the phone for a few minutes contemplating whether or not to come clean, but what other option did I have at this point? Then this nigga wants half of the fucking cut! I had only five bands left in cash. My bitch ass sista emptied our joint account and she dipped out on me. Since I still haven't been able to get up with Candy's ass, that account was also low. That heifer left the exact amount of money I gave her the first year we was together. I talked her into us getting that account hoping she was going to put her money from the will and the insurance policies into them, but she didn't. She only put money she made from the salon in it. I still had my emergency stash spot no one knew about, but that was the very last resort.

My main stash houses got hit a few weeks ago. I'm almost certain Omari and Dovirs had something to do with that, so I was in a bind right now. I had no other choice to get shit back under control and back the way it should be.

"Yeah, I was behind that missing shipment. I had some goons from Miami come in and help high-jack that shit. Afterwards, I sold that shit on the side and made a profit off it so that I can make my come up without Marcus. It was time to move from under him and that was the only way. If it looked like he messed up the shipment, then we could come up with him out of the way," I explained.

"You honestly thought that was gonna work?" Dovirs asked.

"Yeah, nigga."

"Aiight then. That's what it is. Thanks for finally coming clean about it. Yo, check it. I'm throwing a birthday party for O this Saturday night at the Spot. You already know, it's gonna be a block party. Come through and break bread with us niggas. We can chop it up then. Bet? Now what about the fifty-fifty deal?" He asked.

"That's a bet." Fuck! I did not want to agree to that but had no choice.

"Then that's what it is. The party starts at nine. I'll get at ya then."

We disconnected the call. I felt a bit better knowing I was gonna finally have my day ones back on my side. But I was having a lingering feeling that was telling me to skip the party. I rolled over in the bed and wished I had Candy lying next to me so I could slide up in her wet, tight pussy. It still pissed me off that I wasn't able to get to her at Shanell's funeral since it was impossible to snatch her up from where she was staying. I'm still wondering who the fuck she living with. Had her ass not passed out in front of the congregation, I would have been able to snatch her ass up. Since that day, she has been M.I.A. I even tried to get to Trinity's room, but they increased security and had them guarding her room around the clock.

Sleep crept up on me. I smiled a as I thought of how my reign on top was getting closer and closer. It was time to get all these muthafuckas back in line and let them know no matter how it may seem, I'm still the HNIC.

Dovirs

"What he say?" Omari asked as soon as I hung up.

"This nigga really thinks shit is gravy. He gonna come through for your party Saturday night. He did finally admit to taking that shipment. But check it. He wants us to go see Verna and he's willing to go fifty-fifty on the deal."

"Word? You know that nigga is down bad if he's hitting us up, admitting to taking that shipment, and agreeing to give us half of a cut! Naw, I'm not believing that. He's up to something."

"Yeah, and said he had some niggas from Miami help him. O, this is going to be our only chance to get at him for all the bullshit."

"Yep. I'm with ya bruh, and you know the only goons savage enough to do some shit like that was Stone and Crimson."

"Exactly what I was thinking. Let me hit up Marcus and put him on."

"Put that shit on speaker so I can hear his reaction."

I was just about to dial Marcus number when I spotted Candy, Jevar's girl walking towards us.

"Yo, what's up Candy? I haven't seen you in a minute," I said giving her a hug. She then gave O a hug.

"Hey, Dovirs, Omari. How y'all doing?"

"Shit, I'm good, shawty. How you been tho?" O asked.

"I'm doing alright. I was driving past here and saw y'all so I turned around and came back to chop it up for a few minutes," she said.

"Oh yeah? What's up?" I asked tilting my head to the side.

"Have y'all seen Jevar?."

"Naw, I haven't seen his ass in a minute either. I just got off the phone with him tho," I told her.

"Ok, so I'm sure y'all heard I dipped on Jevar some months ago." She spoke as if she was contemplating what she wanted to say to us. Quite frankly I'm glad she finally left that nigga. She deserved better than him. He dogged her ass out, but I learned from previous incidents not to get in between couples issues. I tried to help a chick who was getting her ass beat by her dude at the park, but her dumbass turned on me. After that, I said never again.

"Yeah, I heard. Mona told me how you came to the shop with a bruise on your face and that you hadn't been back to the shop since that day," O told her.

"Right. That night I went home and found him in bed with Sheree's nasty ass."

"Damn, that's fucked up," I exclaimed.

"That's some fowl shit, and with that nasty hoe," O scrunched his nose up.

"My feelings exactly. Anyway, I took off and been keeping a low profile ever since, except to attend Shanell's funeral."

"My condolences to you. I saw story on the news," O said.

"Do they know who did it?" I asked.

"They don't, but I do. It was y'alls boy."

"Are you serious?" O asked in shock.

"Get the fuck out of here," I said just as shock. "Why?"

"I believe he was trying to find out where I was and thought Shanell knew, but she didn't. I never told her where I was staying because she has told him in the past where I was. I didn't want that this time because I'm done with him. That's what I came to talk to y'all about," she explained.

"I'm listening," I told her.

"I heard yall were beefing with Jevar and not fucking with him anymore."

"Shid, you heard right," O said nodding his head.

"I also heard about your infamous block party this Saturday," she continued.

"You know how we get down," I hyped up.

"Yes, I do," she chuckled before turning serious. "I want to use the party to set Jevar up." O and I looked at each other before looking back at Candy.

"Keep talking," O said.

"Yeah, tell us what you had in mind," I told her.

"I need to get him there, and somehow tied up. I am willing to be the bait. You can call him back and tell him I'll be at the party to guarantee he will be there. I'm tired of running and hiding. It's time I take my life back. I can't get it with Jevar chasing after me."

The poor woman looked like she was on the verge of a nervous breakdown. The anguish on her face and the tears that were on the verge of falling from her eyes tugged at a G's heartstring. I know I said I didn't get in other people's shit and usually I don't, but this was a situation I was more than happy to get in the mix of. This was the perfect opportunity to take that nigga down.

"I'm with it," I said.

"I'm down like four flat tires," O exaggerated.

"All you need to do is just show up. O and I will handle the rest," I explained to Candy.

"I already know it's not going to be that easy. As soon as Jevar sees me, he is going to flip out. He's going to act a fucking fool and fight me."

"He ain't that dumb to do that shit in front of everybody," I said not believing that shit myself. The look she gave me said the same thing.

"Jevar has something to prove. He thought he had control over me, so he is going to do something to try and embarrass me and put me in my place. I'm telling you he's going to go crazy. But don't worry, I'll be very prepared for him."

"We got your back, lil mama. As long as what you got planned don't fuck up my shit, we good, you heard me?"

"Yes, I hear you," she smiled.

"That's what's up then. The party kicks off at nine."

"Okay, cool. I'll see y'all then, and thanks for your help." She gave us both hugs before she turned and headed back to her car. I pulled my cell out and snapped a picture of her just as she hopped in and peeled out.

"This party is about to be a lit," O said.

"Yep. Let's just hope shawty isn't in over her head. That nigga Jevar is going to be in beast mode when he sees her. "

"Hell yeah, bruh. We just got to make sure he don't kill her," O replied.

Me: Picture of Candy with the caption 'I just ran n2 your girl n talked her into coming to the party'. I lied n said u won't be there

Jevar: did she believe u

Me: yep...told her we been beefing over business

Me: she said she heard about it

Jevar: how da fuck she hear bout it

Me: IDK but after O told her to come celebrate wit him 4 his bday she agreed

Me: I kno y'all having issues....just want shit 2 get back 2 the way it used 2b

Jevar: That's what's up....good looking out

Me: Ain't nuthin

I then dialed Marcus number. He answered immediately. Shit I don't think the phone rang a whole ring before he answered.

"Speak," Marcus demanded.

"Yeah, I just got off the line with Jevar. He admitted to taking that missing shipment and he thinks we cool again. He'll be on deck Saturday night for O's birthday party at The Spot."

"That's good news. I'll be touching down. Don't let that nigga out of your sight and don't tell him I'm in town."

"Bet, but you should also know, he said he had help from Miami. My bet is on Crimson and Stone, and he wants to go see Verna."

"You'd won that bet too. That nigga Crimson hit me up and let his mouth run about the shit."

O and I were in shock by this bit of info. Something had to go down if he turned on Stone. Those two were like two peas in a pod. They did nothing apart and always had each other's back. So, for him to let it rip on Stone, shit got real.

"Damn! You can't trust no man in these streets."

"Especially when you dealing with grimy, greedy muthafuckas. No need to worry about Verna because he won't make it there to see him. I'll see you niggas soon."

"Bet."

Chapter 21

Candy

I scrambled around my room getting dressed. I finally invited Verdell over to meet Mrs. Piercing. I was nervous as if he was meeting my mom for the first time. I saw her as a second mom and wanted her to like him just as I wanted my real mom to like him. Verdell has become such a big shining ball of light in my life. He has shown me everything I desired and deserved in a man. He has been patient with me when I was 'bout fed up with myself. He has always kept it real with me and hasn't given me a reason to doubt him. His actions have been in line with his words, and for that I am grateful. But in order for me to continue on with my life and be with him completely, I had to close this chapter of my life with Jevar forever.

That was also another reason I was nervous. I planned to tell Verdell and Mrs. Piercing about my plan to set up Jevar. I went over it in my mind for several days since I passed out at Shanell's funeral and believe it was my best option; my only option. I was tired of hiding and tired of innocent people getting hurt by him. First, he killed my best friend, and then he almost killed Trinity. Even though I felt some kind of way at how Trinity approached me at the gas station that day, I didn't want to see her hurt.

Never in my life did I ever think I'd have this type of trauma going on in my life. I'm not sure how I found myself in a situation like this. Even though my dad cheated on my mom, I never witnessed him abuse her. I still haven't figured out what really caused him to cheat on her and with Betty. I've always wanted to ask my mom what happened, but I was afraid of what she would say as well as how it would make her feel. I've always felt things didn't add up, and even when I tried asking my sisters, they brushed me off.

Whatever it was that went on, my family has shielded me from it. It made me think that was why I found myself in shitty relationships with shitty men. Maybe it was daddy issues I suffered from. Maybe it was the divorce and having to split my time in between my parents' homes.

This relationship with Jevar has taught me one hard lesson. Never will I ever ignore the signs showing who a person is. I will no longer push my well-being and feelings to the back to make someone else happy. Once a person shows me who they are, I will believe them from that moment and distance myself from anyone is not about being positive or kind. I am learning to love every aspect of myself and whoever comes into my life will have to accept me as I am, flaws and all.

I stood in front of the bathroom mirror, putting on some lip gloss that had a hint of pink to it when the doorbell rang. My belly started doing somersaults. I looked over my appearance once more then headed out of the room. The smell of the green bean casserole, baked chicken, homemade mashed potatoes, dinner rolls, and made from scratch peach cobbler I prepared whiffed through the air. Those somersaults turned into a growl with that mouth-watering aroma in the air.

By the time I got the door, Mrs. Piercing and Verdell were in deep conversation. They were speaking as if they already knew each other, which surprised me. I took in the two people who have made big impacts on my life in this past year, and it made me misty-eyed.

Who would have thought a girl from the hood would be in the presence of not one, but two millionaires, who were not obnoxious assholes but were kind and generous, down to earth people? There was no doubt about it that I was an around the way girl. They both were dressed in nice slacks and crisp, collared shirts, where I was dressed in a pair of ripped, hip-hugging skinny jeans and a baby tee that had the word diva written across the front.

"Candice didn't tell me it was you she's been dating," Mrs. Piercing's voice brought me back to the now. She then turned to me and placed her hands on her hips. "Candice, so he was who you were on the phone with the day you got the call about Shanell?"

"Yes ma'am."

"Isn't this something? You got with my cousin who I always thought would be a good fit for you," she gushed.

"Wait. What?" I looked between them, confused as hell.

"Yeah, babe. Marion is my cousin on my mom's side."

Verdell walked over to me and wrapped his arms around me. He pecked me on the lips and my panties immediately became moist. I had to pull out of his embrace to help calm my throbbing coochie.

"I didn't know y'all were related for one, and for two, I had no clue we would be at this level of a relationship."

"Well, I'm glad you two are together," she waved a hand from me to him. "I can't tell you how happy I was when Lisia told me you and that woman, Trinity, were no longer together. Something always seemed off about that relationship," Mrs. Piercing frowned with a head shake.

"And to think all this time, you've been staying out here with my favorite cousin. Cuz why didn't you tell me you had a sexy, single lady staying with you?" Verdell teased.

"To be honest, I was going to call you but not until Candice was rid of that lunatic for good."

We all sat at the table that was already set, and food waiting to be served and eaten. Since living with Mrs. Piercing, I had become accustomed to having breakfast, lunch, and dinner at the table with her and making sure we said prayer before even touching a fork. After Verdell led us in prayers, we dug in the dishes, filing out plates with everything. We ate in silence for a few minutes before Mrs. Piercing spoke.

"Like I was saying earlier, Bryant, I was going to call you once I knew Candice was done with Jevar for good. When I first met Candice, I thought of you for her, but once she told me about Jevar I left it alone.

Even though you were with Trinity, I was willing to steer you away from her. I never knew what you saw in her."

I chuckled at the way her face contorted when she said Trinity's name. She looked as if she had just bit down into a lemon.

"Marion, you don't have to tell me. I know. I know. None of the family liked her, but she was loyal until she got hooked on the drugs. Our relationship was just a happen stance," he shrugged.

"Did you ever have any idea that she was on that stuff before you went to her house and found out?" I asked.

"Nah, I had no clue about the drugs or her sleeping around on me. I guess it was because I was so engulfed in work since I had just really taken over the family business."

"Mmm."

I took a sip of water before placing a fork of mashed potatoes in my mouth. My mind was on overdrive as I gathered my thoughts to tell them my plan. I knew it was about to be mayhem once I told them what I had in mind, but nevertheless, this was what needed to be done so I could get Jevar Jackson out of my life for good.

"Okay, so here me out on my plan to take Jevar down," I started. That immediately had Verdell and Mrs. Piercing's heads snapping in my direction. He gently sat his fork down onto his plate, while Mrs. Piercing continued to eat, but was paying attention to me.

"Word on the street is that Jevar was behind a shipment of drugs and guns that were sent down from his connect in Chicago. His connect is big time dealer Marcus Armstrong, and he isn't too happy about his stuff being missing. On top of that, he fell out with his two best friends behind the missing shipment. Jevar always thought he was the top guy and talked down on Omari and Dovirs like they were minions, but after this last incident, they went their separate ways."

"So, what does all of this have to do with you and your plan?" Verdell asked.

"I saw Dovirs and Omari earlier, and they agreed to help me set up Jevar this weekend at Omari's birthday block party they throw every year. They're going to tell Jevar I was invited and agreed to come if he wasn't there. The thing though, is that Marcus and his guys are going to be there, too. My plan is to contact have Detective Shingles and APD on standby so they can take him in."

"Have you lost your damned mind?" Verdell belted.

"Wh—"

"Hell no! It ain't happening, Candice. You're going to get yourself killed. Detective Shingles ain't no damn good cop," Verdell slapped his hand on the table causing me to jump.

"And you expecting him to just go with the police in silence, without putting up a fight? Not to mention, there is going to be a major drug dealer who has connections with the Cartel in the mist of this," Mrs. Piercing chimed in.

"How do you know you can even trust those guys not to turn you over to Jevar? Huh, Candice?"

"Stop yelling at me." I stood to my feet knocking over the chair I just occupied. "Look, Dovirs and Omari have been feeling bad vibes from Jevar for a long time and had been waiting for the right time to make their move. Jevar knocking off that shipment was their window of opportunity along with him giving Marcus the run around about it. They need me to bring Jevar out of hiding since he's been laying low after he attacked Trinity and his face has been plastered all over the news. The only way he's going to climb from under that rock is knowing he will be able to get at me. This is the best way."

I looked between Verdell and Mrs. Piercing with now tear-filled eyes. They both have been hounding me about handling my business and dealing with Jevar and this is the best way I knew how. I held on to the edge of the dining table with my head hanging as the tears streamed down my face. I rocked back and forth not knowing what else to do.

"She's right, Bryant. This is the best way to catch Jevar. He isn't going to come out from hiding unless he has a guarantee he will be able to get to Candice. She made a fool of him by disappearing while still living in the city, but he can't seem to find her, or he's broke and just about low on money if not wiped out already."

"I am not letting you go in there and get yourself killed. It ain't happening," Verdell said forcefully.

I looked up to find him standing next to me. He was breathing so hard, his breath was hitting me in my face. His chest heaved up and down with every breath he took. The rage I saw in his eyes scared the shit out of me, but I wasn't going to let that deter me from what I had to do.

"Bryant, you don't have a say in the matter. This is my life, and it's time that I take it back. You may not like my plan, but this is what it's going to be."

"Oh so, now I'm Bryant? And I do have a say so. The day you came into my life I had a say so. And what I say is law!" He pointed a finger in my face, and his eyes bucked.

"You are not my daddy! He is dead so you can't tell me what to do. And that is law!" I rolled my neck with much attitude.

"Hey, hey, hey, you two need to calm down. You're taking your anger and frustration out on each other for no reason," Ms. Piercing blurted out as she ran and got in between us.

She grabbed one of our hands in each of hers, looking back and forth between us. Verdell and I glared at each other like two fighters who were about to duke it out for the championship belt. I was so pissed and hurt he came at me the way he did, talkin' bout what he say is law. Nigga please! I'm glad I finally got to see his true colors while we were still fresh in this relationship because as of now, I was done.

"Nah, Mrs. Piercing, Bryant just showed me why I am going through with my plan. I left Jevar and have been dodging him for damn near a year because of his controlling and abusive ways. Now, the moment I do something Bryant doesn't agree with, his controlling behavior come out. Like I just said, this is my life. Now that I finally found my voice and strength and know my worth, I will never go down that road again. So we are done!" I snatched away from Mrs. Piercing's hold and ran to my room.

"Candice, wait," I heard them both call out to me.

I ignored them as I slammed my door and locked it. I quickly grabbed one of my duffle bags and tossed some clothes in them. I heard a knock on my door but ignored it as I ran into the bathroom and grabbed my toiletries and tossed them in the bag.

"Candice, open the door," Mrs. Piercing called out to me.

I continued to ignore her as I made my way inside the walk-in closet and felt inside one of my purses and pulled out the Springfield Armory HELLCAT OSP 9mm Semi-Auto Pistol I'd purchased a couple of days after Jevar murdered Shanell and having that conversation with Mrs. Piercing. I really didn't care for guns but knew I had to pack some heat just in case Jevar caught me slipping. If I was going to go through with this plan, I sure as hell was going to need that fire.

"Candice, open this door!"

I swung the door open startling Mrs. Piercing and rushed past her. I made it to the front door but was halted by someone yanking my bag right off my shoulder. I turned around to Verdell standing there with a look of horror on his face. It quickly turned into worry, followed by anger.

"You just gonna leave my cousin's house like this after everything she's done for you?" he asked credulously.

"No dumbass, I'm not running away from her. I'm getting away from you so I can handle my business. Now give me my bag so I can go."

"Candice, please don't go like this. Calm down and think this through," Mrs. Piercing begged.

"Look, I'm sorry for how I came at you. I never should have said that to you. It just pissed me off that you are putting your life in danger with a plan that is not airtight. Baby, we just want you to think this through some more. Please don't go."

"Please, Candice."

Bryant

When Candice said she was going to let these guys use her as bait to get at that fool, I lost it. All common sense left me as I went off. No grown man would be okay with his woman putting herself in danger. And if she thought I was just gonna sit back and just let her go out on her own, she was out of her damn mind!

Nah, I shouldn't have told her what I said was law, but I needed to get my point across to let her know that plan of hers was too dangerous. I love Candice and would burn this city down if something happened to her. So when she went off on me and told me we were done, my heart sank to my gut while at the same time I was turned on. I stood there with my mouth open in disbelief. That newfound confidence Candice had was sexy as hell. Damn!

"Let's all just think this through rationally," Marion's voice cut off my explicit thoughts of Candice.

We all sat in the living room in silence, minus Candice sniffling. I slid to the edge of the sofa and reached for her hand, but she moved it.

She sat with her head turned away from me, elbow propped up on the arm of the chair resting under her chin.

"Baby, listen. I'm sorry for going off on you a few minutes ago. I'm not trying to control you. I just want to help you and keep you safe. I want you to have a plan B in place. That's all. I cannot let anything happen to you. I wouldn't be able to live without you in my life."

I watched as the tears streamed down the side of her face I could see. Marion stood and left the room. I moved so that I was on my knees on the floor by Candice and grabbed her free hand, holding it tightly in my hand to keep her from snatching away from me.

"Candice, look at me."

She reluctantly turned to face me. My heart broke into a million pieces seeing her like this. Hurting my lady in any way is not the business I'm in. I ran a hand down my face and sighed.

"Baby, I'm sorry. Please just understand I want what you want, and I understand what you must do. I just want you to be careful. Detective Shingles is not going to help you. If you tell him what's going on he's going to alert Jevar."

"How do you know that?"

Marion returned with a box of Kleenex and handed it to Candice. She took the box and pulled a couple out to wipe her face and nose.

"Because he is in Jevar's pockets. He's been a crook a long time. You remember how Ma Fe told you about her son. He even tried to hem up a friend of mine who lived in a who other state."

I stood and began pacing the floor. I had to tell Candice about her dad and didn't know how she was going to take it. I rubbed my forehead before sitting back on the sofa next the chair she sat in. I leaned forward with my elbows resting on my thighs.

"There's also another reason I know those two are in cahoots with each other."

"Okay, what?"

"What I'm about to tell you, you need to have your sisters and your mom present for this."

"Why? What is going on?"

"Yeah, Bryant, what's going on?" Marion asked, concern in her voice.

"Babe, just call and get your people on facetime or on speaker, please."

Candice reached in her bag and pulled out her tablet. She pressed on it a few times and then it began to ring. She propped the tablet on the coffee table against a vase. One by one, three angelic faces filled the screen

"Hey pumpkin," the woman I knew off the bat was Charlene. She smiled brightly but that quickly disappeared as her eyes roamed Candice's face.

"Candy, what's wrong? Why are you crying?" one of her sisters asked.

"Yes lil' sis, what's up?"

"Hey, y'all. Um, there's so much I need to tell y'all."

"Who is that man standing beside you?" the other sister asked.

"Oh, this is Bryant McIntosh and I have Mrs. Piercing here also. Bryant, this is my mom, Charlene, my sister, Cassandra, and my other sister Michelle." Candice pointed to each of the ladies as she made her introductions.

"Wait a minute! I know you are not talking the Bryant McIntosh! The billionaire software guru Bryant McIntosh," Cassandra said.

While Charlene and Michelle looked puzzled, Cassandra was gleaming. Marion and Candice both laughed and shook their heads at her excitement.

"Yes, Sand, that's him and we're dating."

"What?" they all asked in unison.

"Wait lil' sis, what the heck is going on? Is this a good idea with that fool Jevar still looking for you?" Cassandra asked.

"You're moving too fast don't you think?" that was Michelle.

"Will you two shut the hell up and let her speak?" Charlene fussed. They both became quiet but were clearly agitated. "Now, Candice, baby, what is going on up there in Atlanta? I have to agree with your sisters. You seem to be moving too fast and you still have unfinished business with Jevar."

"Well Momma, that's why I have y'all on this conference call. And if they will shut up I can finish what I was about to say."

I rubbed my baby's back because I could feel the frustration steaming off her body. The pressure and all the drama surrounding Jevar has reached a boiling point, and Candice was about to explode. She looked up at me and a gave me a half-hearted smile before turning back to the tablet. She let out a sigh then let it all out.

"Y'all know what's going on with Jevar and me and why I've been staying her with Mrs. Piercing. Before all of this happened and what I thought was us in a better place, I thought I sent a text message to one of Jevar's burner phones, but the text went to Verdell, um, Bryant instead." She pointed her thumb back at me.

"What kind of text, sis?" Cassandra asked with a smirk.

"The kind that was meant for my man at that time."

"So, you were what y'all young folks call it, uh, sexting? So, you sent Jevar one of those things but it went to him instead?" Charlene asked.

Everyone broke out laughing at her question except Candice who buried her face in her hands. The Carson women were all beautiful and are a version of their mother in some way. But Candice was a carbon copy of her mother.

"Ma, what do you know about sexting?" Michelle asked between giggles.

"I was watching divorce court and the wife was going off on the husband because she found nude pictures and raunchy text messages from several different women in his phone and Judge Tavern said 'oh so you got other women sexting you'."

We all laughed even harder because Charlene was so serious with it. We shared a few more laughs behind that before getting back to the subject at hand.

"Okay, so I'm not sure how long it was after I mistakenly texted Bryant, but he texted me out of the blue one day and we began a friendship."

"It took four months of us texting back and forth every day before she finally agreed to meet me in person," I told them.

"That long? Are you for real?" Cassandra asked.

"Yeah. I didn't know he was Bryant McIntosh until the day we met in person. Plus, he gave me his middle name when we began texting back and forth."

"Okay so how long has this been going on?" Michelle chimed in.

"A total of six months now."

"That long and you just now telling us? That's fowl, Candy," Cassandra said with an attitude.

"Cassandra shut your damn mouth! Do you call us and tell us everything you're doing?" Charlene scolded her. "I didn't think so. Hell, I'm surprised you even answered this here conference call, since you don't seem to have time for your family anymore."

"Momma, it's okay. Look, I haven't told anyone really except Shanell and that was because she went with me to me him. I have been under the radar until Shanell got killed."

"Have they found the person responsible? I spoke to Gertrude, and she hasn't been doing so well since Shanell's been gone," Charlene said.

"That's tied into all of this mess with Jevar. He killed Shanell because he believed she knew where I've been staying but lying about it. But she didn't know. I never told her for fear if she knew, she would end up telling him. I didn't tell her thinking it was for her protection but as we saw, nothing was going to protect her from Jevar's rage."

"Where in the hell did you find this man, Candy? I mean, damn, he is literally the devil!" Michelle fussed.

"Candice didn't find him. Jevar set out to find you because you were a target," I told her.

"What are you talking about? I met Jevar at a club one night." She frowned up at me.

"Yeah, you did but that was a set up. You and your family are a target. He's been playing you all this time because he's trying to get that insurance policy your dad left you."

Chapter 22

Bryant

"What? How do you know this, Bryant?" Marion spoke for the first time in a while.

Sitting on the arm of the chair Candice occupied, I let out a sigh before breaking the bad news to them.

"When Candice sent me that text message, I had a very extensive background check done on her, or at least, the person whose phone number that text came from. Being who I am, I have to be extremely careful and cautious about people and things, including random texts from numbers I don't know. Well, my guy who did the background dug up so much stuff and so quickly about you all."

"What stuff?" Candice interrupted me.

"The basic background information, your names, where you live, social media accounts, where you work. But like I said my guy, Aaron, somehow finds stuff you may have buried in the desert when no one was there to help you. Anyway, he had information about Michael and his wife Betty."

"Tread lightly, Mr. McIntosh." Charlene's voice was stiff and strong, but more than anything, powerful.

"I think it's time she knows, don't you think, Ms. Charlene?"

She turned away from the camera. Michelle and Cassandra's eyes grew at the realization of what I was about to say. Candice caught on to it and slowly looked up at me. She tilted her head to the side with a look of confusion. It's a damn shame all this woman's life she didn't know the truth about her father and what he did.

"It's not your place to tell her," Charlene said through tears.

"Tell me what momma?"

"Mommy, no, don't," Michelle begged.

"It's time she knew. I should have never shielded her from this. Candice, even though your father was not happy you didn't turn out to be a boy as the doctor told us you were, you were the apple of his eye. Yes, he loved you Cassandra and Michelle, but he had a connection with you, Candice, that I still cannot explain today. After you were born, he was home more often, being with his family. He had even given out positions to some of his top men to keep his organization running smoothly so he could be home every night with you girls. That was, until he started messing around with that wench, Betty, and got her pregnant."

"Mom, what is it that you're not telling me?"

"Your father was a major drug dealer. He was one of the most notorious drug king pens in the country. You wouldn't know if you didn't know him because of how and where he lived. He kept us in the hood so that wouldn't bring a lot of attention to him and what he was doing. It also was his way of keeping us safe, by having us close to where he operated. After Betty got pregnant with his son, that is when he left me, us. But that baby would never even get to take a breath because he was stillborn."

"This is a joke, right? You can't be serious right now," Candice stood and began pacing.

"Sis, unfortunately, mom is telling the truth. Our daddy was a gangster. His name reigned in the streets even now. That is why I left home and joined the military. I needed, wanted to be as far away from that place as possible.," Cassandra admitted.

"Luckily, he kept us shielded from that lifestyle so not too many people know of us. Plus, once he got with Betty and married her, we were pushed further in the background since she wanted nothing to do with us," Michelle stated.

"He tried to come back to me after they lost that baby, but I filed for divorce. I delt with a lot of Michael Carson's shit for a long time, but the day he walked out on me to be with my best friend, I was done. Because of his connections, the custody arrangements of how your time was divided between the two of us was mandated by the courts."

"So, all my life, y'all been lying to me about daddy?" Candice stopped pacing and placed her hand on her hips.

"It's my fault, Candice. Your sisters were going through it, knowing what he did and getting picked on by the other children in school behind it who knew he was your father. When you came along, I decided I was not going to put you through that. So, I told you he was a businessman who owned several different businesses in town."

"Technically, it wasn't a lie. You just left out the part about him slanging drugs," Michelle quipped.

"Okay, but what does all of this have to do with Jevar, Bryant?" Cassandra asked the million-dollar question.

"Well, it turns out Jevar is Betty's little brother, and they are responsible for killing Michael."

Gasps rang out amongst them all. I knew this was going to be a heavy bomb to drop. I don't know if Candice will ever recover from knowing she had been sleeping with the enemy for years and not have an inkling.

"No, no, no, no. You're lying!" Candice shouted.

"I'm so sorry baby, but it's true."

I went over to her and grabbed her just as her legs gave out under her. She let out a wail that pierced my ears. I scooped her up in my arms and walked over to the chair and sat with her in my lap. I rocked her the way a parent would rock their child to sleep.

"It's okay, baby. You didn't know," I did my best to comfort her.

"Bryant, how did your friend find this information?" Marion asked.

"He has been keeping tabs on Jevar since Shanell's funeral. He placed a tracker on his car that also serves as a listening device. He is on a recording talking to Betty about them finishing up the job. Betty is pressuring him to do whatever he had to do to get the money from Candice."

"I knew Betty was a bitch, but I see now she's also certifiable, too! Candice, baby, don't let this break you. He has tried all this time and didn't succeed, and he can't now. I know you're hurt, but you will heal. You're broken, but you got a new man that will help put you back together. Right now, you feel weak, but you are stronger than you know. You have your father's blood running through your veins. You may look like me, but you are every bit of him. You just have to channel that which is within you. You got this, baby."

Charlene's words were so on point. She made me stick my chest out more, and she wasn't even speaking to me or about me. Her words seem to resonate with Candice. It was as if she was a blown lightbulb that had been replaced. Her energy illuminated and sparked a brightness in her eyes. I could tell the wheels in her mind began to turn.

"Thanks, mom. I needed that. I can always count on you to bring me out of my funk. So, this is my plan and I need y'all to listen," she said with confidence before turning to face me.

"Bryant, you said you can help. What help do you have I can use?"

"Well, my beautiful lady, I'm glad you asked. My best friend since childhood is, how can I put this? Well, basically he's in the same business as Jevar."

"What?" Candice asked.

"Seriously?" that was Cassandra.

"Lawd," Charlene shook her head, then burst out into laughter.

"It's true," Marion told them. "They've been thick as thieves since they were about nine years old, right after Bryant and Bradford kicked his butt along with several other boys' butts during a birthday party in my old neighborhood one summer," she laughed. "Those boys underestimated them because they weren't from the hood. They didn't think Bryant and Bradford could fight."

"Well, Bryant, you and Candy have something in common. She used to get into fights a lot when she was little," Michelle chimed in. Both she and Cassandra laughed.

"Nobody asked you to volunteer anything, Chelly," Candice chuckled.

"I knew she had some feistiness in her," I told them. "But check it, Dontae has also been keeping his ear to the streets about Jevar. He also informed me about the party that's going on this weekend. Instead of involving Detective Shingles as you suggest, we can get Dontae and his guys to watch your back instead."

"Bryant, you got more hood in you than you think," Cassandra said.

"Yeah, I am my mother's child. She taught me street sense, whereas my dad taught me the boardroom sense."

"A deadly combination," Charlene declared.

"I wouldn't call it deadly; powerful, yes but not deadly," I retorted.

"Oh no, Bryant, it's deadly as I said. You are so much like Michael and probably why you and Candice connects so well. Mike could have been a millionaire or possibly a billionaire like you, had he used that knowledge he had to create legit businesses. Instead, he used all that knowledge to run the streets. For many years he ran it like a fortune five hundred corporation, and it worked until the competition took him out. Betty wasn't just after his money. She was working for Vinny DeLuca. He and Mike were big rivalries. He could never understand how this Black man reign so deep in the drug game. Vinny tried so many times to take Mike out, but none of his men would turn on him. So, for Betty to set Mike up, either Vinny had something on her or he paid her a lot of money," Charlene explained.

"But Jevar is working with this dude named Marcus from Chicago," I told her.

"Trust me youngblood, I know more about this game than you think. He may be working with Marcus Armstrong, but Betty is working with Vinny DeLuca."

"Ma, why haven't you told us any of this?" Michelle asked. She looked a bit frightened by her mom's confession.

"It was and has always been for your protections. Your father and I did our best to shield you girls from that life. I wasn't just a stay-at-home mom. Who do you think kept track of the cash flow and inventory for your father? I made sure he, we, were straight financially. I was still handling his finances even after our divorce. Why? Because of the three of you, and he didn't trust Betty with his money."

"This is just crazy," Candice shook her head.

"Look, girls, I know this isn't what you were expecting to hear from me of all people. Y'all are grown now and need to know this, especially with Baby girl's situation. We thought we were doing the right thing by keeping that life away from you, but I see now it was wrong. Y'all should have been made aware once you were old enough. Maybe you wouldn't be in this predicament now, Candice."

"No need crying over spilled milk now, Mom. It's okay, but thank you for finally telling me, us, the truth," Candice said.

"Ditto," Cassandra replied.

"Exactly," Michelle chimed.

Candice turned back to me and smiled. I returned one back to her. "Let your friend know, I'd like his help. Come Saturday, this mess will be done and over with."

"Y'all leave Betty to me. I'll handle her," Charlene said. By the way she said that, I knew she was about to bring the pain to Betty. I would love to be a fly buzzing around to see that.

"Ma, you are not going after her! No ma'am," Melissa scolded, shaking her head.

"Child, hush your damn mouth! I'm not weak. I do what I must to live under the radar, but when it comes to my children, all bets are off! I sat back and quiet when Candice told me what was going on with Jevar because I saw she was trying to handle it on her own. But now, with all of this going on and to know Betty's sorry ass is behind this and Mike's death, your momma is coming out of retirement to handle what should have been handled years ago." Charlene had leaned forward in the camera.

"Ma, I'm not trying to hear what you're talking. You haven't been in the game for a long time now. I'm not okay with you going all Annie Oakley to get yourself hurt! Candice got herself in this shit, so let her get herself out of it!" Michelle went off.

"Who in the hell do you think you are talking to, little girl? You think because you are living over there in Jonesboro, working at that hospital, with the trifling ass husband of yours, that you think you're untouchable? Well let me school you some more; little do either of you know, people still keep tabs on all of us because of the lifestyle Mike lived. But because neither one of you fell into that line of business, no one has stepped to you until now. And Candice didn't intentionally get herself into this shit, the shit rained down on her. And you know what else smartass? They will come at you and your family, if need be, to get what they want! So shut your damn mouth and do what you have to do to support your sister in any damn way!"

Silence fell amongst us. Charlene look liked she wanted to reach through the screen and smack the shit out of Melissa. Tears were now streaming down Melissa's face. Cassandra looked on in awe, and Candice ran her hand down her face. They all looked exhausted behind all the drama. Marion and I looked at each other as if to ask what now?

"Okay, ladies, let's all just take a breath and calm down. This is a stressful situation for everyone. We are here so we can get this thing with Candice and Jevar resolved." I said in a soft tone.

"Well, count me out of this shit! I am not supporting my mother who is in her late fifties, going rogue over some shit Candy got stuck in. And I'm telling you now, if something happens to my momma because of you, Candice, Jevar is the last person you will have to worry about because I'm gonna kick your ass!" Michelle threatened before leaving the chat.

"Ma, I'm coming home. I'm gonna let my Major know I have a family emergency and get on a plane as soon as possible," Cassandra said.

"No, no, Sandy. You don't need to get involved and get yourself in trouble with the military. Just—"

"No, Ma, I'm coming home no matter what you say. I need to be there to support you and my baby sister. Chelly is tripping, and I'm not just gonna sit by and not do something. You say you can handle Betty. Well, I'm gonna be there to assist you. This is not up for discussion. I love y'all and I'll see you soon."

"Okay, baby. I love you, too," Charlene said.

"Love you, too, sissy," Candice replied.

"Momma, you go ahead and get some rest. I'll talk to you tomorrow, okay?"

"Okay, baby. Bryant, please take care of her, and Marion, thank you for being there for my baby."

"It's no problem at all. I've seen Candice as a daughter since the day I met her, and she began doing my hair."

"And trust me, she's in great hands with me," I told Charlene.

"Thank you both so much. I'll talk to y'all tomorrow."

"Goodnight, Ma. I love you," Candice told her.

"And I love you more."

"Love you Sandy," Candice called out to her sister again.

"Right back at ya, sis," she replied.

Both ladies ended their video call.

Candice stood and looked around the room at nothing in particular. She rolled her head twice then rolled her shoulders. She turned to me with a weary look. "Can we go to your place?"

"Sure," I told her.

"Cool. I'm going to go repack my bag," she said picking up the bag she packed earlier.

"Okay."

Marion and I watched her until Candice disappeared from our view.

"Bryant, she's going to really need you to hold her down until all of this is over."

"I know, Cuz. But if she let me, I'm going to hold her down not only until this is over, but forever."

"I'm glad to hear that. You two make a cute couple."

"Thanks. I can't wait to introduce her to Mom. I know she's going to love her."

"Oh yeah. They are going to get along just fine."

Marion had just finished that statement when Candice came walking back into the living room with a pink and black bag hoisted on her shoulder. I met her halfway and took the bag from her shoulder. I couldn't help myself when I grabbed her waist and pulled her close to me before I leaned down and pecked her twice on the lips. She smiled up at me and I rocked up.

"Okay, Mrs. Piercing—"

"Child, we are family now. You can call me Marion." Marion waved her hand at Candice.

Candice pulled out of my embrace and went over to Marion. The ladies embraced in a hug. When they pulled apart, we all headed towards the door.

"Y'all be careful now," Marion said as she watched us from the porch.

"We will," Candice and I said in unison.

I held the passenger door open for her and closed it once she was seated before tossing her bag in the back seat and making my way to the driver side. Once I started the engine, Candice and I waved at my cousin as we pulled off heading home.

Chapter 23

Charlene

The next night...

I always knew the past was going to come back and haunt my girls and me one day. I'd only hoped it wouldn't get them hurt or worse, killed. Mike and I had a well-kept oiled machine in place during our run the streets. Like I told the girls, their father ran his set just like that of a fortune five hundred firm. He treated everyone from his right-hand man, Louis, to his corner boys, with the upmost respect. That's why he was untouchable for a long time. The men and women who worked for him were loyal. Some have even had their lives taken because they refused to turn on him. They all loved and respected him because of his love and respect for them.

It was the reason I fell in love with Mike. He treated me like a queen. When we met, he was up front with what he did. He made it clear he wanted me, but couldn't be with me if I couldn't accept what it was he did. It wasn't hard for me to decide to be with Mike, because of his respect for me and my feelings. He didn't force that lifestyle on me. I chose him so I chose that lifestyle.

As I said, I kept the books straight with the finances and product. I kept an account of all the trap houses, who worked them, and when product came in and went out. That was how we lived until shit went left. That was when Louis started shooting up our product into his veins and could no longer function. Then all hell broke loose.

One of our trap houses kept coming up short with money and product. I ran the numbers many times before I made Mike aware. When I did, he exploded. He went off on the guys running that house, but they swore everything was accounted for. I suggested to Mike to have someone sit on the house to scope out the activities. Come to find out, it was Louis, his righthand man, who had been taking product and cash. Because of the love he had for Louis, Mike couldn't kill him, so I did it for him; shot his ass right between the eyes.

Even though majority of everyone was loyal to Mike, there were a few who were just as loyal to Louis, and Betty was one of them, being they were siblings. After he died, she went to Vinny Deluca and gave him what intel she knew on Mike's operation. Betty was recruited to seduce him, which he fell for. How do I know this? Well, Vinny called me after Mike was killed and told me so.

She had always been money hungry on top of jealous of my life. Many times, she would say I had it made with that man of mines and the way we lived. I didn't understand that because Mike always felt living in the hood, right in the mist of everything was where we needed to be. We had money where we could have moved in any neighborhood celebrities lived at in, in the metro area, but again Mike wanted to close to the action so he can see with his own eyes what was going on.

It wasn't until one day Betty came to me boldly to tell me she had been sleeping with Mike that everything changed for me. It wasn't that she slept with my husband but was supposedly my best friend. No, that wasn't what bothered me. It was the threat she made to kill my children that was the issue. And to show she was true to her word, she showed me live surveillance of someone watching all three of my children as they played at the park. She also had several videos of them at different school events as well. I had to divorce Mike and allow her to marry him in order to keep my girls alive.

Mike came home later that day and gave me the news of him leaving me for Betty. I had to go along with the shits to keep my girls safe. And well, we divorced and made it seem as if we had a horrible divorce with the judge mandating I remained in the same neighborhood as Mike and Betty so we could share custody of our children. He also took his name off all bank accounts he and I shared together and removed all money from spots Louis was aware of and placed it in different bonds and certificates for me and the girls. He made sure Betty's trifling ass has no access to anything we built together.

We went along with the facades for a long time. Betty's threat to kill our children was the deciding factor for Mike to step away from the drug game. He loved that life but loved his children more. During their marriage, she made several attempts to change his will and insurance beneficiaries, but Mike was always several steps ahead of her. A few months before Mike died, Betty even attempted to take out an insurance policy on him making herself the beneficiary. Somehow, he got wind of that and changed her name and made Candice the beneficiary.

I always thought she had something to do with his death but didn't have any concrete proof until now. This was the day I've been waiting for. Betty Jean Jackson honestly had no clue she had been living on borrowed time only because I allowed her to. And now, her time was up.

I sat in the dark and silence as I patiently waited for her to return home. Looking at my watch, the time read 11:37 p.m. I had been there for about three hours before I heard the garage door open, and a car pull inside it. My leather-gloved hands balled into a fist with anticipation. I grabbed my Glock with the silencer screwed on it and sat up straight when I heard the keys jiggling in the locks. My body became jittery with excitement as the door opened and she walked in.

"I could have sworn I set the alarm before I left," Betty said.

"You straight?" Someone's voice blared through the speaker of her cellphone.

"Yeah, I'm good," she said flicking on the light. When she turned around and saw me, she gasped.

I held my finger up to my lips and my gun pointed at her head.

"Sis, you good over there?"

"Y-yeah, Jevar. I'm good. Look I'm about to turn in for the night. I'll talk to you tomorrow."

"Oh aiight. Later," Jevar said, and she ended the call.

"Long time, Betty," I told her as I watched her sit her purse on the counter.

"What the hell are you doing in my house, Charlene?"

"I thought it was time you and I had a reunion. Don't you agree?"

"You need to leave before I call the police!"

"Go ahead and call them. You'll be dead by the time they get here anyway," I hunched my shoulders and stood. "Now, let's go ahead and get this over with. I've already missed Golden Girls sitting here waiting on you."

"You are out of your fucking mind!"

"Bitch, what did you expect when you have been coming after my family? Huh? You trying to set my baby girl up and for what? For money that isn't yours?"

"Fuck you, Charlene and those bitches you pushed out! You always thought you were the shit when you and Mike were together. You always thought you and your ugly ass children sat on a fucking pedestal. That's why I took the one thing away from you, I knew would hurt you, Mike. And I would have taken those three bastard bitches from you, but I was instructed not to do so!" Betty spoke with so much venom.

"You really thought you took Mike away from me? No, you didn't. Gone and have a seat so I can give you the real tea," I motioned for the chair closest to her. She reluctantly sat down, phone still in her hand. "Slide that on over here. You won't be needing that anymore." I held my hand out for the cell. She slid it over to me, and I smashed it on the floor before stepping on it, never taking my eyes or gun off her.

"Now, let me tell you this before I send you to meet your maker. Yeah, Mike and I divorced and yeah, you did marry him. But Betty, you and I both know that was all you did. You thought you were getting your hands on the empire he and I built together, but you got nothing but air and opportunity. You could never break the bond Mike and I shared. We did what we had to do to protect our children. That included making sure your ass couldn't get your hands on our money. But let me also tell you this," I aimed my gun at her, and my laser beam lit up right between her eyes.

"You thought you were running things, but Vinny DeLuca told me the deal after Mike died. He explained to me he had you set him up so he could take over Mike's turf. He also told me he had nothing to do with Mike's death since he got out of that line of work once our girls' lives were threatened. For the longest time I always felt you had something to do with him being killed."

"I had his bitch ass killed because he owed me for my time and for killing my brother! I wanted to take everything from him the same way he took from me. Louis told me about all the places they kept the money. I went there looking to take every dime of it after Louis was killed but the spots were empty. I did what I could to drain Mike for everything he was worth, but no matter what I did, he was always two steps ahead of me. So, I had Jevar kill him so I could get the insurance money. But to find out, that motherfucker found out about it and took my name off and added Candy's name was devastating! You motherfuckas owed me and I wanted what was taken from me!"

"Is that why you had Jevar seek out Candice? To get with her and take her money?"

"Of course." Betty hunched her shoulders not fazed by what she just said.

"Well, for the record, Mike didn't kill Louis. I did."

PEW!

PEW!

PEW!

I put a bullet in each one of her eyes and the third in her heart. Afterwards, I went over to the microwave and set the timer for five minutes before leaving out of the house the same way I came in. I pulled my mask back over my face and made my way through the wooded area that led to the back of a convenience store on the opposite side of the woods. Being that they had no lights in that area and I was wearing all black from head to toe, I had no problem sliding into my car and driving off without being noticed. I was turning into traffic when the explosion happened. I smiled and jammed to Mary J Blige radio on Pandora all the way back to Macon.

Chapter 24

Jevar

Tuesday morning....

My mind ran a mile a minute as I thought about my sister. Last night after we ended our call, something wasn't sitting well with me. When I heard her gasp, it made me think something or someone was at her. I ignored the feeling when she told me she was fine. Now I wish I had followed that gut feeling.

When I turned on the TV and the local news was what was on, I just about lost my damn mind when I saw her house up in flames. Was Betty in the house when the explosion happened? Who the fuck could have done some shit like this? How the fuck did they even get in when she had a high-tech security system? Why would they want her dead? All these questions flooded my mind, and the news wasn't providing the fucking answers.

I hopped in my ride and sped over there to see it with my own eyes. When I made it to her side of town, I had to park a couple of blocks away because they had the street blocked off. I jumped out and ran down to the house. Debris from the explosion was everywhere. I prayed for the bastard's sake my sister was fine. If not, they better hope I don't find out who was responsible because the muthafucka was going to die a slow and painful death.

Remembering I was a wanted man, I couldn't go up to a cop and find out if they found a body or not. But I didn't need to ask because a few seconds later, they were rolling out a gurney with a black body bag on top of it. I knew then Betty was gone.

"Fuck!" I ran a hand down my face. This shit could not be happening. Now that I had my answer, I took off back towards my car before someone could recognize me.

When I got back to my car, I punched the steering wheel letting out my frustration. A couple of tears ran down my face. I sat pondering on who could have done this, and I narrowed it down to Vinny DeLuca, Omari and Dovirs, or either Marcus. Deciding to just go with the process of elimination, O and D were the first on my list. This party on Saturday was when it was going to go down. Niggas was about to feel my fuckin' wrath. And once I'm done with this shit, I'm going to get at Candice and that bitch nigga Bryant McIntosh.

I ran a hand over my face before starting my engine and pulling off. I nodded my head as I ran my plan in my head.

Bryant

"How is she?" I asked Rachel as I entered Trinity's room. It had been a couple of days since she was attacked, and I wanted to check on her progress.

"She's been in and out of it because of the meds, but she seems to be doing okay. I'm just glad she's alive, Bryant."

Rachel looked so weary. Even with her dressed in an expensive outfit and her makeup done to perfection, I could see she hadn't had any sleep. Adding to the fact that she had been crying, the makeup couldn't cover up the puffiness of her eyes.

"Have you found out any information as to why that Jevar guy wanted to do this to her? Was he her dealer or something?"

"No, I haven't found out anything. He's been M.I.A. since his pic has been splattered across the news outlets. He's going to slip up soon, and when he does, we will get him."

"I hope so. I want him to pay for what he did to my baby." She began to cry.

I walked over to her and placed a comforting hand on her shoulder. I gave a light squeeze. "Don't worry, Rachel, we will find him. And he will pay. I promise you that."

At that moment Trinity's eye fluttered and opened, landing on me. I needed to get her alone so I can ask her some questions Rachel did not need to be privy to. So, I suggested she go to the cafeteria and get some tea or take a walk outside to get some fresh air. After a few minutes of persuasion, she finally agreed to go get some fresh air.

After Rachel left, I took the seat she previously occupied and looked into Trinity's one eye. For a few moments I said nothing but only stared at her. She was the poster child for a don't do drugs commercial. She had a wonderful life before she began dipping into that shit. If only she had taken the advice and help I tried to give her to get clean, maybe she wouldn't be lying in this hospital bed all fucked up.

"Hello, Tri. Blink if you can hear me."

She blinked once.

"Good. I need to ask you some questions. Nod your head to respond, okay."

She nodded her head up and down.

"Was Jevar your dealer?"

She shook her head.

"Were the two of you messing around?"

She shook her head no.

"Were the two of you working together on something?"

She hesitated but nodded her head.

"Did it have anything to do with Candice?"

She frowned at that question. For a few minutes she just stared at me with that one eye.

"Answer my question, Tri. Were you and Jevar working together on a plan about Candice?"

She reluctantly nodded her head.

"Did you go to him?"

She nodded.

"Okay. One more question I need to ask you. Did you tell Jevar about our little secret?"

A tear fell from that one eye at that question. She closed her eye not responding to me. There was no need since her crying had given me confirmation. I was grateful at the moment that she couldn't speak, he'll move for the most part. I sighed then stood. I leaned down and whispered in her ear before kissing her on the cheek. When I straightened up the tears were flooding down that one eye. I used her finger to press the medication drip so the morphine can get into her system, then I left out.

I gave a nod to the nurse sitting at the nurse's station as I made my way towards the elevators. The doors parted just as I made it to them, and Rachel stepped off.

"Oh you're leaving already?" she asked.

"Yeah, she had fallen back to sleep not too long after you left."

"Oh okay. Well thank you for stopping by. Your mom called me earlier to check on her. It was good talking to her a few minutes."

"That's good. I'll tell her to keep in touch with you—"

"What is going on down there?" Rachel's question cut me off.

Already knowing what she was referring to, I played along. She took off down the hall, and I followed behind her. The nurses and doctors were scrambling into Trinity's room. When we made it there, all we heard was the heart monitor's long single beep.

"Time of death 10:48 a.m.," the doctor announced.

"No!" Rachel cried out.

I grabbed her before she collapsed on the floor. I held her tightly in my arms as she cried out for her daughter. I looked on as one of the nurses pulled the sheet over her face.

"My baby! Bryant, not my baby!"

My heart broke for Rachel, but little did she know Trinity was in a much better place now. Had she remained alive, her life was going to be a living hell. Rachel fought to get out of my embrace, then ran over to the bed and fell on Trinity's body bawling her eyes out. I grabbed my phone out of my pocket and called Lester. I gave him the news and he said he was on his way.

Chapter 25

Candice

Friday, the day before the party...

"I don't believe you, Mom!" Chelly said.

"Do you think I give a damn, Michelle?" my mom retorted.

"I'm just upset you went all vigilante without me," Cassandra folder her arms over her chest and pouted.

"Oh my God, Cassandra! Are you serious?" Chelly turned around to look at our sister. She placed her hands on her hips and glared at her.

"Hell yeah, I'm serious. That bitch has been a thorn in all of our sides for as long as I can remember and knowing she is responsible for Dad's death, was more than enough reason for me. What I want to know is why the hell are you not feeling the same way?"

"Yeah, Chelly, I have to wonder the same thing," I chimed in.

"Y'all know she was always the do-gooder as well as the soft one amongst the three of ya. I really thought it was Candice because she's too nice to people, but nah, this one right here is just lame," my mom explained.

Both Sandy and I laughed at that. It was refreshing to see my mom smiling and joking around with us. For a long time, she seemed unhappy so to see a smile on her face as she teased my sister was refreshing.

"It's bad enough our dad was a drug dealer. Now our mom is a killer, and y'all acting like it's just another day in the neighborhood! There ain't nothing funny about this!" Chelly began to cry, and we all laughed louder.

"Okay, okay. Y'all stop laughing at your sister," mom waved her hand around. "She's being serious right now. Let's hear her out. Go on Michelle, speak your mind." My mom stood in front of her with her head tilted to the side and her hands on her hips waiting for her response.

"All I'm saying is you shouldn't be running around shooting people and blowing up their houses! You are not that person, and I don't understand why you two are in cahoots about it. Something could have happened to you while you were trying to be Foxy Brown, and we wouldn't have known shit!"

"For your information, Miss Smarty Pants, I ain't new to this. I'm true to this. I was the Bonnie to your father's Clyde. I was his right, left, and back hand. A lot of the times your father needed to set an example when someone got out of hand, it was me who took care of the dirty work, not him. Now, that is the part of him you took after. The both of you were softies when it called for an iron fist. Well, little girl, I was that iron fist."

"But momma—"

"Don't but momma me. Listen to what I'm saying Michelle. The lifestyle your father and I lived was not for the soft. Your father was able to reign as he did because of me. No one ever expected me to be the muscle. If it wasn't your Uncle Louis before he started shooting up that shit, it was me. I had a good coverup being I was a 'housewife.'" She used the quotations marks with her hands emphasizing housewife. "They never saw me coming."

"This is unbelievable," Chelly shook her head. She began pacing the floor.

We were all at my mom's house in Macon since Cassandra was able to get emergency leave and come home. We were discussing the news of Betty's house blowing up, and my eldest sister Michelle asked my mom if she had anything to do with it. My mom proudly admitted she put three bullets to her body before setting the timer on the homemade bomb inside Betty's house.

For a brief second, I was in utter shock, but that quickly wore off and turned into admiration. One thing I have always known about my mom is that she said what she meant and meant what she said. That's why I don't know why Chelly was taking this so hard. I decided to voice my thoughts.

"Chelly, I do not know why you are so flabbergasted by what mom did. You should know she means what she says and says what she means."

"Exactly," Sandy agreed.

"That one time you snuck out to go to Erica Petty's party, and ma came and got you, she told you in front of everyone she was going to whoop your butt from then until we made it back home, she did just that."

"Oh yeah, baby sis, I remember that!" Sandy laughed.

"Her dumbass didn't know we had cameras around the house. We told this child good she couldn't go to that party, but no, she wanted to defy us. So, we sat and watched her on the camera as she climbed out of her bedroom window, run down the block, and hop in Jalisa's car. Mike was livid. I never saw that man get so angry at neither one of you until that day, but I calmed him down and told him I'd handle it." Mom said in between chuckles. "I made sure when I got to Erica's house the party was all the way live. I walked in, walked through the house, and found this heifer in the corner with Rashad Jones, puffing on a blunt in one hand, and had a cup of something I learned was some liquor in the other hand."

"Nah nie, Chelly!" I exclaimed.

"Not Miss Goody Goody," Cassandra laughed.

"Mama, why you got to bring up old stuff for?" Chelly whined.

"Because you trying to act all high and mighty like your shit don't stink, so I needed to bring you back down to earth. Rashad saw me first, and damn near pissed on himself. He was so scared; he couldn't even speak when I walked over to them and tapped Michelle on her shoulders. She turned around with an attitude until she saw it was me. This girl wasted all the liquor on Rashad and damn near burned a hole in the palm of his hand when she shoved the blunt in it. When she saw the belt in my hand, this girl took off to running towards the door, thinking I wasn't going to catch her."

Sandy and I laughed so hard, we both had tears in our eyes, while Chelly sat there red as hell in the face. I can tell she wanted to say some choice words to my momma but thought better of it. We all knew Charlene didn't play.

"When I got my hands on her, I tore that ass up, then put her on punishment for two months."

"That made me do my best not to get into any trouble. I didn't want that embarrassment, no ma'am," Sandy shook her head.

"Me neither," I agreed.

"Yeah, well that taught y'all to understand me when I say what I mean and mean what I say. So, Michelle, it was either I take Betty out, or I continue to allow her to harass my family for shit she was never entitled to. Is that what you want, to have to look over your shoulder for the rest of your life?"

"How do you know we still won't be doing that, momma? You know better than me, the code of the street is a life for a life. Jevar is still running loose and he's going to want revenge for his sister's death."

"You're right, baby girl, but I've been doing this long before either of you were alive, so I know how to cover my tracks. Your mother isn't an old senile sickly woman. I'm very vibrant and in great health at the fabulous age of fifty-two. I get hit on by men your ages all the time when I'm at the gym, grocery store, and gas station."

"With all that junk in the trunk, do you blame them?" I joked.

"Anyway," Chelly fanned her hand and rolled her eyes, "Candy is everything set up for tomorrow night?"

"Yeah. Last night before I came here, Verdell, uh, Bryant and I talked with his friend Dontae as well as Omari and Dovirs to make sure everything was set up. That man is something else. It kind of scares me how he switches up from this business mogul to this hood nigga."

"Sis, he did say his mom is from the hood, so that may have a lot to do with it," Sandy said.

"Yeah, I know, but y'all didn't see him last night talking to Dontae and Dovirs. It was like he turned into a whole different person."

"I don't know, Candy. Did you talk to him about it afterwards?" Chelly asked with a look of concern.

"No, I didn't. Afterwards, I just got on the road and came here."

"Baby, that man cares for you if he's putting himself out there for you, especially knowing he's a world-wide known businessman. Ain't no man going to put his business in jeopardy like he's doing if he didn't love you," my mom explained.

"I know he loves me because he said so. But it still has me on guard a bit. I don't want another Jevar, not that I think Bryant will hit me, but a man who's in the streets dealing that crap. I don't want to deal with that anymore. I'm trying to establish myself as a reputable businesswoman, and I can't continue to associate or be in relationships with hood niggas. I've already lost several clients because of the way I've had to maneuver. My revenue has dropped because I'm not in the shop to keep an eye on my employees. They've been doing whatever the hell they want in my absence, and I can't blame anyone but myself."

These past few days have shown me a totally different side of Verdell that has me on edge. It worries me because I love him, and I know he loves me. But do I really want to be with a Dr. Jekyll and Mr. Hyde personality?

"Candice, I understand about your business, but do you honestly think Bryant will hurt you? I mean, I saw how attentive he was the other night when we facetimed, and the way he spoke of keeping you safe, I think that would be the only time you see that side of him is when he's protecting you," Chelly stated.

"Yep, I agree," Sandy replied.

"Mm hmm," my mom nodded.

Chapter 26

Candice

Saturday night...

I sat in an old Ford Focus with tinted windows down the street from Omari's house. I watched as people stood around in the yard and on the porch, drinking, smoking, and shooting the shits with one another. I had yet to see Jevar pull up. My nerves were a wrecking ball with anticipation. I prayed to the most high everything went off without anyone else getting hurt. I wanted this to be over with so I can get my life back.

"Baby, you okay over there?" Verdell's voice came through the earbud placed in my ear.

Earlier as I was getting dressed, he came into the room holding a small box and his tablet. At first glance I thought he was about to pop the question and my anxiety started to kick in. I wasn't sure I was ready to make that commitment to him, even though I was in love with him.

There was still a lot we had to learn about one another, and I didn't think us becoming engaged was a good thing to do so soon. When he opened the little black box and sat it on the bed next to me, I let out a sigh of relief when I saw a pair of diamond stud earrings and an earpiece. But then curiosity gave way.

"Those earrings are beautiful, but what's up with the earpiece?"

"The earrings have a listening chip in one and a camera in the other. The earpiece is so we can communicate with each other. I'm not letting you go in there alone. I'm going to be with you this way," Verdell explained.

"Wow! How the hell did you get a listening chip and camera inside of them? That's some James Bond type of shit," I exclaimed. I picked up one of the earrings and inspected it before doing the same to the other one.

"This is something my team has been working on for a while. You're the first to try it out."

"How did you come up with this? I mean this is genius, Verdell."

"That's a story for another day, babe. I'll tell you all about it after this shit is over with."

"I'm gonna hold you to it. Now, how does it work? I mean, how do I know everything is on? Are these real diamonds?" I shot off question after question.

"Once they are secured in your ear, they automatically are on. They're linked to an app that allows me to hear and see what you hear and see, and yes, they are real. Put them on," he instructed.

I placed them on and to my surprise they didn't feel heavy. I walked over to the dresser and looked at my reflection in the mirror. The diamonds sparkled brightly. I turned my head from one side to the other, checking them out. "This is pure genius! How much will these sell for? They can't be cheap if the diamonds are real and you're putting software like that inside them?"

"You're right they won't be cheap. These will go for twenty-five grand and will only be available for a select clientele. Here look at this." He handed me the tablet. I could clearly see the bedroom on the screen. It looked damn near 4D, it was so crisp and clear.

"Say something," Verdell instructed.

"Hello." I watched as lines on the bottom of the screen moved across to indicate it detected my voice. My mind was spinning at this new technology. Who in the hell would think to come up with this shit? "Um, Verdell, I am speechless at this. You have to tell me, what made you come up with this?"

"I deal with a lot of rich, powerful clientele that are always looking for ways to ensure their safety and security. They hire men and women to help with that, but they don't want them to always look obvious. They want them to blend in with guests at parties and other events so if some shit pop off, no one would see him or her coming. Think about it; someone at an event tries to start some drama, then you get hemmed up by the waitress who just served you a cocktail. You had no clue she was part of the security team."

"That's brilliant! Just make sure any jewelry you give me isn't equipped with this," I pointed to the table.

"Nah, baby. I wouldn't do that to you. Tonight's the exception since I can't walk into the party with you."

"Okay. I think I'm ready. How do I look?"

I turned around showing off my voluptuous booty in a pair of white skinny jeans, a white fitted tee with 'Prima Dona Style' written in black, purple, and gray letters across the front. I started to wear a pair of heels but changed my mind. Instead, I donned a pair of white Adidas with purple stripes to match the purple in my shirt. I pulled my curly back into a ponytail. I wore no makeup except a purple glazed lip gloss.

"You look sexy as fuck in all that white. You got my man about to burst out of my jeans, baby."

"Ooh. Well, let me help him out until later."

I sat on the bed then pulled Verdell to me by the hooking my finger in the loop. I unzipped his jeans, then pulled them along with his boxer briefs down. His dick sprang out at me and my mouth instantly watered. I licked the tip just as precum drizzled out at me. I sucked him into my mouth and hummed once it hit the back of my throat.

"Sss, baby," Verdell moaned.

I began to bob my head up and down, slurping, licking, sucking that big dick like it would be my last time ever having it. I played with his balls in one hand as my other stroked his shaft while I sucked just the tip. I pulled him out of my mouth with a pop before spitting on it and sucking him back into my mouth.

"Gotdamn! Shit, baby! Suck that dick just like that!"

My panties became moist at that shit talking Verdell was doing, but I didn't stop. I pulled him out of my mouth again, then latched on to his balls. I sucked on them as I stroked his shaft with my hand. I hummed on them and could feel them tighten as he was getting close to climaxing.

"Naw, baby, I need to be deep inside you," Verdell protested and pulled away from me. "Drop those pants and turn around."

I didn't need to be told twice. I stripped out of everything before climbing on the bed on all fours. I arched my back and tooted my ass up at him. I buried my face in the plush comforter and waited for him to penetrate me. I moaned when he smacked my right butt cheek then the left. I could feel my juices flowing down my inner thighs I was so wet for him. Instead of him entering me as I thought, I felt his warm tongue glide along my folds before he latched on to my clit sucking it into his mouth.

"Yes, baby, like that," I moaned in the comforter.

Verdell sucked on my clit as he slid two fingers in and out of my wetness. My pussy hungrily clamped down on them, pulsating around them. I felt my orgasm making way through my body. "Aah, ssss, mmm," I belted. Verdell thrusted his fingers faster in and out of my now soaking pussy, causing the macaroni in a box sound as Cardi B said. I arched my back and tooted my ass more as my pussy contracted on his fingers and I began to climax. "Oh shit!" I cried out in pleasure.

"Damn, your pussy tastes divine," Verdell said.

I felt him shift then the tip of his one-eyed monster at my opening. I pushed back on him forcing him inside of me. We both moaned at out connection. Verdell began long but quick stokes that hit my spot with precision. He smacked my ass and my walls pulsated with pleasure. "Just like that, daddy."

"You like that, huh?" he asked cockily.

I answered him by bouncing my ass back on him, saturating his man of steel with my juices. He thrust faster and harder, knocking against my spot with each thrust. It became too much so I placed a hand on his stomach to get some relief.

"Un un, take this dick. Gotdamn, Candice!"

"Shit, baybee, wait! Damn, ooh, Bry-ant, I'm cumming!"

"Let that shit go!"

Verdell grabbed ahold of my hips and pounded in me. He went so deep, the pleasure started to feel like pain. I tried to scoot forward so he wouldn't be so deep, but he had a death grip on my hips as he thrust inside me three more times before he came.

"Oooh shit, Candice!" Verdell let out in a grunt before collapsing on the bed next to me.

I lay there spent trying to get my breathing back to normal while thinking what the hell? My damn coochie was throbbing something serious from that beat down. Hell, I wasn't sure if I should be mad or happy. It was all confusing to me.

"Baby, you alright?" Verdell asked. He placed a hand on my ass and rubbed the cheek.

I rolled over to face him and said, "To be honest, I don't know. It started to hurt when you went deep."

"Damn, baby, I'm sorry. I wasn't trying to hurt you, but your pussy was feeling extra good and was wetter than usual. You had my dick looking like a glazed donut." As much as I wanted to be mad, I couldn't help but laugh at the serious look plastered on his face. "While you are laughing, I rocked back up just thinking about it." I looked down at his meat and sure enough he was standing at attention again.

"Oh no. Nope. I don't have time to be fooling with you. You're going to make me late." I quickly stood and headed for the shower.

"You gonna leave me like this? Babe!" I ignored him as I hopped back in the shower and began to wash up. A couple of minutes later, Verdell joined me. He stood behind me with his thang poking me in the back. I tried to ignore him, but he reached around and placed his hand on my mound, stroking my clit.

"Verdell, no, baby. Umm, we can't do it again. Shit! I need to get ready."

He ignored my plea as he turned me around and planted his lips on mine, kissing me passionately. Our tongues intertwined as he picked me up. My legs wrapped around his waist as his penis found my opening and slid in. He pressed my back against the tiled wall and thrust inside me, never breaking our kiss. He made fast deep thrusts inside my throbbing tunnel. He broke our kiss and latched on to my right nipple, sucking it hard then soft, nibbling on my swollen pebble before doing the same to my left nipple. I arched my back and threw my head back against the wall with my mouth open, panting from the sexual healing I had no clue my body was craving. Even after the pounding I'd just endured just a few minutes ago, my yonni was contracting and pulsating around Verdell in need, want of him. I felt my orgasm making waves just as Verdell began to come. We both yelled out each other's names as we came simultaneously.

"I love you, Bryant."

"I love you, too."

"Candice."

"Huh." Verdell's voice broke me out of my daydreaming I hadn't realized I was doing.

"Baby, are you okay? Do you need me to come over there?"

"Oh, no, no. I'm fine. I spaced out for a second, but I'm okay."

"Are you sure? I called your name three times," he sounded concerned.

"Yes, I'm fine. Heads up, this is Jevar's truck that just passed me," I told him.

"I see him coming this way. He's going to have to go park further down the street since it's full. Go ahead and get out and make your way inside so you can be in place."

"Okay, babe. You just make sure you stay in my ear so I'll know you're with me."

"Don't worry, I got you and I also have extra eyes on you as well."

I hopped out of the car and headed towards Omari's house. All eyes were on me as I approached the house. I spoke to several people I hadn't seen in a while due to me keeping a low profile because of Jevar. Others didn't know me and had curious looks on their faces. One guy even stepped to me just before I walked inside the house. Of course, I kindly turned him down, but his ego had him calling me all kinds of stuck-up bitches to my back as I entered the house.

I made my way through the crowd until I spotted Omari and Dovirs in the kitchen. There was a group of guys in a circle talking shit over a game of craps, and those two were in the midst. They all were so engrossed in the game that they didn't see me at first.

"O, I know you didn't start without me," I spoke loudly above the men.

"Oh, shit! What's up, Candy? It's been a long time, shawty," Omari said.

"Damn, Candy, you looking good," Dovirs said.

"Thanks, and it has been a long time. What's good?" The two men halted the game to give me hugs.

"It's good to see you. I can't believe you came out to celebrate my birthday with me. You know I know ya boy has been looking for you."

"Yeah, I know, but I wasn't going to miss one of your infamous block parties, especially being it's your birthday."

"I feel special now," Omari said placing a hand on his heart.

"Man, fuck that special shit. Let's get this fucking game going. Shit, I'm trying to win my money back," a tall light-skinned guy with dreads snapped.

"You ain't winning shit back, nigga, cause I'm about to take all of y'all's money," I explained, and they all broke out into a fit of laughter and ruckus.

"Shit, put your money where your mouth is, lil mama. I ain't gon' have mercy on you because yous a bitch. Fuck that," a short, brown-skinned guy looking like a baby Hulk said. Dude had too many damn muscles bulging out for my taste.

"I'm about to show you who's the bitch, my nigga. Let's do this," I said pulling my money out of my cross-body bag. I bent down and tossed a twenty in the pile of money. I looked back up at the men to see what the holdup was. I laughed at the confused and lustful expressions they each wore on their faces.

"Candice, you shoot craps?" Verdell asked in my ear.

"Yes, I shoot craps, guys," I chuckled.

"I think I'm in love," Dude with the dreads said.

"Damn, I just fell in love with you all over again," Verdell said in my ear.

"Nigga, that's Jevar right there so get out ya feelings," Dovirs scolded.

"Stop procrastinating and let's get this shit going. Mama trying to buy a new pair of shoes," I grinned.

The guys had just knelt down in the circle to get the game going when I heard a voice that made me cringe. My body stiffened in anticipation of our little reunion. I gave myself a pep talk in my head to not show fear, to not let his words phase me, but to show him I was no longer afraid of him, and that I would no longer place my life on hold for him.

"Yo, my niggas, what's good?" Jevar said.

"Damn, if it ain't 'most wanted'," Dovirs joked.

"What's up, J," Omari said.

"My nigga. Where the fuck you been hiding at?" Dreads asked.

"You know how I do."

I slowly stood up then turned around. Jevar froze when he saw me.

Chapter 27

Bryant

"Turn to your right so the camera could catch his face baby," I instructed Candice through the earpiece. She did as instructed.

"Hello, Jevar," she softly said.

I watched as his expression went from shock to anger before his hand whacked Candice across her face. She fell against Dontae, and he caught her by the waist. Candice quickly stood upright before he charged her, then punched her in the face. I immediately got pissed off and was about to jump out the car and go whoop his ass, but Brad's hand grabbed my shoulder to keep in place.

"Just calm down, bro. We already knew this was going to happen when he saw her. She told you this. So let it play out for now."

I knew he was right, but it didn't mean I was okay with that asshole putting his hands on my woman. I fell back into my seat and continued to watch everything play out on the tablet. My jaw clinched as I watched Candice's left eye quickly swell up. Being that she was light-skinned, Jevar's handprint was also visible on her face. What really pissed me off was the fact that none of those niggas had the curtesy of trying to help Candice, seeing a man beating on her. Those was what I called bitch ass niggas.

Dovirs reached in his back pocket and pulled out a taser and pressed it against Jevar's back. His body started convulsing as the electricity zipped through his body.

"Oh, shit!"

"Goddamn!"

A few of the onlookers said. He held the taser to Jevar's body and continued to shock the hell out of him before he fell to the floor then stepped back, looking down at his limp body.

"Yo, grab his ass and take him to the basement. Dipset, shut this shit down," Dovirs instructed.

Omari walked over to Candice and placed a hand on her shoulder. "You did good, ma," he told her before Dovirs tased her, knocking her out.

"Just wait, Bryant," Brad instructed. My little brother knew me too well. He knew I was ready to go in and set it off. "Let's see where they're going. They don't know they're being filmed so give a few minutes. Plus, Dontae isn't going to let them do anything else to her. He knows how far to let it go."

"This is some bullshit, Brad!"

"Man, I know, but we have to be extra careful. Would you rather she gets bruised up or get killed?"

I hated when he was my voice of reason or had the level head at times. I knew what he was saying made sense, but it didn't negate the issue of her being hurt at all. I didn't want anything done to her. I felt like my manhood was being tested for just sitting by and watching that bastard hurt my woman. I tried to calm down to see what they had up their sleeves. If it was some bullshit, fuck what Brad was talking about, I was going in to get my woman.

I looked up to see a couple of the guys that was in the kitchen, were now outside instructing everyone the party was over and to leave. No one seemed to protest and began departing. Within minutes the street was clear of people and most of the cars parked up and down the street. Brad and I sat quietly as we watched Candice and Jevar being dragged down the steps to the basement.

Dontae placed Candice in a chair then tied her hands behind her back with a rope that laid next to the chair. He then stood behind her with his arms crossed and watched as a couple of the other guys tied Jevar's hands and feet with zip ties. They then wrapped a chain around his hands then used a hook to hoist him in the air to a rail built into the ceiling. The men then stood off to the side and waited for Dovirs and Omari to enter.

"Where the fuck are they?" I asked out loud.

"The same thing I was thinking," Brad replied. "Look," he said tapping on my arm then pointed towards the front of the house.

A couple of SUVs pulled up to the house and several men stepped out. Omari and Dovirs came out of the front door and met the men on the porch. They shook up with the one guy who seemed to be the one in charge. They said a few words before everyone filed into the house except for four of the men. Two of them began canvassing around the house while the others stood guard near the cars.

"How the fuck can they have all this shit going on and no one has called the cops?" Brad asked.

"You know we in the hoodest of the hood, and ain't no cop gonna come around here like that. Besides, the people living in this neighborhood are more afraid of those types of men rather than the cops." I pointed towards the house.

"Mmm," he nodded his head in agreement.

I turned my attention back to the tablet. Jevar was starting to gain consciousness. His head rolled a couple of times and he moaned. Just then, the door to the basement opened. Dovirs, Omari, and the guy they shook up with on the porch came walking down the steps. Everyone, except Dontae seemed to come to attention once they saw the guy.

"Who the fuck is this bitch?" the man asked.

"That's Jevar's old lady," Omari asked.

"I figured you'd want some extra collateral," Dovirs told him.

"Wake that muthafucka up," the man instructed, pointing to Jevar.

Dovirs took the blunt from the short guy and placed the lit part to Jevar's chest.

"Aaaah!" Jevar screamed from the pain of the burn. His eyes bulged as he flapped around in the air realizing he was tied.

Jevar

I can't believe I was such a dumb muthafucka to think I could trust those two niggas. My gut told me not to come to this party but being the cocky muthafucka I am, I came thinking it wasn't no way they would go against me. No one fucked with Jevarius Jackson. But when that nigga told me Candy was coming, there was no way I wasn't gonna show up so I could put my foot up her ass for dipping on me. I guess the joke was on me, because here I was tied up and hanging while these bitches looked on. I was too pissed when I saw Candy's ass hanging out with them like shit was all gravy. All my focus went on her, and I just wanted to stomp a hole in her ass.

"Jevar, you one hard fucka to get up with," Marcus stood in front of me and spoke.

"I been busy," I told him.

"Shit, I see. You a wanted man by everybody; the cops, these niggas, and me. Oh yeah, Vinny looking for you, too. We had a long conversation about you. He gave me his blessing that I'd handle you and Betty, but I see someone already took care of her."

"Nigga, you know you did that shit! Don't try to play like it wasn't you. If it wasn't, it was those muthafuckas."

"Nah, I unfortunately had nothing to do with that," Marcus said.

"We didn't either," Dovirs said.

"My momma killed that piece of shit," Candy confessed in a groggy voice.

"Word?" Marcus swung around at the sound of her voice.

"Ah hell naw," Dovirs laughed.

"Not, Ms. Charlene," Omari said.

"Bitch, stop lying! Ain't no way her old ass did shit," I said not wanting to believe what Candy said.

"Charlene isn't as sick as you thought. She paid a visit to Betty, put three in her ass before she set that house on fire. You and that bitch didn't think we would find out about y'all, did you?"

"Damn, what the fuck I miss?" Marcus asked.

"Should you tell him, or should I?" Candy asked.

"Tell them what?" I asked. I wanted to slap the shit out of her.

"Tell them how you pretended to be interested in me but all along you and Betty were setting me up to get the money my father left me in his will and insurance policy. Better yet, tell them how you and Betty were behind killing my father, you piece of shit! Give me the goddamn gun so I can put a bullet up his ass!"

"Damn, ma, that's some fucked up shit right there. Did you really do that?" Marcus asked.

"Fuck that bitch and her pappi. Hell, yeah I pulled the trigger. But her dumb ass knew that. She was with him the day I took his life."

"How the fuck did I know it was you, Jevar? I was in the store you dumb ass! Then when I ran outside, that's when the explosion happened."

"So, it seems to me, Ms. Charlene finally got the revenge she been waiting on all these years," Dovirs nodded his head as he toked on a blunt.

"Fuck that! All you bitches gone die," I threatened Candy.

"Maybe so, but it looks like you gone die before I do," she retorted.

"Oh, so you a bad bitch now? You think because you done got with McIntosh you the shit now? Well let me tell you, that nigga ain't no betta than me. That nigga ain't squeaky clean as you think. If you live, ask that muthafucka about the nigga he killed." I watched as her facial expression changed from smug to concern. "Yeah, ask that nigga about an app the nigga had that was some kind of spyware that McIntosh was hungry to have, he killed for it, then made it seem like that bitch Trinity was the one to do it when she witnessed it. You think you got something better than me. Naw, he just wears a suit. That nigga ain't no better than me!"

I kicked and twisted trying to get loose. I wanted to knock her fucking head off her shoulders. This bitch had me fucked up. She better pray I don't get loose or else I'm gon' to fuck her up.

"Wow, Jevar. You're that pressed about me not wanting to be with you anymore that you'd say whatever to try and make yourself look good, huh? Well, if Bryant did any of what you're saying, he is and will always be better than you. You ain't shit and will never be shit. You think you are because you beat on women, but I don't see you jumping bad to these niggas that got your ass tied up like a pig that's about to be slaughtered. It took me a long time to realize this about you, but I guarantee you this, if they let me loose, I'm gonna be the one to send your sorry, tied, trifling, no good, poor excuse of a man ass directly to hell."

"Damn, baby, I just might take you up on that offer. But before we do I need to ask you, Jevar, where is my shit?" Marcus asked.

"Shid, gone. I took it, sold it and reaped the benefits," I shrugged. No need in lying about it since I knew I wasn't going to survive.

"Thanks for your honesty, my nigga. I already knew that, though. I just needed to hear the words come out of your mouth," Marcus said before pulling his gun out and shooting me in both legs.

"Arrrgggg!" I cried out in pain.

"Untie her," he commanded.

Dontae untied her, and she stood. For the first time since knowing her, I saw hatred in Candy's face. For a moment I felt guilt for how I played a part in the fucked-up parts of her life. Then I recalled her saying her momma was behind Betty's death, so fuck her and her momma and daddy. Marcus handed her a gun then stood off to the side. I watched her hold it up towards me. I laughed so hard, tears ran down my face.

"You don't have the balls," was the last thing I got out before she pulled the trigger.

Chapter 28

Candice

"You don't have the balls," Jevar said.

I pulled the trigger and let it rip on his ass. I kept shooting even after the clip was empty. It wasn't until I felt someone grab my hand that I stopped. The guy they called Marcus gently took the gun from my hand. I watched as the blood spilled from Jevar's body to the floor, making a puddle beneath him.

"Lil mama, you good?" Marcus asked.

"I'm more than good; I'm great," I replied.

"Well, that's what's up," he patted me on the back.

"As long as you keep your mouth closed, you won't have to worry about this gun getting into the cops' hands, being that your prints are the only ones on this gun," he politely threatened.

"That's cool so long as you know, I have you on recording and would hate for this to get in the hands of the cops as well," I came back with.

"The fuck!" Dovirs choked.

"Yeah, no need in worrying about this getting out. I want this to be done and over with just like you do. Am I right?"

"You a cold bitch, you know that?" Omari asked.

"Maybe; maybe not. Who's to say?"

"Damn, ma, my dick just rocked up. I know you got a man and all, but what's up with you and me?" Marcus smiled deviously.

"Not a damn thing. I'm about to go home and do to my man what you wish I would do to you. Goodnight gentleman," I said and made my way towards the back door.

"Hold up. How we know she won't go to the cops, though?" the short guy from earlier asked.

"Really? You really gonna ask some dumb shit like that?" Marcus asked before pulling another gun from his waist and putting a bullet in dude's head. "I can't stand a dumb muthafucka. Get this shit cleaned up, and find a dumpster to put that nigga," he pointed towards Jevar's body.

"Hold up, Candy, is it?"

"Yeah."

"I want to meet your dude. Can you make that happen?"

"I don't know. Babe do you want to meet him?" I asked.

"Yes," Bryant said into the earpiece.

I relayed his response to Marcus, and they agreed to meet up the next day. I left out of the back door and headed towards my car. Questions ran through my mind as I wondered about the reality of what Jevar said about Bryant. Being that he was so quick to say yes to meeting Marcus didn't help matters either. I needed to have a conversation with him to see what was really up with him. No longer was I going to be blind-sided by a man I was in a relationship with. In that moment I felt so liberated and empowered. No more would I run from any man. No more will I tolerate another man putting their hands on me in an abusive manner. No more will I allow someone's words to affect me in a negative way. It was a new day and a new Candice Larae Carson.

Bryant

I wish I could have been the one to pull that damn trigger and put one right between Jevar's eyes. I was pissed he told Candice about what I did to Gerald. I only hoped this didn't cause her to leave me. I was in love with her and didn't want to lose her. It didn't help matters that the app Jevar was referring to was the very app we were using tonight. I muted the mic so Candice couldn't hear me loudly use every explicative possible of what Jevar told her.

"What are you going to tell Candice when she asks you about what Jevar said?" Brad asked.

"I'm going to tell her the truth," I ran a hand down my face and sighed.

"Are you sure that's a good idea? I mean, look at what happened with Trinity."

"Trinity was a liability and should have been dealt with a long time ago. I allowed her to live as long as she did because I was attracted to her in the beginning. I didn't want to kill her, and she would still be alive had she not let the drugs consume her. She should have just gone to rehab and went on about her life. But nope, she wanted to make shit difficult. On top of that, she threatened me. I wasn't having that."

"Bryant, you are one cold motherfucker," Brad admitted.

"Touché, my brother."

"Do you think she will leave you once she knows the truth?"

"I don't know," I sighed.

Candice came walking from the back of the house with one of the guys following closely behind her. We waited until she was in her car and pulled off before we pulled off behind her. Brad and I rode in silence the entire way to my house. Once we were in the driveway, Candice quickly hopped out and stormed inside the house.

"Good luck, bro," was Brad's parting words before exiting the car and heading home.

I got out the car and made my way inside the house. There was nothing but silence as I took the steps one at a time. Once I got to my room, I stood at the closed door to see if I heard any alarming noise but there was none. When I opened the door and entered the room, I didn't see Candice anywhere. I heard the shower going and let out a sigh of relief. I honestly thought she was in here packing her clothes to leave. Instead of joining her in the shower as my hard dick was trying to coerce me to do, I took a seat on the bed and waited for her to finish up. About ten minutes later, the shower turned off. I heard Candice mumbling under her breath something I didn't understand before she finally emerged from the bathroom.

Wrapped in a towel, she went over to the dresser where she kept her things. She opened one drawer and pulled out a pair of panties, then opened another drawer and pulled out a nightgown. Once she had those items in her hand, she took the body butter off the top of the dresser then walked over to her side of the bed and began applying the body butter.

"Do you need some help with that?" I asked trying to break the ice.

"No," she said sharply. "What I need you to help me with is what Jevar said about you and this app. And please don't lie to me or leave any details out." She put emphases on the word any. She didn't even bother to look up at me. She just continued to slather that great mango scented body butter over her body.

I let out a sigh, ran a hand over my head then down my face before letting it all out.

Chapter 29

Candice

"Gerald Carlyle came to me about an app he wanted us to work together on. He ran down the details of it and I became interested in it. We agreed on the terms of the deal and on my end, everything was good to go until he started making outlandish demands. I tried to reason with Gerald and to make this a joint business venture when he originally came to me with it. However, he wanted me to pay way above the market value of the app's worth. Basically, he was trying to scam me. At that time, the app was worth a few mil, and I was okay with that. But then he got greedy and wanted more after I agreed upon the set price he quoted me."

"So, you killed him, took the app, and pulled it off as your own intellectual work," I stated.

"Well, sort of," Verdell said.

"What the fuck do you mean, sort of?"

"Can you let me finish explaining?"

"I'm trying, but I feel like you're trying to bullshit your way out of this." I snatched my panties off the bed and put them on.

"Candice, I promise you, I'm not. I'm telling you the entire truth. There are only two people alive that knows that, and that's me and Brad. Please, let me finish," he pleaded.

I pulled my nightgown over my head then took a deep breath to try and calm my nerves. My head hurt and my eye felt like it was going to explode. I needed a shot of Patron and a Xanax expeditiously. I took a seat on the bed and looked over at Verdell then waved my hand for him to continue.

"I say sort of because his death was an accident. I didn't go there with the intent to kill him. The day I met with Gerald in his office, Trinity showed up unexpectantly. Gerald attacked me and we began to tussle. The gun went off, and he ended up dead. To keep Trinity from calling the cops and saying I killed him, I forced her to hold the gun in her hand so her prints would be on it. Being that I was wearing gloves, my hands prints weren't there, but being that she was a witness, I had to do something to keep her quiet."

"But if it was just an accident, why didn't you call the police?"

"I never want anything to tarnish the reputation of my father's company or our family name. The media would have had a field day with that if they ever found out about that. I couldn't take any chances." He stood and began pacing back and forth. "I did what I thought was best for my family and our business. I had Brad erase the security footage of that night from the time I entered the building up until a few hours afterwards.

"I began a relationship with Trinity to keep an eye on her in hopes she would keep quiet. It worked until she got careless with the drugs. I was happy when I caught her and Matthew in bed because I was never in love with her and didn't want to marry her. I don't know; I figured it was better to be miserable with her than to let that night get out."

"Why did you and Trinity break up then?"

"She started dabbling in heroin more and more, then I walked in on her screwing a colleague. They had no idea I was there because they were both so doped up. They had that shit laying out on the table while they were fucking. The next day, I gave her an ultimatum to either go to rehab and get clean or we were done. She went but checked herself out the next day."

"So, you broke it off?"

"Yeah. It was pretty much a done deal anyway."

I folded my arms over my chest and sat thinking of everything Verdell just told me. Did I believe what he said? For the most part, I did. But I could tell he was leaving something out.

"You know, I believe the story you just told me but not your innocence. You see, there's a totally different side of you I know you're trying to keep from me, and I need to know that Bryant Verdell McIntosh in order for us to move forward."

I watched him continue to pace back and forth, looking over at me every so often. I never took my eyes off him. I needed, wanted him to know I was serious. I had to show him I wasn't backing down, nor was I going to just accept anything. I wanted to know every detail of him, the good, bad, and ugly, if he expected me to remain in a relationship with him.

He finally stopped pacing and stood in the middle of the room glaring at me. I watched his eyes turn dark and his whole demeanor switch to, something, someone different. I started to rethink wanting to know that part of him for second.

"Okay, Candice, here's the deal. I'm a man who gets what he wants, when he wants it, and will do whatever it takes to make it happen. Gerald had something I wanted but when he tried to bullshit me, I came at him with a demand he gave me the app or else die. He tried to get cocky when Trinity showed up and it got him killed. Trinity was always a liability. To keep from killing her, I made her my woman. Catching her with dope and Gerald was my out, but she wouldn't let go.

"You, you were different though. That picture you sent me did something to me internally, and I needed to know why. It was something in your eyes that grasped my attention. Don't get me wrong, that pussy shot was a plus, but it was what I saw or didn't see in your eyes that held my attention. They were dead, and that intrigued me. Why would a beautiful woman have eyes that were lifeless?" He was now sitting on the bed next to me.

"Because of the man who made them that way," I answered as a tear ran down my cheek.

"I know that now and why I've tried to keep this side away from you. I don't want to ever be the reason your eyes were like that, how they are looking now. I want them to be bright and filled with life."

He used his thumb to wipe away my tears. I stood and backed away from him.

"Tell me this and I'm done. What happened to Trinity? Did you have something to do with that or did she have a complication like they reported on the news? You went to see her the day she died, right?"

"I did go see her. I needed to know if she told Jevar what happened with Gerald. A while back she came to me and threatened to tell what happened if I didn't take her back. When you told me she came at you about us, I had a feeling she was going to try and get back at you by linking up with Jevar. When her security camera caught him at her house, I knew then she told him. So, I went to the hospital to ask her about it. She admitted it. I used her fingers to press the morphine drip. It only allows a certain amount, but I have a cousin who works at the hospital who was one of her nurses. I gave her the money to pay off her house and she went in and shot more morphine in Trinity's IV to make her overdose. "That's it, Candice. That is everything. I have no more secrets. You have me by the balls, baby."

"Not quite, when you have dirt on me and my family as well."

"True, see we are a match made in heaven," he smiled deviously at that.

"I'm pregnant," I blurted out.

"What? Are you serious? I'm going to be a daddy?" He placed a hand on my belly.

"Mm hm," I nodded.

"Wait. Did you know this before we went there tonight?"

"I wasn't one hundred percent sure and didn't want to say anything until after everything had settled down. Plus, it was painful when we had sex, and I never had an issue taking that dick before. So, I took a pregnancy test once we got back.

He picked me up and spun me around with excitement. I squealed with excitement as well. We've been through so much in such a short amount of time. This was too much too soon. Who would have thought, a text sent to the wrong damn number would bring a lot of drama and a lot more love along with it? I loved this man and, yeah, he was stuck with me for life.

Epilogue

Bryant

Seven and a half months later...

"Push, baby! Push," I coerced Candice.

We were in the guest room of our house. Due to the spread of the coronavirus, and our family not being allowed at the hospital, I paid for around the clock medical care for Candice her last month of pregnancy. There was no way our moms were not going to be there for the birth of their granddaughter and my wife.

That's right! Candice and I got married two months after she told me she was pregnant. I would have married her the next day, but she refused since she hadn't met my parents at all, and she wanted to me to meet her mom and sisters formally. So, we had a big family dinner meet and greet at my house the next day.

Our families meshed well with each other. Bradford and Cassandra even made a love connection and are now dating. When we announced Candice was pregnant, both of our mothers began planning baby showers, gender reveal parties, and some other shit that had me scratching my head. It didn't matter though, as long as my baby was happy.

With the coronavirus shutting everything down, that halted the big plans for the baby's arrival. Candice and I had to adjust to being at home together every day, and sometimes that wasn't easy with a hormonal, emotional pregnant woman. I couldn't keep up with her mood swings! One second, she was hungry, the next she was horny. Then she got pissed off if she didn't get what she wanted in that moment. All I could do was shake my head and take a shot of Jack Daniels to keep calm. It was easier making business deals than dealing with Candice's mood swings at times.

Speaking of business deals, I met with Marcus Armstrong, and was pleasantly surprised at his business sense. I didn't know what to expect our meeting to be about, but when he came in talking about a joint venture for a media company, I was all in. Realizing he needed to begin the process of transitioning from the illegal mode of financial gain to getting it the legal way; his words, not mine. However, the business plan he laid out along with what his financial contribution sparked a business deal, and AM Media was birthed. We already received a few scripts that has piqued our interest. Soon, AM Media will be invading a small and possibly the big screen.

"Okay, Candice, give me one more big push," Dr. Baker told her.

"I can't, I can't push anymore. Just pull her out," Candice moaned.

"Come on baby, you got this," I told her. "Give it one more push. Malika is ready to meet her mommy and daddy."

"On this next contraction, give it all you got, Candice," Dr. Baker instructed.

Candice's face contorted as she took a deep breath and began to push. "Aaaaggghh!" She screamed.

"There you go. Keep it going. I see a head full of hair! Alright! Okay, you can stop pushing. Good job," Dr. Baker shot off.

"She is adorable," Nurse Morgan squealed.

Candice fell back on the pillow, face moistened from sweat. She closed her eyes as she tried to get her breathing under control. She was so exhausted she fell right to sleep.

"Daddy, do you want to cut the umbilical cord?" Dr. Baker asked.

I moved over next to the doctor and cut the cord. Tears filled my eyes as I looked down at my first-born child, my beautiful daughter. She looked just like her mother as she whaled for the first time.

My life was now complete. I have the woman of my dreams, who may I add is also a boss in her own right. Since Candice had to shut down the salon and spa due to the coronavirus, she started a podcast, Curious Candice, and it has garnered a huge following in a short period of time. She's even done a few virtual speaking engagements telling her story to other women in hopes they won't feel they should remain in an abusive relationship. Words cannot express how proud am I of her. I love this woman with everything in me, and I am so thankful God blessed me with her. I vow to honor, love, protect, and cater to Candice, now mother of our daughter, Malika Renee McIntosh, for as long as I have breath in my body.

The End

More by the Author

Coming Soon!

www.ingramcontent.com/pod-product-compliance
Lightning Source LLC
Chambersburg PA
CBHW021309250626
47155CB00002B/453